Collingwood's Club

After reading History at UCL, in 1970 Stephen Bibby departed for Malawi where he worked as a VSO teacher. Although he later followed a career in the UK civil service he was able to continue travelling widely and in his late thirties undertook a two year secondment to Lesotho in southern Africa.

Having visited many distant countries, he has written a large number of travel articles, as well as short stories and entertainments for his grandchildren. 'Collingwood's Club' is his first novel.

Stephen is married with two children and four grandchildren and lives in Hampshire.

Collingwood's Club

Stephen Bibby

Collingwood's Club

Olympia Publishers
London

www.olympiapublishers.com
OLYMPIA PAPERBACK EDITION

A CIP catalogue record for this title is
available from the British Library.

ISBN: 978-1-84897-306 0

(Olympia Publishers is part of Ashwell Publishing Ltd)

This is a work of fiction.
Names, characters, places and incidents originate from the writer's
imagination. Any resemblance to actual persons, living or dead, is purely
coincidental.

First Published in 2013

Olympia Publishers
60 Cannon Street
London
EC4N 6NP

Printed in Great Britain

Dedication

To my wife and family with sincere thanks
for their suggestions and encouragement.

1

I hate heights.

That was the reason, I told myself, that I felt slightly queasy as the glass elevator ascended swiftly up the exterior of the bank's soaring glass tower thrusting heavenwards above the daily toil of Docklands. The gilded light on the button '37th floor' glowed invitingly as the manicured trees, the sad grass and a few huddled hurried figures appeared to slip away from me down into the wintry dullness.

But to be brutally honest I was intoxicated by the culture. I shared the collective schizophrenia: unbridled anticipation of massive reward and uncontrollable worry of impending humiliation. No, it was not fear of heights that brought on the slight wave of nausea, it was the nagging dread that there might be only the mocking figure 'one' before the six noughts of my bonus.

London was grey and wet. Bonus week – the first in February – was always dark, damp and chilly. The O2 Arena sulked way down below, shabby in the nondescript murk. I was still at Warwick University when an astonished monarch uncertainly linked uncrossed hands on millennium night and the pristine white dome welcomed the new century. Now it receded from me, begrimed and grey, as I glided towards my golden reward.

This was only my third year of international trading. I worked long days for a salary amounting to more than my parents would have earned in a lifetime, had they survived. But Mr and Mrs Turner senior would never know what became of their son; a criminally careless lorry driver hurtling into their braking Ford Focus crushed the life out of them on the M40 as they drove home from my graduation.

The six figures guaranteed by my contract were insignificant compared with the year end bonus. Business was booming. My employers, Hazzard Brothers, were hugely profitable. In the language of our deals we were well in the money.

The bank's accounting date was 31st December. There was a fervid post Christmas rush to close off positions, to encourage the back office to complete paperwork. Then the accountants on the 23rd floor enjoyed temporary mastery as they telephoned to check figures or clarify details. The provisional results were presented to the Board; a summarised unaudited profit and loss account was published internally. We laughed at this arcane description. It was never a loss but unfailingly and emphatically a profit.

The annual secretive bonus allocation came next. There was a week of expectation and occasional ecstasy as generous rewards came tumbling like cup cakes from a fat boy's table. The accountants would expect 20 per cent. The back office staff received flat rate sums sufficient to purchase cars or foreign holidays. Even the girls on reception picked up a four figure sum. Only the cleaners and security guards remained glum, but they were invariably from overseas and employed by an agency.

Those of us on the trading floor did best. It was rumoured that some operating in the riskiest markets and contributing most substantially to the string of noughts in the bank's thick black profit figure were awarded as much as £25 million. Certainly for the last two years I had received a satisfying £1 million bonus. Already I owned a spacious apartment and a bright red Porsche. Like the other international traders I was fired up, filled with a consuming enthusiasm to succeed. I wanted to make as much money as possible without much thought of what I might do with it. My mind did not dwell on the monumental evil or little parcels of good which wealth would enable me to dispense. It was merely a symbol. There was only one sign of success in my world – the quantum of your bonus.

Of course I put in the effort. I would be at the computer screen at 6 a.m. catching the tail end of business in the eastern markets. I would stay late into the evening, adrenalin still surging if the American markets were coming alive. I had cultivated my telephone contacts in Tokyo and New York. I became quick, sharp and decisive.

My apartment – literally bought lock stock and barrel (there was even a small keg of real ale in the kitchen) from a departing American – was simply a place to sleep. If I wanted a meal I phoned for a takeaway or went to a restaurant. Someone cleaned twice a week.

Every year I had a luxury holiday in the Maldives. It was easy to get one of the office girls to come. We would have a fortnight of sun, champagne and sex and they would then go back to their East End boyfriends saying that the bank had sent them to an overseas conference. The Porsche stayed in the garage, coming out at Christmas when I would dodge the speed traps of the M3 and alarm Pam and Gary – my sister and her husband – by screeching to a halt outside their terraced house in Eastleigh. Sadly on the last occasion, nearly five months into a queasy pregnancy, Pam had been singularly unimpressed.

This last year I had been lucky. Late one evening I had just settled a run of the mill American trade when something flashed onto the computer screen. It was garbled and obscure, from one of the agencies off Wall Street, but implied there was to be an issue of collateral debt security by a little-known American bank. I picked up the telephone and dialled New York.

"Ben Turner, here. How are you doing?"

The unmistakable Manhattan drawl of Art Feinman came clearly down the line. He sounded just the same as when I had met him the previous year on a bank jaunt to New York. They had sent a group of promising young traders to learn some trans-Atlantic tricks from the old hands at Grossman Brothers, with whom Hazzards had some reciprocal links. Art had been my mentor.

"Not so bad." But he was alert, inquisitive. "You still on the lookout for juicy debt packages?"

"Something has just come up on my screen. It looks as though Chicago Commerce might have an interesting offer. What do you know?"

"Geez, you must be on the ball. I heard half a whisper – nothing more. I'll poke around to see what I can find and get back to you. Usual terms?"

I agreed. Half a percent was a small price to pay if I could get in first.

Within an hour I had the lowdown. Chicago Commerce had a package of mortgages to sell. It was an eclectic mix. There were Great Lakes mansions, fishermen's retreats, downtown apartments, condominiums, car workers' dwellings and newer cheap mass housing from the burgeoning suburbs of middle America.

It was now 10 p.m. and my trading floor was deserted. Art had an intricate network of insider contacts and had proved a reliable source over the past few months. He told me that he had picked up the suggestion from an old Wall Street snout that the bank was hoping to sell for $750 million. What the market didn't know was that Chicago Commerce had severe cash flow problems. These were only temporary – a forward position would right them within three months – but just then the bank was anxious to generate some immediate liquidity. I chanced my arm. I authorised Art to act as agent and buy for $700 million.

I had to trust him. Having never dealt directly with this bank I relied on his intercession. It was nearly 11 p.m before he got back to me. If I was prepared to close the deal and arrange the transfer of funds we could settle on $725 million. Done!

I tapped the numbers into the computer taking extra care. It was late and I was both exhausted and exhilarated. This was just the moment when tired traders were known to succumb to fat finger syndrome. This was not going to happen to me. Very deliberately I entered the correct number and the correct currency. I could not afford to slip up and overexpose my budget by maybe $100 million. Having left instructions for the back office, I went back to the apartment, rang for a pizza, downed a Peroni and went to bed.

Next morning the phones were buzzing with talk of the Chicago deal. Harding and Co., our main rival – we could almost see into their trading floor from ours across the grey dockland basin – was beside itself. Hazzard Brothers had stolen a march. A rumour quickly spread that Hardings would have gone much higher to grab a slice of the Chicago action.

This was where my luck came in. I remembered reading that in the late 1970s another bank in that same city – First Chicago – had to be rescued when it found a large tranche of its debts were disastrously doubtful. There was something unnerving about the haste of this recent offer; something unsettling about the ease of my late night deal. I decided to take no chances. Barely twelve hours after the deed was done I put in a call to Declan Faulkner, a former colleague who had

15

left Hazzards two years earlier after an unfortunate miscalculation and who now worked for Hardings.

I feigned panic. I hinted strongly that I urgently needed to divest myself of North American debt having over extended my position. Declan would obviously understand this dilemma having similarly over extended his. I told him we were fortunate to have acquired a lucrative Chicago package but I had unbalanced the portfolio. I was reluctant to let it go, but I needed to move quickly before my quarter's trading account was closed off. The securitised debt could be his for $800 million.

Of course he was not a pushover. We haggled for half an hour, my apparent desperation increasing by the minute. Finally I threatened to offer the package to one of the boutique merchant banks, subsidiaries of massive reinsurance companies, who we both secretly feared. He offered $775 million. I closed the deal.

We owned those American mortgages for less than a day. In 24 hours I had generated a profit of $50 million, less of course a half a percent commission to Art Feinman on Wall Street.

My boss was interested only in cash flow and profit margins. No one paused to calculate whether we should have held the investment long-term and taken the interest. But in any event it was only exceptionally that Hazzards operated like this. We acted as wholesalers, snapping up assets, putting them in fancy wrappers and passing them on to other wholesalers or the investment arms of the high street banks.

Then, six weeks later, I became the talk of the trading floor. Chicago Commerce had to be rescued. It was bailed out and subsumed into another eastern seaboard conglomerate. Not only had I made a profit out of the bundle of debt; I had done so before anyone realised just how toxic it was.

Yes, it had been a good year. I had done well for Hazzards and knew I deserved recognition. I should have been confident, but the bonus committee could be capricious. They had their favourites. No one knew what anyone else received or how the bonus was calculated. Nevertheless there appeared to be a clique, a loose coterie of certain select individuals who always did particularly well. There was an indefinable smugness among a dozen or so on the trading floor whose confident bearing, whose hint of a swagger, identified them as amongst the elite.

I carefully avoided looking down as the lift stopped and I stepped out. A secretary sat outside the boardroom door. She was disarmingly attractive, wearing a smart black jacket and pristine white blouse. Giving a standard red lipstick smile she picked up a telephone.

"Ben Turner has arrived." She enunciated clearly.

Brushing her skirt down, she rose and turned the gilded handle on the padded double door, holding it aside as I stepped into thick carpet and made for the solitary chair opposite a long rosewood table. Behind it sat the chief executive, the finance director and the head of personnel.

The ritual commenced. Firstly the chief executive, urbane and expansive, gave an overview. Hazzards had indeed experienced an exceptionally good year. He acknowledged that a major contributory factor had been the expertise and dedication of the international traders. Indeed it was a series of splendid foreign currency transactions that had, as it were, constituted the icing on the cake, significantly increasing the bottom line to close on £1billion.

Then it was the turn of the finance director. In assessing individual bonuses comments had been received from trading floor managers. Details of any major achievements had been noted. My Chicago Commerce profit was commended in glowing terms with no mention whatsoever of the toxicity of the asset.

Finally the suspense was broken by the head of personnel. The directors recognised that because of my contribution my bonus should be increased significantly compared with the previous year. My award would be £5million.

Immediately I was shown the door. They were obviously well practised in letting the bonus figures slide softly through the rarefied air then smartly ushering you out, denying both thanks and protest.

It was left to the secretary to hand me a formal paper which I had to sign to acknowledge that I had been notified of my award. I was required to keep the information confidential and not to disclose it to anyone including other employees.

Then I stepped back into the lift and sped away downwards to safety away from these Olympian heights.

Back on my floor, I did what everyone else did after these interviews: I went into the Gents. Once I had seen a colleague in his late 30s sobbing in a cubicle after a boardroom encounter; on another occasion someone had been physically sick. But today I smiled at myself in the mirror, punched the air with relief, urinated happily, went back to my desk and left work early.

Work could not stop in bonus week. The markets did not go to sleep because, temporarily, we were more interested in the digits on our bank statements than on the stock exchange screens. But amongst most there was an air of elation. Despite the secrecy there was still celebration. A few of us might go out and blow a few thousand pounds in an exclusive restaurant or in the hospitality suite of a Premier League football club. It was in one of these weeks that I bought my Leica camera and my Porsche.

But I had absolutely no idea how I would spend my latest reward. The culture of secrecy did not encourage wishful speculation and it was dangerous to develop detailed plans in case of disappointment. I still had a mortgage on the apartment but no other debts. Quite simply from now on I was in the unenviable position of being able to regard even £10,000 as petty cash.

Then Crispin Collingwood approached me.

I realise now that he had a perceptive insight into the minds of colleagues. But at the time I was startled by his invitation.

He too worked on the trading floor but was a few years older than me and definitely not my type. Somehow we all knew that he had been educated at Eton and then Oxford. It was not that he said anything in particular but rather that his general demeanour and sartorial statements consistently identified his background. He was tall and blond with a handsome bronzed face. His suits – vying to be the most expensive even amongst a floor of Jermyn Street trousers and jackets – were emphatically striped; his crisp shirts sat comfortably on an athletic torso now just losing the firmness of youth; his ties were loudly colourful. He always appeared more relaxed than other traders, never crumpled at the end of the day. He was generally one of the first to leave, striding from the floor with an aristocratic effortlessness. I guessed he was part of a charmed inner circle for, although he never appeared to strike spectacular deals, he never appeared uncomfortable at bonus time. Above all he seemed to know everything that was going on.

It was a few days after my summons to the boardroom. I had shut down my computer just after 7 p.m. to see Collingwood looming over me. He must have been waiting for this moment, standing there, the tips of his long fingers interlocked and then tapped together impatiently as he eyed my end of day ritual.

"Ben Turner," he gushed. "It's time we became better acquainted. Let's go for a drink."

I was so taken aback that I agreed. I could not remember him ever speaking to me directly before. Indeed the only time we had been close to a conversation had been a few months earlier in a merry group chortling about my Chicago deal. Without addressing me directly he had commented haughtily, "Yes, not a bad coup for a comprehensive boy."

He steered me into the lift and then out of the building to a nearby wine bar. It was packed. I noticed a number of colleagues were drinking there, some at loud tables tucked into exclusive corners, others all elbows and mouths annexing lengths of the light oak bar. But, arm around my shoulder Collingwood navigated the bustling room. At some imperceptible signal a young waitress opened a door, a cleverly concealed section of the light oak wall panelling, and we were in a small dining room, the table already set, a white cloth stiffly starched holding a silver platter of lobster and tiger prawns. Next to them, chilling in an ornate ice bucket, a bottle of champagne lay ready to be uncorked. Seeing his nod the waitress gingerly lifted it, revealing the name Dom Pérignon.

He waved me to one of the seats.

"Here's to you Ben," he said clinking his champagne flute against mine. He was thoroughly relaxed and suddenly, unexpectedly, very pleasant. "You know your trade was very brave. It takes a certain something to pull a coup like your Chicago deal. I think I may have underestimated you."

Slightly nonplussed I could think of no response other than a mumbled, "Thanks."

"Yes, word in Hazzard Brothers has it that you are very much the coming man." He sounded vaguely wistful.

"Am I?"

There was a pause and then he said, "You received a handsome bonus."

I was cautious. "I won't deny that I was called to the boardroom but I can't give any details."

"I was making a statement, not asking a question."

For a moment the arrogance showed through. Then once more he was silk. "There are, at this moment, some high numbers in your bank account – and that's another statement."

"How do you know?"

I was unsure of his game. I wondered if he was spying on me. Had he been sent to test whether I had the fidelity to abide by the declaration signed before the boardroom secretary?

He tapped his finger on his nose and leant forward conspiratorially. "Let's not play games Ben. I know everyone who trousers £5 million or more. You're part of a very elite club now. It's time to issue your membership card."

"Membership card, what do you mean?"

For a moment I was apprehensive, even a little frightened. I was not sure whether 'elite club' was a euphemism. I wondered if perhaps there was some arcane custom of which I was ignorant, some public school ritual that I would be forced to endure. I had heard that at Eton the heads of new boys were held down the toilet while the flush was pulled. It occurred to me that any ritual humiliation of a new millionaire would be far more unpleasant than that. Crispin evidently detected a shiver of distaste.

"There is nothing to worry about Ben," he said reassuringly. "It's just that we have – how should I put it – a dining club. Everyone at our income level is a member and now it's your turn to join."

The press had recently published photographs of certain members of the shadow cabinet, in their Oxford days, dressed in evening wear arrogantly posing at the commencement of a Bullingdon Club engagement. Was this what he had in mind? Was there some exclusive society of people like him who would wine, dine and behave outrageously in one of London's expensive restaurants?

To buy time I took another sip of champagne. It was truly delicious. I had to acknowledge that Crispin and his cronies knew how to live and eat well. I had tasted fine wine before but was no expert. It would be enjoyable to dine on gourmet food and in the process absorb the savoir-faire of some of my colleagues whose varied life experiences were more privileged then my own.

He seemed to be very genuine, anxious that I should feel included. I put down the tall, long stemmed glass and asked, "What sort of club is this? Which restaurants do you patronise?"

"We are very select. We do not of course patronise restaurants. We have private catering from exclusive chefs in some discreet and sumptuous residences. You will dine on truly exotic morsels; you will sample the most succulent of savouries, the provender of princes, the sustenance of kings."

He selected a particularly large prawn, peeled back the scaly pink casing and sucked a huge mouthful of flesh into his large soft lips.

Possibly because he was warming to his theme, becoming fluently poetic in his description of food, possibly because I was hungry and the champagne was stimulating a desire to eat, I found myself intrigued, even salivating slightly. But still I was uncertain.

"I appreciate this Crispin," I said hesitantly. "But you know I'm not sure that I will fit in. After all ..."

I tailed off, not wanting to do myself down, desperate to choose the right words.

"What I mean is that you and many of our colleagues have different backgrounds from mine. We may not always find it easy to get along socially."

"Don't worry about that, dear boy. There are all types in the club. We have about 250 members, a great variety of interesting characters. They are not confined to Hazzard Brothers. This is a club that transcends territorial boundaries. We are truly a gathering of the princes of the profession."

I was impressed. His network obviously extended across the entire merchant banking sector. He had inside knowledge of who earned what on our trading floor and his tentacles reached also to the plush boardroom floors of other Dockland towers. He mentioned a couple of vaguely familiar names from other merchant banks adding, in explanatory rather than derogatory tone, "Both of them were comprehensive boys too."

"Every trading floor holds a diverse cultural mix," he continued. "You will be quite at home. As I said you are one of an elite now, a £5 million man."

Despite his blandishments I remained sceptical. Although there was a superficial attraction I was not certain that I had sufficient élan to slip effortlessly into this plutocratic clique. Besides I had never belonged to any sort of club. Although tempted by wine and fine dining I was cautious about committing myself.

Then I noticed the silk slip aside momentarily and a glint of steel crept into his eyes.

He said coldly, "Of course you do not have to join. But you will be the first £5 million man not to. They will all know. Don't expect any favours. Remember you have a reputation. Faulkner is still smarting because you offloaded the Chicago deal on him. If it becomes known that you wish to remain an outsider just wait for something to be dumped on you."

What he said rang true. In the trading world behaviour could be both ruthless and unforgiving. If I did not conform, if I did not play my part as one of the elite, then my descent could be as rapid as my rise. More had changed than simply my bank balance. I had broken through an invisible ceiling; I had been propelled into the superior set. There was no going back. I would have to do what was expected of me.

I raised my glass. "You commenced this conversation by offering me a membership card. How do I accept?"

"Good man." The hardness dissipated. "Come on. Have some of this excellent lobster."

I sank my fork into the yielding white flesh and took a mouthful. It was pleasant, but slightly disappointing.

"You like it?"

I nodded.

"This is nothing to the cornucopia of delights that await you."

He reached inside his jacket pocket and extracted an envelope.

2

Collingwood's envelope was not just any envelope. It was completely different from those used by the back office to send letters of confirmation or contract notes. Neither did it resemble the white envelopes used exclusively by the directors. It was heavy and substantial, deep cream in colour with a tasteful gilt edging. The back flap carried an embossed monogram. I eased it up carefully as it seemed sacrilegious to tear it open.

Inside was a similarly gilt edged card. At its head again I found the embossed monogram and noticed that it was a clever design of scrolls and whorls extending outwards in artistic flourishes from the letter E. The printing, elegant and formal read: 'This is to certify that Benjamin Turner Esq., having met the qualifying conditions, has been admitted to membership of the Epicureans.'

"Named after the Greek philosopher, Epicurus, with whom I suspect you are not acquainted," he observed patronisingly.

Ignoring the tone I said, "Qualifying conditions? What does this mean?"

Collingwood obviously sensed my suspicion. "Don't go looking for a catch," he replied, "I've already explained – you're a £5 million man. Conditions met."

I relaxed a little and, as if in reciprocation, he leant confidentially across the table waggling a tiger prawn by its tail.

"There's only one other condition as you might expect," he said softly. "Naturally every club has its entrance fee. Ours is quite modest. Any of us can easily meet it – merely a minor disbursement from our recent rewards – but obviously if the club is to deliver the sensory delights to beguile and enthral the financial elite of the country, then it has to have the wherewithal to function. Don't pay me now: here's what you need to do."

He extracted from his pocket a correspondence card bearing the name of the prestigious Coutts Bank. On the reverse there was no writing, simply two strings of figures – a sort code and an account number.

"You just need to transfer to this account and, voilá, membership is duly subscribed," he added with a flourish.

He raised his champagne flute, swiftly swallowing the final drops of the Dom Pérignon while picking at the remaining pieces of lobster, now a sad carcass fractured on the platter, its noble pincers cracked and splintered, errant flaky remnants of flesh sullying the stiff white cloth. Our meeting was clearly at an end. He stood up, shook my hand and turned to leave, ushering me out through the busy bar and onto the damp pavement, slippery with a cold London drizzle.

"Of course your highly desirable card is not valid until the transfer comes. But I have never known anyone let us down. The amount by the way is £100,000."

Suddenly he could not get away quickly enough. He turned swiftly and was gone leaving me alone with my astonishment.

I walked slowly through the chilly gloom of Docklands back to my apartment, at first feeling flattered, them bewildered, but finally as I turned the key, triumphant.

Of course I had no option. I need not make the bank transfer but Collingwood had made it quite clear what would happen if colleagues took an aversion to me. The Epicureans extended across the city so that not only would my non-conformity damage me within Hazzard Brothers it would also make me a pariah amongst alternative employers.

The triumph was in acceptance. I had known there was a hierarchy; subtle and undefined it existed in deference, in cliques and connections, among wine bar companions and in social invitations. Doors were being opened to me and I relished the opportunities which I would encounter when I walked through.

Shaking off the dampness from my coat, I switched on my laptop, tapped at the keys and transferred £100,000 to the account number shown on the monogrammed card.

It seemed an extortionate amount to pay to join a dining club, but then I could afford it. In any event I simply had to regard it as a levy, my union dues, my club subscription. But these blue collar metaphors were inappropriate. Instead the outlay was a modest payment for a passport to even greater wealth.

The next day I saw little of Crispin Collingwood. I did get a nod across the trading floor at one point but no other acknowledgement. However over the succeeding week I noticed a perceptible change in the attitude of a clutch of senior traders. More were bothering to speak to me, making a friendly comment if we passed in the corridor. On one occasion I encountered Quentin Foorde in the Gents. He was at one of urinal bowls, his arms resting on the modesty panels, splashing noisily, hands-free.

Like Collingwood before him, Quentin was not someone with whom I ever had a conversation. He was a brutish bull of a man, a former rowing blue, who tended to ignore newer arrivals like myself. But today as I took my place discreetly next but one to him he said with a guffaw, "So, you think you can hang out with the big knobs now!"

I also found that I made several lucrative trading deals. There was still lively competition, the approach, as ever, being to maximise individual profit at all costs. But on the odd occasion, when trading was hectic, people like Quentin would refer a client on to me if they were heavily preoccupied with other business. Somehow it became easier to attract the big ticket trades, to handle even larger numbers, to generate even fatter commissions. Success was breeding success.

It was about three weeks later when I received my first invitation to a gathering of the Epicureans. A monogrammed cream envelope, the only mail of the day, was lying behind the door of the flat when I returned late one evening. It gave a time and date together with an address west of central London. There was no indication of expected dress or proposed menu, simply an assumption of acceptance. At a suitable moment the following day I sought out Collingwood and requested an explanation.

"Dear boy, don't be so provincial!" he said with friendly amusement. "No one declines and part of the frisson of pleasure is in the identification of the dishes, the recognition of the repast."

I stood by his desk slightly bewildered until he rose, clapped his long arm across my shoulders and said confidentially, "You are in for a rare experience; relax and enjoy yourself. But as it's your first time there are two other things you should know. One: wear evening dress. Two: come by taxi and alight two streets away. We like to keep these occasions discreet."

The date of the event was a Friday evening towards the end of March, just after Easter. That day Collingwood disappeared after lunch and I noticed that in mid afternoon a handful of traders were shutting down their computers a little earlier than normal. Quentin Foorde swaggered out with Justin Rhodes and Nick Forsythe. We all knew they were wine bar companions but I realised now that they were inseparable, bonded together by a strong financial cement. To my surprise none of the colleagues with whom I was most familiar showed any sign of leaving and I felt slightly embarrassed, slinking out as quietly as possible independently of the haughty Foorde set.

Although I owned several good suits I did not possess a dinner jacket. My inclination had been to hire one but it was hardly worth the trouble. Several good tailors had small outlets in Docklands. It took me 30 minutes one lunchtime to purchase everything I needed including dress shirt, suit and tie. The whole outfit came to about £500 which I regarded as petty cash even before my bonus. On the appointed evening I was dressed immaculately, even sporting a white silk scarf.

But puritanically I still balked at travelling all the way across London by taxi. The address I had been given was in Knightsbridge. I took the Jubilee line to Green Park and then emerged into Piccadilly alive with early evening bustle. Orange 'For Hire' signs bobbed into the distant traffic as a stream of taxis unloaded their passengers, guests for a function in the Ritz, then sought new fares in Regent Street or Shaftesbury Avenue. I hailed one of these cabs giving my destination as Harrods.

We were soon moving west, zooming under the ground at Hyde Park Corner then emerging past Harvey Nichols and turning into Brompton Road. The familiar sandstone bulk of the vast store studded with several thousand light bulbs loomed into view, an exclusive liner in a sea of luxury craft. I ignored the liveried commissionaire holding the door open for me, thrust a £20 note into the taxi driver's hand and dashed across the road.

I did not have far to walk before I found the address. It was one of those substantial townhouses about four storeys high with an imposing classical frontage, not overly wide but hinting at surprises behind the facade. Indeed the windows on the lower floors were barred and shuttered so that prying eyes even from straying tourist coaches could not discern the activities of the interior.

There was no sign of any function taking place within. For a moment I wondered if I was mistaken, if I had the date or address wrong. But as I mounted the three stone steps leading to the entrance, the heavy black front door swung open. It swung shut again behind me, clicking securely, as I stepped into a narrow porch. Ahead at the lobby door a smart young man, muscular, but the epitome of politeness, examined my membership card. He took my coat and with a "This way, sir," he ushered me up a beautiful Georgian stairway.

The reception room on the first floor was teeming with people. There was a babble of animated talk, the chink of glasses, an intense atmosphere of anticipation. There were perhaps seventy or eighty men aged between their mid thirties and late forties congregated there, all in evening dress, many sporting shirts with pearl buttons or diamond encrusted cufflinks. My £500 outfit appeared subdued and second rate compared to theirs. To my surprise there was also a handful of young ladies. They were part of a small minority and the subjects of considerable attention from the male guests. All wore beautiful silky gowns which clung sinuously to their figures. Many revealed generous breasts, their slender necks hung with diamonds or pearls drawing your eyes towards their pale skin and then downwards to the provocative curves.

Fortunately Crispin Collingwood was looking out for me. Almost immediately he came striding through the room, glass in hand, eager to introduce me. For an awkward minute I wondered if, as a newcomer, I would have to engage in some childish induction ritual, perhaps glugging a glass of champagne straight down or something similarly foolish. But immediately he was solicitousness itself.

"Am I late?" I asked indicating the throng around me.

"Not at all," he responded. "As I told you, we don't believe in drawing attention to ourselves. We stagger the arrival times and our departures are similarly staggered, though sometimes a surfeit of

Chablis might be the cause of that! I've been here since 6.30. Champagne?"

He clicked his fingers and a demure young waitress offered me a flute on a silver salver. I noticed that on a side table there was a regiment of bottles labelled 'Krug' with the vintage year 1996. I took a sip, the bubbles fiery in my dry, slightly apprehensive mouth. Then Collingwood guided me into the Quentin Foorde clique. Justin and Nick were there talking animatedly to a beautiful girl in a stunning bright blue gown matching the colour of her flashing eyes which flickered over me with a quizzical gaze. Nick introduced her as Sabrina St Clair, a Duke's daughter, and she smiled with mock coyness as he exaggerated her charms saying what good fun and a terrific sport she was.

The gathering was becoming noisier, my fellow club members becoming increasingly garrulous with the consumption of champagne. Fascinated, I glanced around the room. Never before had I seen such rich furnishings. There were curtains, soft and flowing, with delicate oriental floral patterns. Much of the furniture was occupied by guests, but I could see gilt arms and legs and the distinctive ball and claws of Chippendale. On the ceilings there were ornate chandeliers. My shiny shoes sunk into a soft carpet exquisitely patterned with exotic birds and beasts fleeing from oriental huntsmen. On the walls elaborate frames held striking portraits of statesmen or generals in tight red uniforms.

"You don't have a wife to worry about do you, Ben?" Justin Rhodes had obviously decided that I was worth talking to.

"No I'm a free agent at the moment." I tried to sound nonchalant.

"You lucky bugger. Even though she has everything she wants, Melissa can't understand when we have a club night. She doesn't have to graft for all hours. She just doesn't appreciate how tough this job can be – or how you have to drop someone right in it from time to time."

Mention of this made me wonder if Declan Faulkner was among the guests. Inconspicuously I executed a swift visual survey but spotted neither the familiar florid face nor the reddish hair. But then of course following the Chicago deal he had probably not met

28

Collingwood's 'qualifying conditions', especially as Harding and Co were known to be somewhat less generous than Hazzards.

Apart from the colleagues present from my floor most of the other members were totally unfamiliar to me. The more I looked the more I noticed all the subtle signs of opulence. Beside the dress shirts with pearl buttons and diamond cufflinks there were silk handkerchiefs, fob watches on heavy chains, gold signet rings.

Collingwood noticed my gaze. "You're here with the elite, Ben; with fellow traders from the most prestigious establishments in the city. We deserve the opportunity for a modicum of indulgence. After all it's what we do that makes the world go round."

Perceptibly the crush in the room was now beginning to thin out but I had seen no one descend the staircase. I realised that the full-length mirrors at the rear of the room were in fact the doors of a discreet lift. Collingwood put a protective arm around my shoulder, coming close enough for me to notice the fragrance of his expensive aftershave, and guided me towards our reflections, mine somewhat tense and alert, his relaxed and expansive.

"You might have become an ace trader but I can see that you are in need of a little mentoring. I may have a further task in mind for you – but let's see how you get on tonight, first. Now onward the Hazzard team – and of course the delectable Sabrina."

The elevator easily held the six of us. I noticed that the birds and the beasts of the carpet continued their flight across the lift floor and up to waist height. From here to the ceiling the wall was mirrored, showing the lovely long slender bare back of Sabrina. Silently the lift began to move, its motion only vaguely discernible. To my surprise I sensed that we were going downwards. The tiny green light flickered 0, -1, -2.

"Stop looking alarmed," hissed Collingwood.

Then I remembered. This part of London is full of listed buildings. The facades are preserved so that outwardly the stately Georgian appearance is retained. Sometimes interior features such as elaborate staircases are the subject of preservation orders but apart from that owners can do what they wish within their property. If they require an extension they cannot protrude upwards and so disturb the balance of the facade. Instead they build downwards. You would not know it but beneath the streets of Knightsbridge and Mayfair there are ballrooms, dining rooms, swimming pools, sunken garages, vast wine cellars, offices, studios, cinemas and private theatres.

The lift panel glowed on -3 and the doors parted silently onto a sizeable dining room comfortably filled with a table in the shape of a large U. It was covered in a thick white cloth, each place setting a miniature armoury of cutlery. There were several delicate wine glasses rising imperiously like tall trees above the weaponry, vying for superiority with ranks of starched conical napkins standing like neat combatants' campsites. The room was humming with conversation, a hint of excitement hanging in the air as if each and every one eagerly awaited the prospect of some rare delicacy.

At this point Collingwood left us, muttering something about getting to his place. Quentin was deep in conversation with a distinguished looking man who I had never seen before.

"Look at Quentin working his contacts," whispered Justin. "That's the head of international trading at Hardings who he's talking to."

Then he gestured to a seating plan. Justin obviously knew the procedure for after a cursory glance he motioned to some seats at the extremity of the U. Our names were on place cards apparently hand written in a flowing italic script. I hardly recognised mine for usually I saw it abbreviated in the Arial font of e-mail and never as a florid *Benjamin Turner Esq.*

I took my seat with Sabrina to my right, Justin on my left. At the centre of the U was one of the young directors of Harding and Co., recognisable from his photograph in numerous financial magazines. It was Sebastian Picard-Syme, known colloquially as 'Kick Arse Swine', for he was ruthlessly ambitious with an arrogance to match. Although barely 40 he had seized some opportunities in the wake of the Barings collapse and reputedly now possessed a personal fortune of over £150 million.

Collingwood took his place next to him. Justin nudged me.

"Crispin's a crafty bugger," he whispered nodding towards the pair. "He keeps well in at director level."

At some indefinable signal an army of waiters and waitresses filed into the room taking up positions behind the chairs as the diners occupied their places. Each uniformed foot soldier held a plate covered with a brightly polished silver dome like the top of a gleaming St Paul's. In unison they bent forward, deftly placing their miniature cathedrals in front of us. In unison they lifted the small gilt acorn at the pinnacle of each dome theatrically offering our first course. It was revealed as a miniature concoction of smoked salmon and caviar moulded and sculpted into a trio of exotic tropical fish. It was a creation of sheer beauty. We all hesitated before inserting our forks to prise away the melting flesh mingling with the tiny translucent spheres, black as night. The first of the forest of wine glasses was filled with an elegant Puligny-Montrachet exactly matching the subtlety and delicacy of the piscatorial tableau now attracting muttered approval from around the room.

No one hurried. Everyone savoured the exquisite, subtly salty melange, pausing to sip the wine, allowing it to play on their taste buds. I remained alert, covertly scanning the room to ensure I conformed, that I displayed no ignorance of the elaborate rituals. My solitary meals were invariably hurried down. Even at a restaurant, although I required good food, I also required quantity and speed. Now I was with people brought up to refined living, gregarious in their gourmet inclinations, confident in consumption, appreciative of artistry.

When the last globule of dark roe had been dusted by the last napkin, when the last drop of straw coloured wine had been slowly swallowed, the army returned. Imperceptibly they materialised behind each seat and with gloved hands deftly removed the used cutlery, the first spent weapons of the opening skirmish, followed by the naked plates.

Next the glass forest was tended. The small emptied vessels were removed and gloved hands slipped the elegant crystal tumblers to the fore. We were offered a choice of waters – Italian, French or British. The selection switched from nation to aeration. The still water came in white bottles; the sparkling in green or deep blue. I chose the latter abandoning myself to the exotic even in the humblest of refreshment.

The diners became more loquacious. Sabrina loudly informed us, "Of course I've been here with Daddy. When he was allowed to sit in the Lords they had a club that came here, just like us this evening. But he doesn't come much now since this lefty lot kicked him out."

At an indefinable moment there was a perceptible hiatus and immediately the regiment returned holding another set of miniature cathedrals. This was the soup course, a light clear consommé, a piping hot sea on which floated tiny croutons in the shape of battleships. Wine waiters dispensed a lovely light burgundy into the next sparkling goblet discreetly selected from the thinning copse.

Then a voice proclaimed loudly that Mr Picard-Syme would take wine with our esteemed Treasurer. Crispin Collingwood raised his delicate glass by its slender stem and a glance of approbation passed between the two men as for a moment all eyes turned to focus at these two notables at the head of the U.

Nick and Justin were evidently expecting the next announcement. Picard-Syme was now to take wine with members of Hazzards' trading floor. They were ready promptly to raise their glasses still holding a mouthful of light red liquid. I hastened to follow suit.

"Collingwood is so well in with Kick Arse that Hazzards had to be next," Justin whispered to me.

The taking of wine continued, steadily moving from trading floor to trading floor, interspersed with a glass lifted to each willowy female guest. It did not cease until well into the next course.

The consommé having been duly sipped and savoured, there was a pause. Some diners rose and disappeared towards a well disguised exit at the back of the room.

"Don't go blundering in," Sabrina giggled. "Remember it's always Ladies on the right, Gentlemen on the left."

I saw Collingwood leave his seat and come across to us. He was slightly flushed but exuded bonhomie. He placed his arm confidentially around my shoulders.

"Having a good time? Enjoy the main course," he said with a curious hint of irony, giving me a playful shake.

Once again the silent cohorts filed into the room, this time each with a silver salver holding a wafer thin china dish no larger than an egg cup. It contained a pure white substance like a delicate wisp of frozen sea foam. I watched as my dining companions selected metal from the array in front of them. This time we evidently needed a tiny spoon such as my mother used to have in the mustard pot. The icy froth was an innocent sorbet, but it cut into the palate like a blade.

In a moment the emptied vessels were spirited away. Wine waiters were again at our elbows, this time dispensing a Château Mouton Rothschild into a broad vessel selected from the diminishing spinney. Suddenly the loud voice boomed, "Silence for Mr Picard-Syme."

The dapper figure rose. "I will take wine with the entire assembled company before the arrival of the pièce de résistance."

We all sipped the most exquisite deep red Bordeaux. Picard-Syme appeared to be immensely self-satisfied.

The black and white battalions, now like swift military engineers, erected circular emplacements of steaming vegetables. There were delicate cubes of diced potatoes, browned, sprinkled with parsley; asparagus; French beans and miniature carrots. A tactical withdrawal and then they were back with their silvered cupolas, standing to attention behind us. Once more there was an imperceptible signal, plates were on the table and with a flash of silver the domes disappeared to reveal the centrepiece of this orgy of self indulgence. In front of us were three modest strips of meat in a light red jus adorned with sprigs of thyme and a juniper berry.

The foot soldiers spooned modest portions from the vegetable tureens and then silently withdrew. The assembled company advanced eagerly on the latest course.

Sabrina muttered half to herself under her breath, "I'm sure I've tasted this before."

I cut into the yielding strips of flesh. They parted but not as easily as a tender beef filet. I dipped a piece into the warm jus and put it to my lips. The taste was strange, a little bland, definitely requiring the tartness of the sauce to please the palate. I took another mouthful and complemented it exquisitely with the Château Mouton Rothschild. The green accompaniments, al dente, were a delightful counterbalance, rich with flavour themselves but also highlighting the tone and texture of the meat. I began to realise what it was like always to dine off the finest food and drink of exclusive labels. This was living.

There was a subdued but excited hubbub around the room; murmured exclamations of surprise and appreciation. I had the distinct impression that the assembled company had never tasted anything comparable before.

The last plate was finished, the silver knives and forks laid to rest. But strangely the waiting army did not appear. Instead up rose Picard-Syme.

"Ladies and Gentlemen," he announced. "As is our practice, before satisfying the curiosity of those unfamiliar with this evening's culinary delight, we will give our newest member the chance to distinguish himself. Please welcome Mr Benjamin Turner."

A loud burst of applause filled the room. Collingwood motioned me to my feet then he too pounded his hands together vigorously.

"Now Ben," said Picard-Syme unctuously, "would you care to identify our delicacy?"

3

For a moment I froze. Despite my wine induced heavy headedness I immediately recognised that this was the moment of ritual humiliation I had dreaded. Trained as I was to react and think quickly I groped for an inspired guess. What I had consumed had none of the equine pungency of horse remembered from an undergraduate jaunt to Provence. Neither did it have the softness of milk reared veal. With the beads of sweat gathering on my forehead, the sickening sensation of impending disgrace in my throat and the realisation that my pause for reflection was about to expire, I lowered my eyes.

It was then I noticed that next to me Sabrina had been surreptitiously scribbling on her removed place card. Two words provided my salvation. Raising my brow I looked directly at Picard-Syme.

"Guinea Pig," I answered.

Surprised, he made a suitable comment of approbation while Collingwood looked on grinning mischievously. There was a further burst of applause, the doors swung open and the serving regiments reappeared.

I remember little more of the evening. There were cheeses; a diverse selection served French style before dessert with a heavy Châteauneuf-du-Pape. There was dessert itself, a meltingly light fruit filled pastry accompanied by a few mouthfuls of Château d'Yquem poured into the last standing sapling of the glass forest. There was coffee and petit fours. But, after that revelation, all I remember is a sensation of profound relief and gratitude to my saviour.

As the diners drifted from the table I turned to Sabrina. I felt overwhelmed both with gratitude and desire. Not only was she beautiful, she was ruthless and quick witted. I could have kissed her there and then but I was being congratulated by an inebriated Nick

Forsythe garrulously introducing me to an acquaintance from another trading floor. The elegant bare back, graceful and serene amidst a sea of black evening wear, was slipping away firmly steered by the hands of other admirers, disappearing towards the lift. When I broke free and hastened back to the reception room Sabrina had gone.

Throughout the next day – a dull windy Saturday – hubris surfaced through my hangover. It had been a near thing but I had survived. Not only had a door opened for me but I had stepped through it with aplomb. I had truly arrived.

Curiously on the Monday morning nothing was said. I received no more than the usual non committal grunts of post-weekend greeting from the other traders as they drifted in to work. It was evident that most were completely unaware of the gathering on the previous Friday evening. As I settled down at my screen I could see Quentin Foorde across the floor. He appeared to be his normal boorish self but I noticed both Justin Rhodes and Nick Forsythe looking tired and rather pale. None of them spoke to me and, considering it prudent not to revel in my triumph, I concentrated on Far Eastern share prices and remained taciturn, engrossed in an impending derivative trade.

I was still engrossed that afternoon when unexpectedly Crispin Collingwood tapped me on the shoulder.

"I said we needed a further discussion," he announced amiably. "Come tomorrow about 9 p.m." He handed me a calling card bearing his name in a noble script and a riverside penthouse address much further west.

For a moment I thought of refusing tartly, even rudely. Why should I allow him to determine how I would spend my evening? But I realised in the nick of time that such a response would merely provoke a withering riposte and kept my cultivated silence. Collingwood walked smartly away and I found I had accepted by default.

Besides, I was hugely intrigued and eager to ascertain what was in store for me. He had mentioned a little task and I wondered what was in prospect. Also why was Collingwood so anxious to cultivate me? There could be no equivocation; of course I would keep the appointment.

The following evening I took a taxi for the long ride west, speeding through Shadwell and past the illuminated Tower of London and thereafter running alongside the Thames. The driver knew the address. He knew exactly where to turn into a tasteful garden just off the embankment and exactly where to draw up outside the revolving doors at the foot of an imposing tower block. It proclaimed its exclusivity with understated nameplates in the lobby where the security guards had a neat military style uniform. My name was on the clipboard clutched by the burly man at the reception desk. I was directed to the lift and invited to press the button labelled 'Penthouse'.

Collingwood was standing opposite the lift on the top floor, his penthouse door flung open. He showed me in to a huge room with a magnificent view over the Thames. I could see tiny dots of red lights bobbing down the river, the silvery gleam of the pods on the London Eye glowing like alien larvae and the flashing blue light of an ambulance racing to St Thomas's Hospital. I had to steady myself slightly but quickly realised that we were safely enclosed and a mere eight storeys high.

I glanced around the apartment spotting on the rear wall two garish paintings by an up-and-coming artist.

"I don't have them for their aesthetic beauty," Collingwood commented, noticing my glance. "The appreciation is enormous."

Besides these minor, rather vulgar works of art there were several framed photographs of a younger Collingwood dressed in cricket whites. He had been captured in various poses, alone or in company, but generally holding a trophy, sitting proudly in the front row of a team. In one, clutching a bruised and tired cricket bat, his blond hair full and flowing, he had a free arm draped around another athletic man, slightly younger but with similar features and the same disarming grin. Next to it the two were pictured together again with their entire team and I could see the neatly printed names beneath each player, including Crispin Collingwood alongside Tristram Collingwood.

"My brother may have been better looking but I knocked up more runs. He always got shaky if he got over 80. 'Tristam's trembles', we used to say and he would get bowled out on 92! I could have been a county player," he continued blandly, "but I got made an offer I couldn't refuse. Besides there's infinitely more money to be made in a merchant bank."

He motioned for me to sit by him on a huge leather sofa and, exuding bonhomie, offered me a drink.

But I refused to be charmed by him. I chose to place myself opposite on another equally large sofa and tried to seize the initiative.

"Why didn't you warn me what would be expected of me on Friday night?" I said sharply.

He appeared to be crestfallen, shrugging his shoulders as if momentarily lost for words. Then he became emollient, even slightly apologetic. He launched into a long explanation.

It so happened that I was the only new member of the Epicureans at the Knightsbridge gathering. It was true that in the past year record bonuses had been paid and a significant number of traders had become millionaires. But membership was restricted to those with a certain cachet. Of course there was total confidentiality but wheels moved within wheels and who you knew mattered as much as what you did. The banks rewarded people with £1 million here and £1 million there. But to be singled out as someone to be entrusted with the greatest risks, to be elevated to the ranks of the elite, you had both to generate an exceptional revenue flow and also impress the directors with your potential. Only those looked upon favourably achieved the magical £5 million or more. I had obviously been identified as the up and coming young man.

I must have relaxed a little for Collingwood grinned approvingly and continued with a brief history. The club was just over two years old. It had been his brainchild and he had lobbied extensively to recruit successful members of the financial community. I was not the only trader to have succumbed to the blandishments of champagne and lobster in the back room of a wine bar.

"But unlike what was said of the infamous prawn cocktail offensive – which you are probably too young to remember," he added as an afterthought, "these crustaceans did not die in vain."

He had recognised that there was a clamour from the rising stars of several different banks to create an exclusive society. After all, we were the individuals who stimulated world trade, forced competition, made efficiency a business imperative. We were at the cutting edge of high finance. It was entirely appropriate that two or three times a year we should gather together. Indeed, if I read any of the literature by modern management gurus I would know that celebrating success is an important part of a healthy commercial life. Accordingly, after the consumption of barely a case of champagne and a creel of crustaceans, an entrepreneurial nucleus had decided to inaugurate a club reserved solely for the crème de la crème of the financial world. It had an entrance fee and thereafter an annual membership fee. In a further stroke of genius Collingwood had secured the appointment of Picard-Syme as president.

A set of rules had been drawn up formalising the membership qualification. However very quickly it had been decided, at the discretion of the president and treasurer, to offer honorary membership to a number of ladies. After all, in this modern day and age, male clubs were no longer de rigueur. But any female member had to have a fortune of at least £5 million in her own right and equally importantly had to have contacts. We would never have had the use of the Knightsbridge house if Sabrina had not known how to negotiate a favour from its aristocratic owner. Collingwood could let me know confidentially that on the day we had enjoyed the use of such splendid surroundings a sum of £150,000 had been anonymously deposited in the Lichtenstein bank account of the owner, a certain Duke of the realm.

He was straying from the point, deluging me with details instead of replying. I repeated my question, but this time more as a mild enquiry rather than a challenge.

Collingwood leant forward and said slowly and very clearly, "My dear boy, you are too young to remember the glorious days when Margaret Thatcher was Prime Minister. But she famously asked 'Is he one of us?' I had to do the same. You are obviously a first-class trader and the directors are smiling on you. You really are that singular phenomenon, a rags to riches character. It was imperative that I ascertained what you are made of.

"There is a rite of passage in any organisation carrying within it a certain cachet. Of course you can hardly expect to know exactly what I had to accomplish to achieve acceptance at Eton. Neither do I imagine that the indulgences of Oxford's undergraduates are in any way similar to those of Warwick's."

I must have registered a look of surprise for he paused, held up his hands in a gesture of silence and said, "Don't worry I've discovered all about you from the Personnel Department. You surely cannot have been so naive as to imagine that there would be no little test; no little something to show what you are made of," he continued. "You passed with flying colours. Picard-Syme was admirably impressed. I thought you might have taken a shot, so to speak, at a guinea fowl but with what confidence you opted for the quadruped rather than the biped – the porcine rather than the avian suffix. That was a demonstration of far greater sang-froid than even I anticipated.

"I told you that I was considering a little task for you; now I am convinced that I have indeed made a highly appropriate selection."

He leant across and patted my knee. "Well done, dear boy – and don't be too hard on me. You would have done the same if you were me."

Despite my irritation at his assumption of superiority, it occurred to me that Collingwood was right. It took time to get to know who you trusted. You gave people little tests to establish how far they would go. That was the way we traders operated; that was how we built up our contacts; that was the way of the world. Then we were ruthless if people let us down.

Realising he had made an impact, he stood up. "Now you must have that drink."

Collingwood strode over to an antique cabinet and poured me a large gin and tonic: the liquor coming from a square blue bottle, the quantity of tonic barely doubling the volume of the drink.

As he handed me the glass he sat himself down on the sofa next to me.

"Now we have cleared the air," he continued rapidly, disconcertingly patting me on the knee, "let me tell you why I asked you to come over this evening. It's time you learnt a bit more."

He launched into a detailed description of the club's finances. Through his contacts Collingwood had quickly amassed the initial membership. Through the contacts of contacts the list had quickly expanded, spreading like a spider's web through Docklands until all £5 million men were enrolled. A few more had joined following subsequent bonus declarations and I would soon discover that although I was the only novitiate at Knightsbridge there would be others at impending events.

In addition to the entrance fee each member paid an annual subscription of £25,000.

"Really quite modest for those who are members of the trading elite. Excellent value for money," Collingwood added.

Then he began to catalogue the numerous outgoings. Hiring of sumptuous venues came at a substantial premium. Besides the £150,000 which had gone to Lichtenstein, a gambling debt at a Monte Carlo casino had also been settled. With these arrangements carefully in place, discreetly out of view of both tabloids and taxman, the desirable property in Knightsbridge had been ours for a day.

"We don't want the paparazzi intruding on our little indulgences do we?" He said rhetorically. "You can imagine the tawdry tabloid headlines timed for the day of the unemployment figures: Knightsbridge Knosh for bankers' bash!"

Somehow he even managed to pronounce the silent K of the contrived alliteration.

Then of course there were the costs of the staff, security and administration. For instance, the substantial club funds were held in a specially designated account at Coutts but naturally such a prestigious bank required a commensurate fee. There was the vintners' bill. Collingwood wondered if I was aware of the cost of Krug, the charge for Chablis?

"In your moment of triumph did you enjoy your generous mouthful of Château d'Yquem? he asked.

"Naturally," I replied with as much insouciance as I could muster.

"Perhaps you have not appreciated that the vintage you imbibed commands a retail price of £750 per bottle."

Then apparently unable to resist he added, "I don't suppose that featured on the curriculum at Warwick University."

But he was not finished. From time to time it was the intention that the assembled company should be entertained by after-dinner speakers. Those invited were not popular stand-up comedians or television stars. No, diners would be introduced to world figures, statesmen, royalty, former leaders of G7 countries. In short the financial elite would, on equal terms, meet the political elite.

Collingwood had done his research. The current going rate for Bill Clinton was $500,000, although he anticipated in due course securing President Bush for somewhat less. However it was rumoured that before long a former British prime minister would aspire to a similar level of fee.

"You can work it all out for yourself, Benjamin," he pronounced conclusively. "The modest subscription to our elite society offers entertainment and reward beyond the reaches of the individual. You are on the threshold of a unique experience."

At this he eased position slightly and patted me firmly on the leg.

"But I was forgetting the most important payment of all. We have to settle up with Ramirez."

As a financial trader I was used to absorbing complex data, but I was beginning to experience information overload. There were several questions demanding an answer and although I wanted to clarify that final remark and in particular his use of the plural, there was a more fundamental query to be satisfied.

Collingwood paused and rose to fill our glasses with more liberal measures of gin and illiberal measures of tonic. Trying to keep a clear head I interrupted his smooth flow.

"Slow down Crispin," I said. "Why?"

"Why what?" he answered.

"Why did you do it? Why did you set up this club? Why go to all of this trouble?"

"I've told you dear boy." He hesitated, handing me the replenished glass, the ice clinking on the rim in a spray of light effervescence. "Ours is a demanding profession. We make the world go round. Without us international trade would grind to a halt. But it takes its toll. You and I, all of us, will be burnt out by the time we are in our late 40s. While we are young and on an upward trajectory like minds should commingle and celebrate their achievements."

"Come off it, Crispin," I responded, unmoved by his easy eloquence. "What's in this for you?"

"My, my, what a cynical comprehensive schoolboy you are," he shot back, although the tone indicated a tease rather than a taunt.

"Very well," he added thoughtfully. "You have rumbled me. Naturally the treasurer who makes all the appropriate arrangements receives a stipend. This is dependent on the surplus which is generated but obviously not less than six figures. Although members undoubtedly receive value for money, the club is what you might colloquially term a nice little earner."

I felt vindicated. My cynicism was not misplaced. Collingwood might exude bonhomie and charm but I had already seen the steel beneath the silk and understood that he was no philanthropist.

"I am sure you receive no more than is appropriate," I said trying to appear unsurprised.

Collingwood shrugged with mock modesty.

"But what I don't understand," I continued, "is why you are telling me all this."

He once again became conspiratorial, replacing his hand more firmly on my knee.

"My dear boy, I like you. I like the way you have demonstrated both skill and daring on the trading floor. I like the way you have consistently risen to the occasion. I have watched you these last few weeks and I have admired what I have seen.

"I know I can trust you – and because I can trust you for the moment what I'm about to say must be kept strictly between ourselves."

Then he announced with a minor flourish, "Wall Street beckons. I am about to be made a director of Grossman Brothers with whom you are doubtless familiar. Of course I'll miss London but I do not intend my sojourn in the Big Apple to be permanent. I'll be back. There is even the possibility that I feature in the succession planning for managing director of Hazzards. Your analytical brain will by now have appreciated that my absence across the pond creates a vacancy for treasurer of the Epicureans. You won't say no will you? It takes someone like you to handle Ramirez. I have made you well aware of the duties. You will write the cheques, consort with class, and have the pleasure of discussing with the delightful Sabrina the terms of the favours we do for her daddy's titled friends who possess premises suitable for one of our little gatherings."

I had wondered what task Collingwood had in mind for me or what errand he wanted me to run. But I had not been expecting this. Absurdly at the same time I felt both immensely flattered and unsure. I was unprepared for this remarkable suggestion. The liberal quantities of gin did not help. I could sense the colour flowing into my cheeks; I was hesitating where normally I was decisive.

"This is your golden opportunity, Ben Turner," Collingwood said benignly, his hand graduating from a pat to a caress. "Remember a skilled treasurer will always generate a margin; a grateful club will always vote a bonus – helpful even though you have a very substantial bank balance. More importantly you will have access to the great and the good. Didn't you notice how Picard-Syme sat next to me, was first to raise a glass to me? If your success is to continue then cultivate your contacts."

Everything Collingwood said was right. The treasurership would offer me access to the elusive inner circle. Doubtless there would be discussions with Picard-Syme, a daily attender in the Hardings boardroom whereas the Hazards boardroom was open to me only at bonus time. Like Collingwood I would know exactly who were the rising stars, who had golden career prospects. I might soon be in a position to award and receive favours.

Furthermore there was an additional source of income. I had been doing my mental arithmetic and even though the picture was incomplete I was confident I could generate a large margin. Of course I did not need the money, but the money was an end in itself, a sign of success. Tantalisingly Collingwood had also mentioned the name of Sabrina.

I seized the initiative. It was too awkward to rise from the sofa, but I swivelled round and shook Collingwood firmly by the hand.

"Your confidence in me is not misplaced, Crispin," I answered. "I will do my best to emulate your success."

"Good man!" he beamed. "I knew I could count on you."

"What happens next?" I asked. "Is there an election?"

"An election!" he exclaimed. "How provincial. No Ben you are in a world of contacts and recommendations now. What happens next is that you will not be on the trading floor tomorrow."

"What do you mean?" I asked, unable to keep the puzzlement from my voice.

"Don't worry, dear boy." His words were soft, his voice an unguent. "Everything is taken care of. You have a bad cold and sadly and uncharacteristically require a day away from work. In reality you will meet me at Coutts in the Strand. Thereafter, there is one simple matter to which your immediate attention is necessary, another equally simple task in which I shall direct you and finally something requiring a little forward thinking."

He was plying me with yet another drink, reaching for a bundle of papers lying unobtrusively on the glass coffee table in front of us.

"Here is the latest statement from the commendable Coutts indicating the current financial health of our little society."

Collingwood now produced a sheet of figures, the bank's famous name printed in refined italics at the head. It showed a balance of several million pounds.

"The first matter is indeed simplicity itself. We will arrange for some sample signatures to be witnessed by our trusty bankers and then you will be treasurer. This accomplished, I will introduce you to Ramirez and we will settle his account. Indeed you will have the opportunity to brandish your newly issued cheque-book."

"Who is this Ramirez?" At last I could voice the question.

"The only person capable of providing last week's delicacy." He answered.

"A butcher?" I asked.

Collingwood roared with laughter. "He would be greatly offended with that appellation. No, Raoul Ramirez has various business interests. Recently he has managed a complex logistical achievement to satisfy our palates and now we must satisfy his account."

"I take it that is your simple task," I responded. "But what needs the forward thinking?"

"The planning for the next event in June," Collingwood said as if stating the obvious. "The venue for Friday's feast could accommodate only half the membership. There is to be a second similar banquet as soon as Ramirez has the supplies. You will have the honour of making the arrangements and ascertaining if another novitiate answers our chairman's question with your panache."

He rose and with his arm around my shoulders steered me towards the door. Despite the effects of the alcohol I looked directly at him and said boldly, "Crispin, be in no doubt that I will carry this off; but tell me, why me, and, more to the point, let me ask you again, what's in it for you?"

"The answer to your first question should be quite obvious from what I have said," he answered in a flattering tone. "You are sharp and streetwise, that's why. You are also shrewd. As I've mentioned, it needs someone like you to handle Ramirez.

"The answer to your second question can be simply stated, but I must preface it with a reminder that for the next few days my transatlantic assignment is confidential. As I have indicated, when in due course, maybe in three years' time, maybe in four years' time, it comes to a conclusion I shall once again take up a position in this city. You, dear boy, will have consorted with those even more powerful and influential. Doubtless you will be here ready, willing and able to welcome back your benefactor, to propel him instantly into the most select gatherings, to assist him to glide effortlessly into the innermost circles and of course if there is a vacancy for president of the Epicureans, to ease him into that exalted position."

I turned to him in the doorway with one further question. "As I will need to make arrangements with Sabrina what are her contact details?"

"All in good time dear boy, all in good time!"

Then he showed me out, past his contemporary works of art, past the white cricketers, past the disarming Tristram and into the lobby.

Silkily he whispered, "Remember 10.30 tomorrow morning at Coutts in the Strand."

4

I arrived early, asking the taxi driver to drop me by St Martin-in-the-Fields in Trafalgar Square. I sauntered into the Strand and approached the entrance to Coutts exactly at 10.30. It would have been unseemly to loiter outside.

Collingwood emerged from a chauffeur driven car, sleek, black and brightly polished, accompanied by someone who I instantly recognised as Picard-Syme.

"There you are, Ben, punctual as I expected." Collingwood was in affable mood. "I'm not sure if you've been introduced to Sebastian Picard-Syme," he added.

Picard-Syme was shorter and slighter than both of us. Although he was a youthful 40 something, his sandy hair was already thinning but his eyes were piercing behind his rimless spectacles. Before I could speak he reached out to shake my hand.

"Pleased to meet you properly – and I'm delighted to accept Crispin's recommendation that you take over the finances of our rather special society. I've heard excellent reports about you. That Chicago deal was quite a coup – and I say that even though Hardings took a hit, although I don't suppose Declan Faulkner will ever forgive you."

"Thank you," I responded unsure whether to call him 'sir', 'Mr Picard-Syme' or 'Sebastian'.

We were ushered inside by a uniformed commissionaire, up an escalator to a small but comfortable meeting room. An attentive young man was already waiting for us with forms duly completed. The first required the signatures of both Picard-Syme and Collingwood; the second of Picard-Syme and myself. In less than a minute I had assumed responsibility for a balance running into several million pounds.

Collingwood returned his cheque-book and immediately I was handed a replacement in an elegant leather case, my name already embossed in the lower right-hand corner.

"It is the convention that only one signature is required to authorise expenditure but our chairman is also a signatory and can accordingly act on our behalf in the event of the indisposition or unavailability of the treasurer," Collingwood announced for my benefit with a nod at the slightly obsequious Coutts official, who then turned again to me.

"I take it that you enjoy the same profession as Mr Collingwood and that your circumstances are similar?" he asked.

When I responded in the affirmative and also to the supplementary questions about salary and bonus, he concluded with a firm handshake and an invitation to open a prestigious account in a personal capacity. More comprehensive services were offered than those were available from my high street bank.

Our business complete, we left him and rode effortlessly down the escalator back to the atrium.

"I expect great things of you, Benjamin," Picard-Syme said smiling at me. "We will speak again well before our June event – and no doubt Crispin will acquaint you with the necessary arrangements. In the meantime here's my card. Feel free to contact me at any time if there's anything I can do for you."

He handed me his business card showing the name 'Harding and Co.' in raised gold print with below that 'Sebastian Picard-Syme, Director' in a deep blue.

"I won't let you down," I said. "I look forward very much to working with you."

The chauffeur was still with his car, pretending to polish the offside wing but actually peering down the busy thoroughfare alert for an approaching traffic warden. With relief he opened the rear door, showed his employer inside and pulled out into the choking traffic.

"That was quite painless," Collingwood announced breezily. "Now we must meet Ramirez. This way dear boy. He is staying at the Savoy."

Deftly he steered me across the Strand through the traffic at a standstill, past the rear of the purring black car, its occupant invisible behind the tinted glass.

"Our society's positive balance is about to be depressed somewhat," he said as we reached the opposite pavement. "I agreed a substantial fee and, within reason, a contribution to overheads."

Then he added conspiratorially, "I've known him since we were both up at Oxford. You need to handle him with care, but it would be difficult to discover an alternative source of supply and he has his uses."

A spring breeze was funnelling down the Strand, flicking discarded newspapers from the gutters, sending fistfuls of dust into the faces of distracted pedestrians, sweeping everything before it, hurrying us past the waiting taxis and round the corner into the embracing inlet of the Savoy Hotel. We took the lift, an opulent art deco construction, up to one of the luxury suites. Collingwood pressed firmly on the bell push and I noticed the briefest flicker at the brass spy hole before the door swung open.

"Crispin! Welcome!" A short rather swarthy man reached out and offered a token embrace to Collingwood trying, but comically failing, to make contact with both cheeks. "Come on in – and bring your assistant too."

We entered a spacious sitting room furnished with comfortable sofas and expensive Indian rugs. The window drapes were drawn back giving a remarkable vista over the Thames. Opposite us, the Festival Hall beamed across the water while the squat sixties brutal concrete of the National Theatre winked from behind Waterloo Bridge as the running lights spelt out the week's productions. A pleasure boat chugged eastwards against the rising tide, the Cockney commentary ('and there in the late 19th century the well known Gilbert and Sullivan staged the Savoy operas') just perceptible through the double glazing.

"Good to see you again, Raoul," Collingwood said with apparent sincerity. "I trust your stay in London has been as congenial as ever."

Then immediately, perceiving the unasked question, he explained my presence.

"I have some news for you. Let me introduce Benjamin Turner. He is not my assistant as you mistakenly termed him, but my replacement. You will have the pleasure of transacting future business with him."

"I'm delighted and charmed to make your acquaintance," Ramirez said expansively, grasping my palm in a handshake so firm as to be almost painful. Even in this first meeting he was seeking to demonstrate who was the superior.

Turning back to Collingwood he asked enigmatically, "What exactly has prompted this desertion of your post – and do you intend to remain faithful to our agreement?"

"In answer to your first question, I assure you it is with extreme regret that I relinquish my treasurership," Collingwood replied, "but I'm shortly off to pastures new. Keep this discreet for a few more days. I am about to depart for a directorship with Grossman Brothers in New York. Instead I'm sure you will find it a pleasure to do business with Ben."

"And the answer to my second question?" Ramirez asked.

But further discussion was suddenly curtailed by a short ring from the doorbell. "Come in!" shouted Ramirez with unnecessary impatience. Inviting us to sit on the sofas and chairs framing a coffee table he explained, "I've ordered us a little refreshment."

A white-gloved waiter produced a small cloth and placed it over the table. He swiftly set out elegant china cups, saucers, a pot of steaming coffee and a plate of miniature croissants lightly dusted with icing sugar.

There was an awkward pause during this brief operation giving me a few moments in which to study Ramirez. He was of indeterminate background, about 40, with brown skin, his face slightly pockmarked. He wore expensive gold-rimmed spectacles and a thick black moustache neatly trimmed so that it did not encroach on his chin in the Mexican fashion. When he spoke he revealed perfectly white teeth except for a slight flash of gold in one corner of his mouth.

You could see at a glance that he did not come from Britain. It was his clothes rather than his colour or physiognomy which gave the game away. He wore a light coloured suit, well cut and of good quality but with wide lapels and gaudy buttons of the sort which would never be touched by a Jermyn Street tailor. His pink shirt collar was buttoned down, but I noticed that he wore cufflinks, each studded with a small diamond. On his feet were expensive shoes, brown brogues but made of thick suede. His tie had stripes in deep mauves and reds rather like one worn by Quentin Foorde. His nationality was not obvious. He could as well have been from Italy or Spain as from Brazil or Nicaragua.

As the waiter slipped away unobtrusively, the door closing with a barely perceptible click, Ramirez beamed at me. "I trust you enjoyed the unusual delicacy you experienced a few evenings ago?"

"Naturally," I responded. "Truly remarkable; I've never tasted anything like it."

"Your delivery fully lived up to expectations," interrupted Collingwood. "I think I might safely add that our little feast was a triumphal success. Of course we left his Lordship's excellent establishment in perfect condition. We are well past our Bullingdon days."

"I expected no less." Ramirez spoke with an impeccable accent. "I take it that you gentlemen of high finance are not bedevilled by squeamishness or sentimentality. You tasted a product of the highest quality. You may not be aware, but I took the precaution of ensuring a delivery timed to the minute. I also personally supervised and instructed those excellent chefs from your most efficient catering company. However I thought it appropriate to keep the nature of the delicacy discreet. No doubt they are still under the impression that the tender morsels were simply fillets of the finest European veal."

He gave a deep, rather ugly chuckle and rocked slightly on the deep leather sofa.

"But now I must present my account. Considerable expenses have accrued since our discussion – when was it?"

The question was rhetorical for he continued with hardly a pause.

"Ah, yes of course – it must have been 6 months ago – the Ambassador's reception in Lima. Such a fine building and Miraflores is such a salubrious suburb. How fortunate I should be there when you needed my services. Just as it was fortunate I was there to assist you that day when you had that problem with that boy in the punt ..."

51

Collingwood cut him short. "Now Raoul let's not stray from the point. We in the Epicureans accept that you have indeed risen to a difficult challenge. We await your account."

Ramirez leant back, smiled as he patted his hands together and commenced a long description. Throughout his narrative he spoke urbanely as if he had merely experienced a troublesome journey. He grinned when he described difficulties and negotiations, the little glimpse of gold becoming more frequent as he stressed the lengths to which he gone to provide such a rare commodity.

He reminded Collingwood that their agreement had been for a fee of £250,000 for himself together with £100,000 to cover the costs of transportation. Additionally there had been a gentleman's agreement that additional unforeseen expenses would be reimbursed within reason should they arise. Such expenses had indeed arisen.

For my benefit Ramirez explained his business operations. He was, as he termed it, involved in 'import and export'. His activities were confined to the southern American continent where sometimes it was convenient for goods to pass across land borders with the minimum of fuss. To facilitate easy commerce he had established a number of warehouses, not only in urban centres such as Rio and Lima, but also in towns or cities near borders. If I travelled extensively I might not distinguish between the ubiquitous corrugated iron constructions in industrial areas. I would certainly not appreciate that these anonymous buildings in places as diverse as La Paz, Montevideo, Iquitos and Puno were all under the same ownership. Ramirez Enterprises SA contributed significantly to the economy of several developing countries.

However, his commodities were never highly perishable. He might handle textiles or hardware, sometimes liquor or unspecified vegetable products. Never had he traded in something destined for a dinner party. Accordingly Crispin had presented him with a challenge; a challenge made even greater as the destination of the goods was not Lima or La Paz but London.

Ramirez paused to savour the impact, having enjoyed the alliterative crescendo.

The easiest part of the task had been to locate a source for the raw material. There were numerous restaurants in Lima and indeed, the very day after the ambassador's reception, Ramirez had made enquiries from compliant waiters as to the location of the establishments whose refrigerated vans daily delivered numerous bundles of grey meat. There was no difficulty in placing a significant forward order with the most reliable of these. Indeed he was able to select the plumpest animals and request that they be set to work immediately, breeding prolifically to produce similarly rotund offspring, succulent for sophisticated western taste buds. Fortunately the encounter with Collingwood had occurred at exactly the right time. The creatures have a gestation period of some two months and then require another two months to develop to full culinary potential. It transpired that even while I was being enticed into club membership by Collingwood, the knives were being sharpened to silence the wheeks and rumblings of this infant menagerie.

During the fattening process Ramirez had studied the rules concerning the importation of goods for human consumption. He now curled his lips, the clipped moustache emphasising his snarl.

"Your stultifying regulations are decidedly inimical to innovation," he scowled. "You require an approved country; an approved supplier; health certificates; a veterinary inspection before importation. Why this should be so when the good people of Lima consume this delicacy on a daily basis, baffles me!"

Once he had acquainted himself with the full extent of the draconian requirements he feared that this enterprise would fall at the last hurdle. What a disaster would be visited upon his reputation for reliability and what a disappointment would be visited upon the salivating taste buds of the Epicureans if his cargo were condemned at the quayside by prying officials. Accordingly he had concluded that the voyage should be clandestine.

It had been necessary for Ramirez to exploit his cunning and his contacts. It was fortunate that to the north of Lima the Pan-American Highway sped past the fashionable resort of Ancón. He knew a number of wealthy businessmen who owned yachts secured alongside the bobbing moorings of prestigious clubs. He had sought out a scheming skipper, eager to earn a few thousand dollars by accepting a covert commission to transport a perishable delicacy. Most luxury ocean going vessels had a convenient area suitable for transporting a reasonably sized refrigerated container. Once loaded, the craft would slip quietly away setting a course northwards through the Panama Canal then eastwards. It might glide unobtrusively into the harbour at one of the quieter Caribbean islands for supplies and then head into the spring squalls of the Atlantic.

As he planned the route it had occurred to him that it might be unwise for a vessel registered in South America to berth, buffeted and bruised, in one of the charming havens of southern England. It would be preferable if all an observant coastguard or inquisitive fishermen spotted was a vessel slipping out on a short voyage – 'having a spin, as you might put it' – and returning unobtrusively a few days later.

Consequently Ramirez had taken a trip to England. "But I never knew," said Collingwood, his brow knotting momentarily. "Why did you not come to see me?"

"Come, now," Ramirez shrugged his shoulders. "Must I tell you my every movement?"

Once more there was the flash of precious metal before he paused, poured himself another cup of coffee and continued with his narrative.

Crispin would recall a certain young man, an acquaintance at Oxford, prominent in the Conservative Association, who was now a successful tax barrister in London. He might also recall that their fellow undergraduate had been brought up on the Isle of Wight. The purpose of the flying visit was to entice him from his chambers to discuss the potential not of a brief but of a charter.

High-flying lawyers enjoy being entertained and a business lunch at Le Gavroche was one of the unforeseen items of expenditure. There was, however, an appreciable return. As Ramirez had anticipated the still airs of the Royal Courts of Justice created an added desire for the smack of the Solent sea breezes. His lawyer friend retained his love of sailing and of course owned a sizeable yacht named 'Son of Ramsay'. ("Curious names you English choose," mused Ramirez. "But perhaps it means something to him.") For much of the year the vessel remained moored at Yarmouth. It was not chartered out but simply kept pristine, its crew assembled solely for Cowes week.

I listened enthralled. As Ramirez rubbed his hands a scornful tone came into his voice. The barrister's attitude to a casual hire had changed remarkably when Ramirez had opened his elegant pigskin briefcase in the Upper Brook Street restaurant. Had the waiters been observing closely they would have seen that the two men took separate taxis out of Mayfair. But whereas the barrister had arrived clutching only a brolly he had left with a briefcase. If we had been alongside him in his cab we would have seen him flick the locks and glance inside for confirmation that it did indeed contain not a pink ribboned brief but £75,000 in crisp £50 notes.

That too was part of the account. A slightly larger sum was now necessary as only a fortnight earlier the yacht had completed its little task. Sadly it had encountered some particularly heavy seas south off the Isles of Scilly and had suffered a little damage. It was nothing too drastic but the vessel had to be restored to its former condition, the broken mast properly replaced and repainted. Unfortunately boatyards were not cheap.

To complete the picture Ramirez explained that a rendezvous had been made at the Cape Verde Islands. The yacht from Yarmouth found itself berthed for the night alongside another from Ancón. It was then a simple task to transfer cargo and commence the two homeward voyages.

The final piece of transportation was the easiest. Hiring a white van and a driver posed no problems. The mooring for 'Son of Ramsay' was adjacent to the little ferry terminal at Yarmouth. On the appointed day the courier from London, ignorant of who had commissioned him and what he was to carry, simply drove down to Lymington, rolled inconspicuously on to the island ferry, collected a container from the Yarmouth wharf side and delivered the goods to the rear entrance of the address in Knightsbridge.

"So there you have it." Ramirez smiled with self-satisfaction. "All the arrangements executed; your exotic consignment delivered; all as you say tickety-boo. Crispin proposes; Raoul disposes. But I am sure you will understand gentleman that it has been necessary for Raoul to dispense to dispose."

As he spoke Ramirez reached forward and placing his soft round mouth with the hint of gold over the last remaining mini croissant, devoured it whole, lightly brushing the icing sugar from his fingers.

We were waiting for him to come to the point, to make his demands on the substantial funds of the Epicureans. But still he hesitated. Outside the riverboat was returning ('… and I hope you will show your appreciation in the usual way for the commentary this morning …'), the lunchtime crowds beginning to assemble in front of the Festival Hall.

Then he stood up. He could not have been above 1.7 metres but as Collingwood and I were still seated in the low leather furniture he created a commanding dramatic moment. He looked down on us, his eyes cold behind his elegant spectacles.

"Now Gentlemen," he proclaimed. "My account is £600,000."

Collingwood stood up instinctively; I followed.

"Sit down please my dear friends. I see you are somewhat taken aback but I'm sure you can appreciate from the narrative with which I have just entertained you that this has been an adventure not without appreciable expense."

Collingwood replied quite sharply, "Now look here Raoul. We agreed on £350,000. Of course I accept that as this was your first engagement for the Epicureans and as there were some unknowns I had to give you a free hand, but this is a bit steep!"

I wondered if for the first time I might see him lose composure. Had he been on the cricket pitch he might have executed an intemperate hook rather than a prudent swerve.

"Crispin, Crispin – and of course Benjamin," Ramirez interrupted, gesturing in my direction. "Be assured that I seek only reasonable recompense. You have to understand that even for an entrepreneur of my skills and experience this has been a novel task. The initial price was never more than an assurance of a suitable reward. You did not wish your March event to be a failure – and I am sure that you anticipate an equal success in June. Do you not agree that the arrangements were the epitome of discretion? Indeed I have strained my financial resources to cater for your requirements."

Collingwood was silent for a moment then, recovering himself, simply played the dead bat. He nodded at me. "Yes indeed. I gave Raoul the authorisation to do whatever was necessary. We have to accept that exotica demands a premium. We will indeed honour our obligations."

Reaching inside his jacket pocket, Ramirez passed me a stiff folded sheet. Opening it, I glanced down at his handwritten instructions carefully set out in list form on the Savoy correspondence paper. Firstly he required a settlement of his substantial room account at the Savoy and the payment to a firm of couriers for transporting goods from the Isle of Wight to London.

He motioned to the desk.

"If you can kindly prepare the cheques now I can have them promptly dispatched," he said, handing me a pen.

This seemed a strange approach. I had anticipated simply settling his fee then commencing a discussion about the June event. Sensing my puzzlement he offered an explanation. "I am afraid that I am experiencing a severe cash flow problem. Some matters require urgent settlement and were I to deposit funds in an account rather excessively in the red, I could not be certain that my facilities would be continued to the extent that I would be able to draw upon them."

I opened the stiff leather cover of the long oblong book and for the first time completed one of the elegant cheques. Several more were required including a sizeable payment to a travel agency.

Thereafter the demands were more substantial, the arrangements more complex. He required a cheque for £100,000 in the name of Elizabeth Goldstein.

I looked up and despite a signal from Collingwood attempting to silence me, said directly, "Naturally I respect your instructions, but may I ask who is Elizabeth Goldstein?"

"You may," smiled Ramirez. "However, I thought that all good English boys looked after their mothers. I like to assist her maintain a quality lifestyle. You will find that as she is a resident of Jersey there is no problem with a sterling cheque. I trust you look after your mother."

I tried to conceal the pain of this remark and continued writing.

Then there were two transfers of funds, one to Ramirez Enterprises SA in a Rio de Janeiro bank and a second to an account in the name of R. Ramirez International, New York. As these would necessitate arrangements through Coutts I promised to attend to them that afternoon.

I was at the end of the list. Rapidly calculating the total of the transfers and the several cheques I realised that I had parted with £350,000. I looked up.

"Was it £600,000 which was agreed?" I ventured.

"Yes indeed. I see that you have a quick mathematical brain." There was a heavy hint of mockery behind the gold-rimmed spectacles and the briefest matching flash from the corner of Ramirez's mouth.

"As for the balance, Crispin will confirm that our agreement was settlement by any means and in any appropriate currency. I require the final £250,000 in American dollars, to be delivered to me in Peru – and in cash."

5

There was a moment's silence.

This was something I had definitely not anticipated. In the brief time since my sudden and unexpected elevation to the treasurership my thoughts had been on arranging venues, selecting wines, engaging caterers and of course contacting Sabrina and establishing both a professional and personal relationship. Carrying cash overseas was simply not on my agenda.

Collingwood spoke first.

"Yes of course. My agreement with Raoul was full settlement in any suitable currency," he explained for my benefit.

"I'm sure it will be possible to obtain that amount of US dollars before the banks close this afternoon," I added. "Then there will be no need for a delivery in Peru."

"Were it so is simple!" Ramirez was shrugging his shoulders again. "I have already alluded to my cash flow difficulties. Alas I also have a large number of local accounts that urgently require settlement and for which only the greenback will suffice. As I have experienced more than one unpleasant encounter with customs officials at Lima, it is far preferable for the delivery to be made by you. Besides I wish to acquaint you with the more sophisticated arrangements I have prepared for the June consignment. Your business trip will be an ideal opportunity for us to enter into an amicable negotiation. After all Crispin had been intending to travel south hadn't you?"

I looked at Collingwood quizzically.

"It was indeed a possibility," he explained, "but nothing definite had been arranged and of course now that the Big Apple calls it is out of the question. It appears that one of your early duties is to be an interesting business trip."

Perhaps I should have realised that the quest for the exotic might take me overseas. Faced with the sudden inevitability of a journey I paused for a moment's consideration of the practicalities. It was normally about this time of year that I would embark on one of my Indian Ocean jaunts. But I had nothing in prospect, having been unceremoniously dumped by my intended companion the previous December necessitating a rather sober Christmas with Pam, plagued by morning sickness, and the ever-attentive Gary. Having never visited that part of the world, I was not unattracted by the notion of a trip to Peru despite its unexpected intrusion into my routine.

"Of course I will make all the arrangements," Ramirez said, "or at least I'll issue instructions to my travel agents. There are one or two things I need to check first but I'll expect you in about three weeks' time?"

"First I need to book some holiday time," I countered, reluctant to give the impression that I was jumping at his command. "But assuming that is no problem I will be delighted to join you – although I would prefer to be regarded as a business client rather than a mere courier."

"Excellent, excellent." Ramirez was beaming once more. "Here write down your email address and I'll contact you again very shortly.

"Now gentlemen if you will excuse me. I have some final packing and of course some errands to attend to before I fly out this evening."

At that he waved the little bundle of cheques knowingly and gestured to the door.

"By the way, Crispin." He spoke almost confidentially just as we were leaving. "You did not answer my second question. Do you intend to remain faithful to our agreement?"

"Of course," was the terse reply as we walked to the lift.

Emerging into the early spring sunshine I had numerous questions for Collingwood. Before I could speak I was distracted by the sound of a ringtone, an insistent tinny version of 'Toreador' from 'Carmen'. It was coming from Collingwood's jacket.

"Hello Charles," he answered. "I see. I'm sorry to hear that." He was now more urgent. "When am I required? Of course, right away!"

Then he turned to me. "Now you can see why I needed someone of your capabilities to handle our friend. But as you can tell I am required urgently. I have to leave you."

The usual two or three taxis stood waiting outside the hotel. He strode to the first and opened the door.

"Just a moment; what's going on?" I demanded. "What agreement have you reached – and where exactly is he taking me?"

The taxi driver was switching off his light, setting the meter and turning for instructions. Collingwood paused.

"It was unnecessary for that to be mentioned," he muttered. Then he added reflectively, "One consequence of that call is that it is necessary to hasten your induction. Come to the Penthouse on Friday evening – about 9 p.m."

He clambered into the cab, calling, "Canada Square" to the driver. He was pressing a button on his phone, already commencing another call, as the vehicle eased out into the Strand, leaving me bewildered before the Savoy.

I hesitated. The morning had certainly not proceeded as I had anticipated. I required a few moments alone, a respite from Ramirez before I executed the remaining financial transactions.

I turned left, weaving my way through the lunchtime office workers scurrying to pub or sandwich shop. Small knots of tourists were emerging from the steps of Charing Cross underground station, cameras poised for a long shot of Nelson's column. Dodging them, I walked on past Trafalgar Square then on impulse entered Waterstones on the corner and made for the Geography section. Finding a large atlas I spread open the South American and Atlantic pages, located Lima in Peru and thoughtfully traced the route that my Friday dinner had travelled.

Feeling a little clearer about my impending journey I stepped out and turned into Whitehall. I decided on a brisk walk to the South Bank for lunch. Then I would return to Coutts and arrange a dollar transfer.

I continued past the Cenotaph and the heavy metal gates to Downing Street. On the corner of Parliament Square I turned and passed Portcullis House noticing the familiar faces of a couple of MPs, one a former cabinet minister, before leaving the shaded streets to be engulfed in a warm flood of sunlight on Westminster Bridge. I turned to look back down river towards the Savoy, imagining Ramirez clicking his fingers as the porters wheeled his luggage down to reception.

While I was lost in this reverie I felt a sharp tap on my shoulders. Suddenly fearful of plunging into the Thames I tensed, locking my legs rigid against the low parapet.

"Relax, relax!" A familiar voice implored in mocking tones behind me. I turned to see the grinning face of Justin Rhodes.

"Don't do it, don't do it!" he cried with exaggerated horror.

"Hello, Justin," I answered, relieved that I was not about to be mugged. "What are you doing here? Why aren't you on the floor today?"

"I could say the same to you," he responded. "Don't tell me you have come over all Wordsworthian – you know 'Earth has not anything to show more fair.'"

"Collingwood had a little task for me in connection with our event the other day," I said, somehow feeling it necessary to justify my absence.

"You, me and Collingwood all off sick. Anyone would think that Hazzards is unhealthy!" he chortled. "Going back to Waterloo? Come with me and I'll tell you what I've been up to. Funnily enough in a way it also concerns Friday's feast. You're not in a hurry are you?"

"No, I've got all day," I answered, unwisely.

We continued over the bridge, turning left in front of the old County Hall, the enormous wheel of the London Eye suddenly towering above us.

"Look I'm in no rush either." Justin was all affability. "It's quite quiet. Let's get tickets for the Eye and then we can sit in privacy, admire the view and you can tell me if you approve of my latest purchase."

"No thanks, Justin," I said instinctively.

He stopped and stared at me. "You're chicken!" he mocked.

"Of course I'm not," I snapped back.

"Come on then. We're sure to have a gondola to ourselves." He was already striding towards the ticket office.

I looked up at the monstrous construction moving slowly, groups of tiny people suspended in glassy pods impossibly high above the

Thames. It was an attraction which I would normally spurn. My amusements were necessarily terrestrial rather than aerial. But I was desperate to do nothing to diminish my standing within this new circle of colleagues. I was acquiring a reputation, becoming accepted. Against my better judgement I acquiesced and allowed Justin to purchase tickets.

We walked up the shallow ramp and stepped inside what appeared to be a solid bubble. Light poured in from all sides and I noticed with alarm that I could look down to the ground below, already slipping away from us. Justin was reaching inside his jacket pocket, withdrawing a tightly wrapped parcel the size of a spectacles case.

"What do you think of that?" he asked. Focusing on the stiff cream wrapping paper rather than the crawling brown Thames, I eased open the package until a slim container of fine leather appeared, the name 'Asprey' inscribed upon it in simple dignity.

I hesitated but Justin was insistent. "Go on, open it."

The elegant gold catches yielded to reveal a necklace nestling on a bed of satin. The chain was pure white gold but suspended from it in a broad band like a thick halter were four lines of exquisitely shaped diamonds. At their apex was a single large translucent pearl. This in turn was surrounded by a circle of more tiny diamonds, glinting vivaciously in the flood of luminosity.

"Don't you think Melissa will adore that?" Justin asked withdrawing the diadem from my hands.

"I should think so," I said hesitantly. "But I'm not the one to ask."

"Of course not. You're not married are you? No need for you to justify a night out!" he said with a note of bitterness in his voice. "That cost £300,000. A small price to pay to enjoy our little indulgences without my wife complaining."

By now the wheel had risen well above the ground. I was becoming uncomfortable, anxious; I could feel the beads of sweat gathering on my forehead. Justin leapt up. "Look we are above Nelson's Column!" he shouted pressing his face against the glass.

He appeared to be too busy pinpointing landmarks to notice that I remained anchored to the bench in the centre of the exposed pod. I closed my eyes tightly. If I tried to concentrate, to pretend I was somewhere else, to rehearse the tasks required of me, I might retain some dignity.

Running through the bank transfers and international currency requirements was indeed a distraction. I was able temporarily to blot out the inane commentary from my unwanted companion, to insulate myself in darkness until I heard Justin urging me with boyish delight to view the roof of Waterloo Station.

"It's like a load of silver fish all packed together," he exclaimed.

But I did not move my eyelids one millimetre until the soft jolt indicated that our circle was complete.

When we alighted I made an excuse about wanting to see the exhibition in the Hayward Gallery.

"That's two things I've found out about you," Justin said sneeringly. "You don't like heights – I saw your eyes were shut when I looked around – and you are an arty type!"

We parted company outside the Festival Hall. He disappeared towards Waterloo Station while I slipped into one of the cafés for a strong coffee and a sandwich.

Suitably revived, I returned to Coutts. It would not have taken me long to walk. Normally I would have enjoyed a stroll over Waterloo Bridge and back down the Strand. But instead I hailed a black cab. If the driver was disappointed at the short fare I assuaged him with a disproportionate tip. He was gratifyingly amazed to receive £20 for less than a mile.

There is certain deference when you arrive at your bank by taxi. It shows in the way the door is held open for you, in the way you are invited to 'Step this way please sir'.

It was a different young man I saw that afternoon to assist with foreign exchange. Nothing was too much trouble. The dollar transfer to New York was a matter of routine. Transfers to Brazilian banks were less frequent but given the correct international sort code and details of the ultimate recipient my wishes would be complied with directly.

This completed, I surprised the assistant with a request to open a personal account. There was more form filling, more solicitous attention as I arranged for £3million, the whole of my bonus after tax, to be transferred to this prestigious institution. The obliging employees even telephoned for a taxi once our business was complete.

But I had the taxi take me only to Waterloo and then took the Jubilee line back to Canary Wharf.

I took it again two evenings later. Collingwood not having appeared in Hazzards all day on Thursday or Friday, I was eager to keep our appointment; eager to be brought up to speed; eager to obtain Sabrina's contact details.

I like the Jubilee line. Its carriages are shiny and futuristic. I like the stations with the protective glass doors along the edge of the platforms where the trains glide to a halt with a satisfying sigh exactly at the designated spot. I like the anonymity. I could crouch in a corner rapt in thought, mulling over what I needed to know, certain that no one would speak to me or make eye contact. Above all I was free of a cockney cabby's banter.

Once again the uniformed security guard gave me access and I took the lift up to the penthouse. Inside was a state of disarray. Collingwood was casually, almost sloppily dressed, his sitting room strewn with papers. His bedroom door was open permitting me to glimpse clothes and suitcases.

"Fear not dear boy," he said with a sweeping gesture. "Rome has not been sacked.   .

"My Savoy summons was to an appointment with the president of Grossman Brothers who happens to be in town. It seems the vacancy in New York has come sooner than anticipated. The director who I am to replace has for some time been suffering from a serious heart complaint. His condition has deteriorated; his immediate resignation has been accepted. His misfortune is my good fortune. My appointment has been brought forward and I am to take up duty forthwith. I fly out mid morning on Tuesday."

"Does anyone on the trading floor know?" I asked, wondering if anything else had been kept from me.

"There will be an announcement on Monday. For some time Foorde, Forsyth and Rhodes – they sound tediously like a firm of provincial solicitors, don't they – have been handling my business. The transition should be seamless.

"But all of this packing is so tiresome. I shall keep this place of course but I cannot appear naked in the Big Apple and I shall want some books, photographs and even the odd picture or two in my Manhattan apartment. The removal company minions arrive tomorrow with bubble wrap and my precious possessions will become air freight."

"I see," I answered. "I take it this is the handover meeting."

"I am sure you are a quick learner," Collingwood responded. "Move those papers, take a seat and I shall guide you – in Latin if would prefer it – through the comparatively straightforward process."

I pushed a few books to one side of the sofa and sat down. He handed me a large folder bearing the title, 'The Honourable Crispin Collingwood'.

Noticing my momentary surprise he said nonchalantly, "It was useful to be so styled at Oxford, but in these egalitarian times modesty is preferable."

He told me that everything I needed to know was in the treasurer's folder. There were details of vintners; contact numbers for caterers; leaflets from companies offering security services.

Then smiling disarmingly, he added, "I have not forgotten. You will find Sabrina's details among the other papers. But remember she is simply one of a number of contacts. Pleasant as the delights of Knightsbridge might be we sometimes have enjoyable events in more bucolic surroundings. There is one particular venue a mere 100 miles from London where our soirées require an overnight stay. Indeed if you exploit your contacts I'm sure you will locate other equally discreet and sumptuous residences. Yes dear boy, the possibilities are endless. I shall envy you from my New York eyrie."

He continued with details of financial arrangements. The initial membership fee was non-refundable. Thus once a £5 million man had joined the Epicureans he had an incentive to remain a member. Additionally it was necessary to draw on these fees to finance the more lavish occasions although of course the interest they earned contributed to the treasurer's stipend.

"That was a strange negotiation with Ramirez," I interjected when he paused. "Why did you authorise me to give way to his demands?"

"I had to agree a substantial fee to secure his services," Collingwood replied. "Such was the timescale that it was impossible to explore all of the logistics beforehand and therefore a margin for unforeseen expenses was not unreasonable."

"But we paid a heavy price," I observed.

"Not at all dear boy," Collingwood answered dismissively. "Ramirez was remarkably cheap. Our previous feast included shark's fin soup imported in even more clandestine fashion through a Tokyo acquaintance. This was followed by the finest kobe beef. Are you aware that exports of this rarity from Japan are officially forbidden? But if you know the right people and pay the right price you can sample a meal fit for a Mikado. Settlement of Raoul's account was trifling compared with the yen transfers I executed on that occasion."

"Who is Ramirez anyway," I continued, "and does he really have a mother by the name of Elizabeth Goldstein?"

Collingwood sighed a little impatiently.

"Let me bring you a drink. Lubrication assists understanding."

He moved to the sideboard returning with an opened bottle of rich yellow wine.

"My choicest collection will of course remain in storage during my absence, but I decided this was one to be consumed. Not the best vintage," he added turning the label in my direction.

I read the year 2002 above the elegantly scrolled name Château Climens.

He sat opposite me and raised his glass. "Here's to us. May we both have success in all our ventures."

Then leaning back he continued his narrative.

"I first met Raoul Ramirez when we were undergraduates at Oxford. It does not concern you how or when; you just need to know that he rapidly emerged as someone who was extremely useful. In case you are wondering he never took a degree. He was asked to leave after a certain incident. If you really want to upset him use the appellation 'rusticated Ramirez'. He does indeed operate commercial enterprises in both Brazil and Peru and possibly elsewhere in southern America. Consequently he was the obvious choice when our tastes progressed from oriental to Latin American.

"I know little of his parentage but am aware that he attended school in this country. He did call himself Goldstein briefly but then reverted to Ramirez. No doubt he liked the cachet of the initials RR."

"What does he want me to see and what did you agree about the next delivery?" I demanded.

"One question at a time dear boy, please. In response to your first my answer is that I'm not entirely sure. Possibly he wishes to demonstrate exactly how he intends to supply the June consignment – and by the way, you will see in the folder that there are contact details concerning a substantial dwelling overlooking Hampstead Heath which may well be suitable for that occasion. Secondly you do need to agree terms. Now that we are well apprised of the logistics I suggest a fixed price so that we transfer any risk from the Epicureans on to Ramirez."

He took another deep sip from his glass encouraging me to do likewise. Even though it was not the best vintage the wine was smooth, sweet and very satisfying to the palate.

"Now dear boy if you will excuse me. 'So little done – so much to do' if I may quote Cecil Rhodes although I refer to my departure not my demise." Collingwood rose indicating that the induction was complete.

But there was something else I wanted to know. There was a question I was saving for the right moment. I had to ask it now or remain silent.

"Crispin," I said decisively. "What exactly is the private arrangement you have made with Ramirez?"

Collingwood flapped his arms in dismissal. "Nothing to trouble you dear boy, nothing at all."

But I was insistent. "It was obviously important to Ramirez," I observed and then, recalling a distant politics lesson, added, "I have no desire to go naked into the conference chamber, if I may quote Bevan."

"You may not quote that socialist rabble-rouser in this household!" he retorted. Then, more conciliatory, he explained, "In the strictest confidence I will tell you that Raoul is registering a new société anonym in Cusco, Peru. I have agreed to subscribe $1 million share capital. That is all. It need not concern you or the Epicureans."

With that he gestured to the entrance, showing me past the blank spaces on the walls devoid of artwork, deserted by trembling Tristram, and ushered me swiftly to the door.

Normally I slept well on a Saturday morning, lingering in my bed until past 10 a.m. But the next day I was awakened when the telephone rang just before 7 o'clock. Sleepily I lifted the handset to hear the excited voice of my brother-in-law, Gary.

"Ben. I hope I'm not too early. But I couldn't wait any longer! You have just become an uncle!"

This shocked me into wakefulness. The baby was not due for another three weeks.

There followed a hurried excitable description of the events over the last twelve hours. While I had been in Collingwood's penthouse Pam had been at home feeling more uncomfortable than usual. Then Gary explained, with rather too much detail, her waters had broken. Contractions having started, they had rushed to the hospital in Winchester and just after 4 a.m., the baby – a little girl – had been born. Pam was fine and was being discharged later that day. The baby was being kept in hospital for a few days until she put on some weight and the doctors were confident that she could go home safely.

"Come and see us tomorrow if you can." He was earnest in his invitation. "We would love it – the three of us!"

Having no other plans for the weekend I took the Porsche for one of its rare outings. In a few places I managed well over 100 mph on the M3, slowing down south of Basingstoke in anticipation of police patrols. The sun was bright, rapidly thawing a late frost, as I drew up behind the humble blue van displaying on its side 'Gary Brown Electrical Contractor – no job too small', parked outside the little house on the estate in Eastleigh.

Pam appeared rather tired, but ecstatically happy. She was glad to see me, not because we were particularly close but because I was her nearest family relative and she did not wish to be monopolised by Gary's parents.

Fortunately I had remembered to stop at one of the motorway service stations and purchase the largest bouquet on display. My offering was just as respectable as the blooms from her in-laws crowding the windowsill of the tiny sitting room.

Before lunch, a rather hurried affair spirited up by Gary out of supermarket packets, Pam became slightly wistful. Our mother and father would have been in their late 50s had they not come to my graduation. They would have enjoyed being grandparents. Instead Pam had a simple request for me. They were naming my niece Hazel and would be delighted if I would be godfather.

I could not refuse, but this new responsibility was more unexpected than the treasurership of the Epicureans. Unsure of what the duties involved I said, "Of course – and you must tell me how I can contribute to her trust fund."

They had already decided to hold the baptism ceremony on a Sunday morning in mid May at the country church a few miles away in the village where Gary's parents lived. There they had been married and there they would christen the next generation.

My visit was not lengthy. By early afternoon Pam was anxious to return to the hospital. She explained that just for the moment I could not be admitted and therefore I could not see or indeed hold my goddaughter until my next visit. I tried to ignore her hurried conversation with Gary about dampness and breast pads. The world of infancy was unknown territory and I preferred to keep it that way.

As there was plenty of time and I was in no hurry to return to my flat I took up their suggestion that I took a deviation past the church. I had forgotten how idyllic was its situation. Unusually it was sited on a quiet lane a small distance from the village. It was ancient, the stone mellowed, the doorway framed by a slightly weathered but remarkably symmetrical Norman carving.

Next to the church was a large field occupied by two alpaca, curious creatures like outsize soft toys. I drew up and lingered by the gate as their heads nodded at me, bobbing above their long necks.

Then I saw that the adjacent plot was occupied by a black and white thatched cottage. There appeared to be no one at home and the garden required some attention although in one corner there was a cluster of bright yellow daffodils. Its charm, its seclusion and its outlook over pasture and church combined to create a property unique and desirable, despite the prosaic name on its gate – Field Cottage.

I was back again on the trading floor fairly early on Monday morning. Things were quiet. During a prolonged lull an e-mail flashed announcing Collingwood's departure. Passing me on the way back from the Gents, Justin Rhodes nodded towards the empty desk and muttered, "Lucky bugger. We all have our contacts but his are gold plated!"

Very little business was transacted that morning. The far eastern markets closed in negative territory and there seemed little prospect of much activity when the American markets opened. Quentin Foorde was complaining of boredom and even had his feet up on his desk. I struck a few routine deals but nothing out of the ordinary.

On Tuesday there was panic. Share prices had fallen in Tokyo and there were rumours of an impending banking collapse in America. Minutes after arriving at work, adventurously, I seized the initiative to purchase in the Far East. I was in the middle of an opportunistic trade when my computer e-mail screen flashed with an unfamiliar sender's name. Glancing down I saw the message was from Ramirez Enterprises SA I was intrigued but it was a full hour before I had time to open it.

When I did I saw that it was addressed both to myself and Collingwood. It read: *1. Benjamin. You will receive your itinerary from my travel agents. Inca Enterprises will meet you in Cusco. 2. Crispin. Our company is shortly to be incorporated. It will be most convenient if your share subscription can come with Benjamin. Cash please. Regards, Raoul.*

But of course Collingwood could not receive it. He was already deleted from the system.

6

Before I had a chance to respond the telephone rang and I embarked on a lengthy, tetchy negotiation with an exhausted contact in Hong Kong. But it was worthwhile. Within half an hour Hazzards held a stake in the expanding oriental leisure industry and a useful put option should we modify our strategy.

I hardly noticed the envelope which appeared on my desk during this burst of activity before the eastern markets finally subsided into silence. Opening it during a lull I found inside a compliments slip with a brief itinerary and e ticket numbers. I was to leave London early on the morning of 19 April flying with Iberian Airways to Madrid and onwards to Lima where I was booked for two nights in the Gran Hotel Bolivar. On 21 April I was to fly to Cusco. Thereafter the only other entry was a return flight to Madrid on the evening of 24 April and onwards to London the next day.

Hastily I typed a reply to the e-mail from Ramirez, indicating that I had received the travel details but would be unable to act as courier for Collingwood. Within a few minutes of pressing 'Send' an out of office reply appeared: *Raoul Ramirez is travelling on business and will not receive your message until his return in 3 weeks' time. If a response is required he will attend to it as soon as possible thereafter.*

This troubled me. I could envisage a poor start to our business relationship if I arrived without the investment he had requested. On the other hand Collingwood could and should sort out his private arrangements for himself. I needed to speak to him urgently before he changed time zones and immersed himself in his New York duties. Again I picked up the telephone. Collingwood was leaving that morning but it was possible his plane had not yet taken off, that I could catch him before he became temporarily incommunicado.

After a moment he answered but the sound was not clear, his words muffled.

"I don't suppose you have seen an e-mail from Ramirez?" I asked.

"No," he replied adding hurriedly. "But I can't talk. Just leaving the gate..."

The sound broke up and I thought I had lost him, but then I heard, "We take off in ten minutes."

"Quick! Listen to this," I continued hastily and read out the message.

"Take him the money," he responded instantly.

I had intended merely to inform Collingwood, assuming he would make appropriate private arrangements.

"What?" I was taken aback. "And where am I supposed to find $1million?"

"From the Epicurean account dear boy ..." The line was breaking up again. "I've not yet received my stipend. It can be an advance on that."

"Are you quite sure?"

"Absolutely!"

"I'll check with Picard-Syme."

"No need. He knows… "

Then the line went dead.

Thus it was some two weeks later that I found myself in the Business Class cabin of an Iberian Airways flight to Lima with nearly $1.5 million in cash in a red attaché case in the luggage locker above my seat.

The Coutts official had reacted as if my request were a matter of everyday routine. The exchange rate was extremely favourable, approaching two dollars to the pound. Consequently the advance on Collingwood's 'stipend' as he put it cost the Epicureans just over £½ million and the £250,000 due to Ramirez and already separately ordered was almost double that amount in US dollars.

There was only one hitch. The briefcase I had taken with me was too small. My cash had to be retained until I made a quick trip to Selfridges to purchase the more solid, slightly bulkier container of deep red leather which now accompanied me. It had cost £375, the smartest case I had ever possessed. Obligingly the assistant had set the combination lock to my usual number – 2912.

There had been a few questions at Heathrow. In fact a minor stir had been caused at the scanner. The bored middle-aged lady staring at the succession of coins, phones, laptops, belts and shoes incessantly passing across her screen almost let the case go. But, just as it was peeping out from the tired rubber flaps, she pressed a stop button and summoned a supervisor. A hurried rewind took place, trays of bags and jackets clunking backwards, and I was ushered into a small room with a two-way mirror through which I could see the anxious glances of other passengers wondering if I were a terrorist bomber. I showed my business card to a hastily summoned Customs Official, explaining my status as an investment banker keen to put money into an emerging enterprise in Peru for which cash was necessary. With questions as to whether it was wise to be physically carrying such a large amount and kindly warnings, I was allowed to proceed but advised not to stray outside the safety of the Business Class lounge.

Iberian Airways served an excellent 1996 Rioja in Business Class. It was the perfect complement to the succulent rare beef flaking from my fork in tender strips. As we dined in airborne elegance my mind turned to the events of the last two weeks. I had become an uncle. I had no real notion of what this meant, still less of what it meant to be a godfather. However, my niece was now home and gaining weight, her parents, relieved and happy, already planning the baptismal party.

On the trading floor things were less happy. For two weeks the atmosphere had been strange. Business had been flat. There were strange rumours that something worse than the infamous crash, when Nick Leeson had stacked up a skyscraper of cards which came tumbling down taking Barings Bank with it, was about to occur in America.

"Crispin might be toast," Justin had quipped.

But then in an allusion to his sporting achievements and his limited opportunity to amass a transatlantic fortune, Nick Forsyth quipped, "Crispy duck more like."

Early one evening I spoke to Art Feinman in New York. He confirmed that there was a strange atmosphere on the American markets and sympathised when I complained about lack of money making opportunities. However he quickly moved the topic from profit to personality and I realised that the unexpected friendly phone call was motivated by his desire to have the lowdown on the self-confident Englishman who had just become his boss.

During this trading lull I made some preliminary arrangements for the June banquet. I spoke to the wine merchants and the caterers and sent an e-mail to Sabrina asking to meet to discuss the venue. Receiving no response, two days later, I telephoned but heard only her husky tones on a recorded message: "I am on holiday in the Bahamas. Please leave a message and I will contact you when I am back in England."

The seat belt sign flashed and the approach to Lima was announced. Glancing out of the window I realised that the descent was into a thick bank of cloud smothering the city, denying the softening light of the evening sun.

After passing through Immigration and Customs with barely an official glance at my red attaché case, I took a taxi to the centre. Following my itinerary I checked in to the Gran Hotel Bolivar, an establishment of faded luxury situated in the very centre of the city.

Having a day of freedom to recover from jet lag before flying on to Cusco, I decided to see something of the city. At the reception desk I left my case in the secure safe and purchased a guidebook, then stepped out into the Plaza San Martin, following a wide boulevard to the cathedral. The day was clammy, the lowering dull grey blanket of cloud creating a heavy brooding atmosphere which exactly suited the muted severe lines of the edifice. It appeared stable and austere, a solid testament to unshakeable values and beliefs. But then I learnt that it had been rebuilt following a tremendous earthquake in 1940. The solid stone pillars were in fact plaster, the walls designed to crumble harmlessly should another subterranean upheaval occur. In a side chapel was the elaborate tomb of Pizarro, the conquistador who had come to this country and shamelessly plundered to satisfy the greed of insatiable Europeans.

I walked on to visit the famed church of San Francisco, a place of worship surviving from the 17th century, more attractive than the cathedral. In the subterranean catacombs I viewed the fragmented skeletons of 70,000 people interred here over the ages. Their mortal remains lay exposed for all to gaze at, the skulls gawping in gruesome rows, leg bones that once leapt or danced spread in cartwheel patterns. It was humankind reduced to amusement for tourists.

With relief I emerged into the street and stood for a moment studying a map, wondering where to venture next. Suddenly my shirt front was spattered with a large foul smelling, greyish green globule of slimy excrement. But in the next instant two helpful youths were sponging me down, warning me to watch out for pigeons. I was about to splutter my thanks when I realised that one of them had his hand in my trouser pocket, the other was trying to locate my wallet.

"Get off me!" I yelled, twisting around.

That brought someone from the church doorway, shouting in Spanish at my assailants, who immediately fled.

"Ah senor," my Good Samaritan exclaimed. "You have fallen for the old pigeon shit trick! Are you all right?"

I was not injured although I stank appallingly. My wallet was still in my buttoned down shirt pocket, but my phone had gone.

Slightly shaken, bedraggled and feeling somewhat humiliated I returned to the hotel, stripped off my soiled clothes, showered and called England to cancel my phone contract.

The loss was a major inconvenience rather than a disaster. Fortunately all my important contacts were recorded in the notebook that I kept in my desk at Hazzards. But I was irritated that my first task on return would be to acquire a replacement and spend an hour of tedium entering numbers.

The city was still damply shrouded the following morning. I retrieved my attaché case, checked out of the hotel and took a taxi back to the airport, this time to the domestic terminal. The Cusco flight was on time. It circled the small city crouching in the enfolding mountains and at 1.15 p.m. touched down on a runway cut into a long strip of high grassland and taxied towards the low terminal building.

As this was purely a domestic airport, all passengers walked from the plane straight into the baggage area festooned with advertisements for Inca sites or the train to Machu Pichu. But before the suitcases began to emerge onto an ancient conveyor belt I began to feel unwell. My head was beginning to pound; nausea gripped my stomach. There was a melee of meeters and greeters, tourists and travellers, all converging in a confusion of luggage. I found myself gasping for breath, staggering, realising I was about to faint. Then, fleetingly to my left, I caught sight of a blurry notice 'Inca Enterprises' and collapsed into the arms of its holder.

I came round in a minibus, my rescuer fanning me with a newspaper. He was not Ramirez but a handsome Peruvian whose chiselled features boasted Inca stock. "Don't worry senor. You will soon be right."

After a few minutes bumpy ride into the city we stopped at a modern hotel just outside the centre. My Inca helped me into the lobby, guiding me to one of the reception sofas.

He reached over to a small table where a silver kettle was gently boiling over a small burner. From a shallow bowl beside it he crumbled a few dried leaves into a cup and added hot water to make a greenish brown infusion.

"Here drink this. You will soon feel better."

I was grateful for any relief, too wobbly to question what I was being given. But within five minutes my head was clearing, my stomach settling; within ten I was feeling amazingly fit, baffled that only shortly before I should have felt so desperately unwell.

As I regained my equilibrium the miracle worker introduced himself.

"I am Ramon. Senor Ramirez sent me to collect you."

I shook his hand. "Sorry to pass out on you. I have no idea what caused that. I don't usually go fainting on people. But what was in that drink you gave me?"

"You must not worry." Ramon smiled. "It happens to a lot of people when they land in Cusco. You have come from Lima at sea level. Here in Cusco we are at 3,400 m. You must take it slowly. The coca tea has done you good."

I checked in and was shown to a clean functional room exactly like that in modern hotels the world over. Ramon waited in reception while I accompanied my luggage. The porter lingered then left obsequiously when I gave him a five dollar bill, his body language indicating that in my ignorance I had proffered well beyond the going rate. But I was glad to be left alone for a moment and anxiously spun the numbers on the lock of the attaché case, fearful that during my incapacity I may have been robbed. The lid clicked open to reveal that the one and a half million dollars were untouched. They stared blankly at me, oblivious to their imminent delivery.

I smartened up then rejoined Ramon. The complaining minibus crawled alongside ancient Inca walls, huge blocks of stone intricately interlocked, darkened with age. We reached a large square dominated by a baroque cathedral. Ramon found a parking place and ushered me up a small side street alongside a busy restaurant, its first floor balcony intricately carved in Spanish colonial style. There was a doorway to the rear with several brass plates at its side. The largest, slightly green with age but bearing an italicised script, proclaimed that this was the office of Guzman 'Business Attorneys'. Beneath this were several smaller, obviously newer plates. Shining with cheap brightness I noticed 'Inca Enterprises SA'.

We went up a short flight of stairs into a small reception area. An uninterested middle-aged lady was folding letters into envelopes. She nodded us through a brown door into a tiny room, dark save for a weak reading lamp. There behind a desk devoid of any pens or paper, swinging slowly on a swivel chair, sat Ramirez.

"Ah Benjamin, how good to see you." He rose, extended his hand then gestured for me to sit on a wooden bench, the only other furniture in the characterless room.

"Wait for us downstairs, Ramon. Mr Turner and I have important matters to discuss."

Ramirez was dressed in a dark suit. He appeared quite dapper, not at all out of place in a lawyer's office. I noticed him glancing at my attaché case as he resumed his swivelling.

"I take it that you have brought what was agreed?"

"Naturally," I answered.

"And you are also making a delivery on behalf of the Honourable Crispin?" he added.

"Everything is in the case," I said. "However we need to discuss more convenient ways of making future payments. I don't enjoy carrying large sums of cash. I was mugged yesterday in Lima."

"Oh, I am so sorry, Benjamin. Tourists need to take care. You're not injured I hope?" he asked, although there was not a sliver of sincerity in his voice.

"No. But my phone was taken."

"You won't need a phone for the next few days. In any case I doubt whether there is a signal where I propose to take you."

"What do you mean? Are we not holding our discussions here in Cusco?" I asked, puzzled at what he was planning.

Ramirez laughed.

"We are here only because Inca Enterprises has just been incorporated here. You are privileged to be the first visitor to its registered office. But like all successful companies its operations take place elsewhere. No Benjamin, tomorrow we embark on an Amazonian adventure."

Before I could ask him what exactly he was planning he began fiddling with the lock of the attaché case.

"Tell me, Benjamin, what is the combination?"

I gave him the number and he swiftly rolled the brass barrels of the lock and flipped up the lid. He paused for a moment almost amorously eyeing the neat bundles of $100 dollar bills, stacked with their obverse upwards, the intelligent gaze of a succession of Benjamin Franklins staring silently back at him.

"Hmm, all in the highest denomination with a picture of your far more illustrious namesake. What a pity. I need some smaller notes. The rental here for this afternoon for example is only $50. I need to visit the bank before it closes."

He stood up quickly and although short, his thickset appearance gave him a degree of command in the little room. While thoughtfully extracting the top $100 bill he asked, "You are comfortable in your hotel?"

I nodded.

"That's good. But don't become too comfortable as it's only for one night."

This time I managed to formulate the question. "So I understand; but where exactly do you want to take me?"

"All will be explained," he answered hurriedly. "But I really must take this timely delivery to the bank. I shall borrow your case.

"Join me for dinner this evening. Over some delightful Peruvian fare I shall describe tomorrow's destination. The restaurant at the front of this establishment is one of the finest in Cusco. Meet me here at 7.30."

Our meeting ending prematurely, he ushered me out past the receptionist whose pile of filled envelopes had barely grown. He paused to hand her the $100 bill which she swiftly grasped. Then she fumbled unenthusiastically in a cash box before shrugging her shoulders.

"Keep it, Maria." He smiled at her. "Remember to look after me next time."

Then he hurried me down to where Ramon was waiting with the minibus. As I was driven out of the square, now thronging with youngsters out of school or college, I caught sight of the stubby figure of Ramirez scuttling into a bank near the cathedral, my attaché case clasped closely to his chest.

Ramon was evidently not at my disposal that evening. I walked the half mile from the hotel, fairly slowly and taking deep breaths, finding progress difficult in the thin air. My head was pounding again when, over 10 minutes late, I arrived at the restaurant. Ramirez was already seated at a corner table, a bottle of red wine open in front of him. Ignoring the waiter, he gestured for me to join him.

"My dear Benjamin, are you still finding it hard to acclimatise? Don't worry you will feel a lot better tomorrow."

It was difficult to know where to begin with him. There was so much I needed to know but I was reluctant to appear ill at ease by firing questions at him.

"Shouldn't we order?" I asked in a matter of fact way.

"It's already taken care of. I'm sure an adventurous young man like you will be more than happy to try a local delicacy. Have a glass of wine."

He poured a liberal measure and invited me to join a toast. "Here's to our future business success."

I responded tentatively, suppressing my instinctive suspicion that taking alcohol was unwise. "Yes. But with whom am I doing business? Is it Inca Enterprises, Raoul Ramirez or even Senor Guzman?"

Ramirez stared at me through his gold-rimmed spectacles, glinting softly in the table's flickering candlelight, and gave one of his sardonic smiles.

"How observant you are! But fear not, Raoul is at your service. Let me explain.

"You will remember that during our most agreeable meeting in London I explained the intricate arrangements that had proved necessary to cater for Epicurean tastes. As my planning proceeded I began to realise that it would be both prudent and expedient to separate my work for the Honourable Crispin from my other more mundane trading ventures. Accordingly, as you shall shortly see, I have created a totally new establishment. This is under the ownership of the newly incorporated Inca Enterprises, your supplier for future occasions."

"You have a shiny brass plate and you paid that lady, Maria, $100," I answered. "But what exactly is the company's function and why here and not Lima?"

"The function is, initially at least, to supply our national delicacy to rich financiers with exotic culinary tastes," he said as the waiter arrived with the first course, hovering attentively until Ramirez leant back and allowed his napkin to be spread over his protruding stomach.

"Bon appétit," he said. "I chose the soup. You Englishmen all like your soup."

I picked up my spoon and dipped it into the thick warm liquid. But I had no appetite, the pounding in my head was increasing and the restaurant was oppressively hot and stuffy.

Ramirez slurped then continued his narrative between gulps.

"As to location, Cusco has so much to commend it. Firstly it is home to Senor Guzman. Sadly, paralysed by a stroke, he has ceased active practice. But he still owns his premises, still retains his accreditation as an attorney and can still discreetly provide necessary legal services. His back room makes an ideal registered office for a société anonyme. He charges a modest fee for companies located there to hold meetings, which given the nature of the enterprises, are usually of limited size. Maria is always willing to assist but as you observed American dollar bills are a useful, how shall I say, lubricant."

He raised his glass to me, smiling yet again, a light dribble of soup running down his chin, congealing on the growing stubble. I was finding it hard to concentrate, forcing a few spoonfuls of the cooling greasy liquid into my mouth, nibbling the bread as a benign accompaniment.

"Secondly, if discretion is required what better location could there be? Prying officials would simply assume that Inca Enterprises offers tours to the Nazca Lines or Machu Pichu. They could not imagine that its purpose is gastronomical rather than geographical.

"Knowing I would complete the registration this week it was essential to arrange the initial share subscription. The authorised share capital is $2 million. The Honourable Crispin has subscribed $1 million. Sadly as temporarily I have a severe cash flow problem, my shareholding is only one dollar. But Benjamin when you have seen the establishment I have created I am certain that you will hasten personally to subscribe the remaining $999,999. You will be assured of substantial dividends."

He dabbed at his face with his napkin, grinning with self-satisfaction.

Despite my headache, now deepening in intensity with every word he uttered, I tried to concentrate. Apparently there was another dimension to my trip; Ramirez had an ulterior motive.

The waiter returned, removed the soup dishes and replenished the wine glasses.

"Of course Inca Enterprises also required a bank account. After all what could be more respectable than a new tour company registered in Cusco and banking in Cusco? The bank manager is indeed very pleased about his new client's instant liquidity. But as you shall see the consignment of cash came not a moment too soon. A number of people who have assisted with the establishment of my venture require reimbursement in hard currency."

Ramirez was positively beaming, his gold tooth glinting in the light playing from the candle on the table. I was struggling to make sense of this torrent of information.

"When the next consignment is dispatched you can make payment to Inca Enterprises. Here I will give you a card with the account number."

He was interrupted by the reappearance of the waiter carrying plates covered in rather battered metal domes, a cheap and crude imitation of the vast collection of miniature St Paul's employed at the Knightsbridge feast. Lifting the tarnished lids he proudly announced the dish, but his thick Spanish was impenetrable.

On our plates there were several strips of grey meat. Trying to ignore my discomfort, to make a pretence of appreciating hospitality, I cut into the unappetising flesh and took a mouthful. The texture was slightly chewy; the flavour was not strong, neither pleasant nor unpleasant. I took a little more then retreated to the safety of the Peruvian potatoes.

I glanced up at Ramirez. I wanted to find out what was in store for me, I wanted to lead the conversation to what he had planned, to where we were travelling, to what exactly I was meant to see which would convince me to make an investment to match Collingwood's. But first I had to know what I was eating.

"What on earth is this?" I asked.

"Another local delicacy, of course," he said triumphantly. "Alpaca!"

At that moment the room started to spin. I made to rise and leave the table. But I was too late. I felt a huge churn in my stomach, an overwhelming wave of nausea, an unstoppable reflex.

Across the white tablecloth, in an arching liquid trajectory, I vomited violently.

7

Before I fainted I glimpsed a look of startled horror race across the face of my dining companion. The reddish brown liquid of the regurgitated soup spread across his jacket; a second wave soiled his bulging shirt front. Then the restaurant spun, there were fading shouts of shock, a clattering of crockery and cutlery and I slumped to the floor.

I suppose it was Ramirez who put me in a taxi back to the hotel. As I regained consciousness in the crisp air of the wide open space outside the restaurant I was conscious of a squat figure scowling, wiping gold-rimmed spectacles, brushing at his shirt with a table napkin, thrusting dollar bills at the cab driver, hurrying me away and out of his presence.

Despite my embarrassment I realised I was a victim of tiredness and thin air, not sentimentality; that I both hated heights and abhorred altitude. But irritatingly the image of Field Cottage came into my thoughts, the beasts in the adjacent enclosure innocently nodding their furry heads.

The staff at the hotel were kind and attentive. For the second time in a few hours they had seen their English visitor collapsing almost comatose in the challenging atmosphere of their Andean city. Ignoring the foul flecks on my jacket, a receptionist sat me down and again administered the soothing coca tea. My nausea subsided allowing the warm reviving liquid to slip down my throat. A few minutes later my head began to clear and I was able to go up to my room and into bed.

I slept deeply but woke early at about 6 a.m., ravenously hungry but still plagued with an insistent pounding across my brow. I rose, shaved and showered then went down for breakfast.

An extensive buffet awaited the hotel's clientele. For a few minutes I avoided the row of heated containers while I revived myself with the invigorating coca infusion thoughtfully provided in tidy sachets along with the Earl Grey and English Breakfast teas. It was only once the headache abated that I warily inspected the warm offerings, selecting only clearly identifiable bacon, scrambled eggs and mushrooms.

Recalling that I was to depart with Ramirez for the destination undisclosed because of my collapse, I returned to my room to pack my belongings. I was almost finished when the telephone rang.

"Senor Turner? You are wanted in Reception."

I hurried down to find Ramirez flashing dollar bills at the receptionist.

"Good morning Benjamin. I trust you are feeling better? I thought 21st century Englishmen had thrown off the traits of their colonial predecessors. But no you arrive and, like a latter day conquistador, despoil what you see!"

"I'm really sorry and incredibly embarrassed. Altitude and I evidently don't mix," I said apologetically.

"No matter." Ramirez flapped his arm dismissively then smiled like a circling shark, the gold filling showing momentarily. "My garments are at the dry cleaners – I'll simply add the bill to the Epicureans' account!"

Then I realised that he was now very strangely clothed. He wore a tropical suit, a light linen jacket with trousers to match which stopped at the knee so that in reality they were well tailored shorts. On his feet were pale, soft leather shoes and on his lower legs, long cotton socks folded neatly at the top of each calf. Not only was the attire incongruous it was highly unsuitable for the chilly Cusco morning.

"I have a good tailor do I not?" Ramirez had obviously noticed my quizzical glance. "My apparel is eminently suitable for our destination."

He could not resist toying with me, teasing my patience to the limit. Trying to maintain my equanimity I simply commented, "I'm sure that had I not been taken ill you would have told me our destination. What are you planning?"

"Our work in Cusco is done," he announced. "The bank manager is happy that Inca Enterprises is solvent; Senor Guzman's professional fees have been met – in cash and in American dollars; a standing order has been set up to pay a modest sum quarterly for displaying our brass plate. Business need never bring you here again. Instead we depart for Iquitos, the true location of my new venture. I suggest you pack while I settle the bill. I trust you have not been profligate in your consumption from the minibar."

Back in my room, my packing complete, I glanced at the tourist bundle on the dressing table and found a map of Peru. My eyes ran down the purple spine of the Andes, noticing names like Cajamarca, Huancayo and Arequipa. Then they wandered off into the long green strip bordering Brazil. In the northwest of the country a block of territory, resembling a misshapen head on a grotesque foetus, thrust itself into Brazil. A black dot in place of an eye bore the name 'Iquitos', a blue streak running from it in an endless tear. This was the Amazon, still youthful in this country but already broadening before sucking in other lengthy tributaries to expand its girth on its long progress westward to the Atlantic.

Ramon took us to Cusco airport, dropping us at the entrance to the check-in desks. He dutifully carried a large leather holdall for Ramirez while I wheeled my serviceable case. My companion carried my borrowed attaché case as hand luggage. At the counter he reached inside his safari jacket, withdrawing a pale plump wallet. He said something in Spanish then counted out $200 in $10 bills to Ramon who beamed at him then hurried away as if anxious to find a quiet corner in which to check the generous payment.

"I don't expect to be here again for some time but Ramon knows it pays to look after me," Ramirez whispered coarsely. "You see how I understand these people. It is easier for him to get nuevos soles for small notes."

We were each handed two boarding cards, the first for the comparatively short flight to Lima, the second for the longer journey to Iquitos. I was relieved to sit down again in the departure lounge, squeezing past three round colourful Peruvian ladies wearing bright red shawls and distinctive squat bowler hats, as again I was feeling slightly breathless. Ramirez positioned himself next to me, his noticeably hairy legs bulging from his short trousers. He spoke quietly.

"We have not had much time to talk, to get to know each other. I am sure the Honourable Crispin must have spoken of me. He must have told you how helpful this poor overseas student was to him in undergraduate days."

My head was once more beginning to ache slightly. Wary, I gave no reaction.

"At least tell me, Benjamin why you have become Crispin's chosen one."

"I am good at my job." I was rather terse. "That's why Collingwood trusts me."

"And I am sure that he is right to trust you, as you can trust me. You have seen how I look after Maria and Ramon. I look forward to doing business with you, to supplying the needs of your gourmet society, to building an ongoing business relationship.

But listen, they are calling our flight. Let's continue our dialogue at 30,000 feet."

Although an aircraft cabin is claustrophobic it is pressurised. I felt better once we were no longer breathing the thin air of Cusco. I would have felt better still had I not had the bulk of Ramirez squeezed in next to me. Once the roar of the engines had subsided and we reached cruising height his oily endeavours recommenced.

"You and I are alike Benjamin. I can tell that like me you come from a modest background. Let me guess, did you go to a comprehensive school?"

"What does schooling matter?" I responded noncommittally. "Life at Hazzards has certainly taught me how to hold my own with the likes of Collingwood."

"I am sure it has. But like me you have had to rely on your wits. Unlike some with whom we are acquainted, we have had to work for every dollar.

"People like us will always succeed because our very circumstances encourage creativity. Your organisation cannot achieve its culinary conquests without my assistance. It is to me that your friend Crispin had to turn as indeed he turned when he was a somewhat indiscreet young man all those years ago at Oxford."

The stewardess brought round a soft drink and a tiny packet of nuts which Ramirez tipped into his hand then palmed to his mouth. Swallowing his drink with a soft belch he resumed.

"You are probably wondering why it is necessary to travel to the westernmost edge of this strange country. Really it is quite simple. Your elite organisation has a current whim to dine on a delicacy unavailable in Europe with its Old World sensibilities. You require a secure and discreet supply. I shall demonstrate how perfectly I can meet both current and future requirements. You may also appreciate the longer term potential of the enterprise. Once you have seen what an ideal establishment has been created I am certain that in your private capacity you will wish to match the investment of your mentor."

I was listening hard to him, nodding from time to time. At first I thought he was telling me what he would have said over dinner had I not been taken ill. But then I began to suspect that he had waited for this flight knowing I would be a captive in an aircraft seat, knowing that he could speak on his terms and that it would be difficult for me to interrupt.

"Sadly I have suffered severe cash flow problems. Business has been going through a sticky patch. But I have high hopes for Inca Enterprises. Now that we're up and running, thanks to Crispin's capital, I anticipate a glorious future. Once I have my director's fees I will again be in a position to look after my mother. I trust you look after yours Benjamin?"

"My parents are dead," I said unemotionally, deliberately not softening the sentence with euphemism to ameliorate embarrassment.

It worked. He muttered something and remained silent as the engine noise changed and once more we headed for the thick bank of cloud rolling over the coastline below Lima.

Fortunately on the longer leg of our trip Ramirez fell asleep. He snored occasionally, his head lolling towards mine, slipping off the narrow, insubstantial headrest. But it was preferable to having to make conversation and eventually, lulled by the drone of the engine I too slipped into a heavy doze.

It was late afternoon when we landed at Francisco Secada Vignetta airport outside Iquitos. By now I was tiring of aircraft, realising with slight incredulity that it was only just over 24 hours earlier that I had landed in Cusco. But the arrival here contrasted starkly with my giddy, gasping reception in the foothills of the Andes. As we stepped onto the tarmac we stepped into sticky hot air, the thick humidity weighing like a blanket on our shoulders. But at least I could walk without fainting despite the perspiration already pouring from me.

I had no alternative but to follow Ramirez, relieved that I had a guide who evidently knew what to do and where to go. Outside the baggage hall there was a hubbub of shouting and gesticulation, a wall of waving placards and signs, a stench of human sweat and stale cigarette smoke. Eager touts thrusting their faces into ours offered jungle tours, comfortable lodges, river cruises. As we tugged at our luggage they tried to grab our bags, running alongside us, urging us to go with them to a taxi. They were noisy and persistent, threatening and confusing. Ramirez pushed them all to one side, scowling, barking out Spanish expletives, bustling his way through the melee, grasping my attaché case tightly to his chest leaving me to bring his holdall perched on top of my wheeled suitcase.

Amid the shoving and dodging we forged a path to the taxi rank. There were few people waiting as most passengers had joined the crowds surging around a packed area thick with motorbikes, all strangely extended by the addition of canvas covered structures so that they resembled rickshaws.

"We will take a taxi, not one of those motokars." Ramirez gestured dismissively. "That's one of the drawbacks of doing business here. It's much more civilised in Brazil."

A battered Peugeot drew up. The driver reached for our bags and Ramirez let him put them in the boot, except for my red attaché case which remained firmly in his grip. Then he gave detailed directions and engaged in a lengthy discussion over the fare. We set off through the slow river of cars, crowded buses, lorries overloaded like wild west wagons, donkey carts and motorbikes all converging on the highway in a deafening cacophony of blaring horns.

"Iquitos is a busy city and there are some good hotels. You shall experience what they have to offer tomorrow. But tonight we must go out of town."

At first we drove with the stream of vehicles making for the city. But gradually the traffic thinned, the whine of accelerating engines and screeching brakes becoming more sporadic as we appeared to be heading away from the urban sprawl. In the fading twilight the lights atop crumbling concrete posts intermittently illuminated roadside squalor. Eventually we passed the last lamp, its casing broken, the neon bulb hanging precariously from its wire. Now suddenly it was totally dark. Only one headlight of the Peugeot was working but this was sufficient to show a road pitted with rough potholes, a deep drain at its side often obstructed with battered oil drums and even on one occasion a ruined refrigerator, its Coca-Cola logo still visible on its side.

Ramirez remained silent but after about 45 minutes he fiddled with the attaché case, raising the lid slightly and discreetly removing a bundle of notes. Shortly after this more lights came into view, the outline of a few buildings, shops shuttered for the night, a couple of petrol pumps. He gestured to the driver to stop, pointing across the road to a snaking strip of red neon shaped to read 'Hotel Rosa'. The doorway was evidently open, the interior screened by strings of large beads.

Our driver was irritable. I suspected he had anticipated one last fare to take him into the city but instead found himself a considerable distance from home. Once again Ramirez counted out notes, holding them up to the light to indicate they were $10 bills. He carefully placed seven bills into the outstretched sticky palm. Then he counted out three more. The driver's irritation was transformed into obsequiousness. With no demur the fawning recipient carried our bags through the clattering beads and into a tiled reception area.

"Ah, Senor Ramirez." The plump proprietress aged about 40, slightly Indian in appearance but light skinned, evidently knew her generous guest.

We were shown up to small bedrooms. Mine had a single mattress on a metal frame hidden by a mosquito net. There was a toilet and shower, the basin slightly cracked but nevertheless clean and satisfactory for one night.

"Rosa makes excellent paella. If you promise to behave yourself this evening, Benjamin, join me downstairs in five minutes," Ramirez called as he disappeared through his bedroom doorway.

I suddenly realised I was hungry and thirsty. But breathing was easy and for revival it was not coca tea that I required but a long cold beer.

We did indeed eat well. The paella was generous with tasty morsels of fish, large pieces of succulent chicken falling off the bone, the attractive yellow rice heavy with savoury juices. Ramirez too needed to satisfy his hunger. He remained mostly silent, helping himself to extra portions, occasionally brandishing a chicken bone and reminding me that he had extolled the virtue of our hostess' cooking.

As we were finishing my eyes wandered to the small bar at the back of the room. A slight movement occurred, the merest dark shadow, perhaps caused by the flickering light. Ramirez noticed my quizzical gaze.

"My dear Benjamin, what is troubling you?"

I looked again. The movement returned but this time to my horror I realised that that the dark shadow was in fact a large rat dodging behind the optics on the upturned bottles of spirits.

Ramirez roared with laughter. "That's nothing to be worried about. We must all learn to cope with vermin – and after all here we are close to the river."

He stood up, wiped his face with a napkin and announced he was ready for bed.

"Sleep well Benjamin. We make an early start in the morning. I assure you that Roaul's endeavours will impress you. Goodnight."

I followed him gingerly up the stairway warily glancing into the shadowy recesses, watchful for movement as I entered my room.

Never before had I used a mosquito net. Not having considered antimalarial precautions, now, confronted with the meshed white tent, I shuddered at the thought of one sly bite insidiously infecting my bloodstream. I checked the material and only when I was certain that it was free from tears did I strip naked, slip under the sheet and tuck the billowing base firmly beneath the mattress.

But there was nothing I could do about rats. Lying uneasily on the bed I strained my ears wondering if I would detect both the scurrying of rodent feet and the tell-tale buzz of the fateful insect penetrating my cocoon. There were numerous irritating noises – a distant television, the electric hum of the hotel sign, the clatter of dishes and after a few minutes, the soft snoring from Ramirez in the next room. Winding the sheet over my head to block out these disturbances, I yielded to the first dreamy driftings and permitted the heaviness of sleep to envelop me.

There were different noises at dawn – the sounds of people calling in the street, bicycle bells ringing, the splashing of water, the occasional motor vehicle already complaining about the day's labours. Then came a loud knocking on my door.

"Rise and shine Benjamin. There is plenty to be done."

I glanced at my watch. It was 6.30 a.m.

We ate a hurried breakfast of bread and a strange type of omelette. Ramirez gobbled greedily.

"Have plenty dear boy. We have a lot to see and do. Take my advice – keep your strength up."

At that he broke off a large piece of loaf and stuffed it into his pocket.

"In England you feed the birds," he stated definitively. "In South America we have more voracious creatures."

This morning the safari suit had gone, presumably folded into the leather holdall. Now he sat opposite me in a light cotton shirt, pale thin trousers and heavy trainers. My polo shirt seemed out of place but it was reasonably comfortable in the damp heat, already oppressive at this early hour.

Ramirez settled the account before we left, again discretely extracting dollar bills from my attaché case. He arranged for us to leave our luggage behind the counter saying we would back for it much later. Then we stepped out into the sunlight and walked a short way down an unpleasant and malodorous street.

Hotel Rosa was the most presentable of the surrounding buildings. Brightly painted it stood in stark contrast to a clutch of shabby shops. Next to it was a hardware store, dark and dusty, the grimy windows plastered with signs for power tools. Rusted pipes slowly decayed outside next to a broken wheel. Beyond that was a food shop, yesterday's stale bread dumped outside, the hardening crusts sniffed at but then ignored by a mangy bitch, her dugs sagging in the dirt.

We stepped on past these dismal establishments picking our way through the detritus in the roadway. Then we turned and ahead of us, just 50 metres away, I saw the huge river, so wide that I could not immediately spot the opposite bank. It was flowing swiftly, a thick heavy mass of forbidding brown water.

"The Amazon," declared Ramirez. "Is this not truly a magnificent river? Delightful as I find the Thames is it not a mere stream compared with what you see before you?"

He did not expect an answer and I did not offer one. We walked a little further towards the swift torrent. I could see floating bunches of vegetation with birds fighting and screeching above them and other pieces of flotsam or jetsam bobbing downstream. Then we stopped abruptly by the open door of a workshop. Ramirez turned inside and I followed, momentarily blinded by the cruel light and shower of sparks as a labourer welded a jumble of metal bars.

The crude building was filled with wood. There were large beams, deep red in colour; lighter planks piled from floor to ceiling; staves and sharpened posts standing in their own shavings along one wall. Next to them was a small office, its glazed door and windows coated with sawdust. Ramirez marched in, surprising a short wiry man bent over a desk also thick with dust which clung to the ancient telephone, ledgers, notebooks, scattered chisels and bills skewered on a dirty spike.

"I've come to settle up with you." Ramirez spoke in English, I sensed for my benefit.

"Que?" came the response and the conversation continued in Spanish.

It was clear that we were in the presence of the proprietor. He scratched around extracting torn and stained papers from desk drawers, speaking agitatedly. Evidently he was complaining about the difficulty of a task he had undertaken, stressing how many materials it had been necessary to acquire, the wages paid, the complexities of transportation across water. I could identify the odd word and his graphic gesticulations told me the rest. He had not had time to work out the total cost and began tapping numbers into a grubby electronic calculator, its keypad encrusted with grime, the numbers almost obscured with dirt so that the display of numerals was barely visible through the cloudy Perspex.

Ramirez cleared a space, pushing the attaché case across the desk in a furrow of filth. He flipped up the lid and began extracting wads of dollar bills. I lost count of how much exactly was handed over because almost immediately, seeing that he was to be paid in full, the excited man slammed the door shut and fiddled with the lock of a small squat safe in the corner. He crammed in the money, thanking Ramirez profusely, almost grovelling.

The transaction completed, we did not linger but emerged from the workshop, the dust furring our clothes. In the flood of sunlight we turned towards the river.

"Yet again you can appreciate how timely was your delivery." Ramirez looked at me approvingly. "I have no doubt that we will witness an excellent edifice – and built exactly to my specifications."

We walked on, avoiding a snarling dog rooting in an overturned dustbin. The sun was climbing higher, the swift Amazon now a bright milk chocolate colour. Just by the edge was a small wooden jetty, its planks lapped by the water, eddies of scum bubbling around the supporting posts. Here a few craft were moored, little more than long dugout canoes but fitted with outboard motors; primitive vessels transformed by a modern device and made suitable for speedy progress on this ancient waterway.

Several ragged boatmen came running towards us, eager for custom. Ramirez beckoned one of them who he seemed to know and commenced a rapid discussion.

"Climb in Benjamin," he said after a moment. "It is perfectly safe."

I placed my feet unsteadily in the designated vessel, wobbling slightly from side to side. Our pilot grinned, his brown mouth revealing wide gaps in his discoloured teeth, and gestured me onto a small box. Then he turned from me. His dirty grey shirt flapped over his torn trousers as he helped Ramirez onto a slightly larger box covered with a faded cushion located just behind me. Then, taking his place at the rear, he pushed off from the damp mooring with a long paddle and yanked the outboard motor into life. Immediately we surged forward, out into the vastness of the incessant brown flow, cutting diagonally across the current then floating with it once we were about 20 metres from the bank.

"Sit back and enjoy the view." Ramirez was revelling in my discomfort. "It will only take us half an hour so make the most of it."

The crude houses on the bank and the remaining boats slid from view. From low on the water the Amazon seemed even more immense. I thought I could distinguish the far bank, a dark strip of shining mud like freshly poured treacle, and above it thick green vegetation, tall trees soaring upwards casting dark shadows on the water's edge. But I was mistaken; rippling waves around an emerging dark spit indicated it was simply a large island.

Moments later the small craft rocked alarmingly. Ramirez was almost upright shaking me firmly by the shoulder. Anxious and unsure of what peril we faced I turned to see him pointing and shouting.

He was beside himself with excitement. Above the drone of the motor he yelled, "Look Benjamin! Look there, to the left!"

8

I turned following the wild gesticulations of Ramirez, wondering with apprehension what I was about to witness. From a mud bank I saw a grotesque scaly creature close its horny jaws and slip slyly into the water. For a few seconds the top of its head and eyes were visible as it glided under the cloudy surface leaving a barely discernible wake. Then it was gone.

"Caiman!" Ramirez was grinning enthusiastically. "You are lucky to see one at this time of day. Take my advice. Do not consider taking a swim."

Instinctively I drew my hands from the side of the boat as Ramirez shouted, "Here is a further reason not to swim!"

I turned again to see him grinning, his mouth wide, his gold filling briefly catching the sunlight. He reached into his pocket and extracted his ball of breakfast bread, crumbling the doughy mess into the brown water. Immediately the crumbs landed the surface came alive with frantic splashing, a frenzy of snapping jaws.

"Much less tame than blue tits." Ramirez roared with laughter, savouring my discomfort. "I thought you might enjoy seeing piranha."

At that moment I recognised that Ramirez was not only demanding, greedy and scheming; he was also sadistic.

The turbulence subsided and as rapidly as they had appeared the vicious creatures dispersed leaving no trace of their unexpected snack.

Our pilot was grinning as he tugged at the starter cord of the motor, silenced during this ugly display. Once more it sprang loudly into life and I felt the craft resist the flow of the stream forcing us back onto our course across the massive merciless river.

Having long since left the large island behind we sailed swiftly past some smaller outcrops completely covered in vegetation, their shores concealed by low dipping branches trailing in the murky flow.

In the distance a vigorous column of smoke was bubbling upwards over the canopy of leaves. Releasing my grip I placed my hand over my eyes and peered at the phenomenon.

"Fires made by one of the native tribes," Ramirez explained, jogging my shoulder. "They are making a fresh clearing for building."

A shaft of sunlight fell through the acrid cloud, glinting on a large vessel about a kilometre away.

"Rather bigger than your Thames barges!" Ramirez yelled. "It goes much further than those tourist tubs that so disturbed our peace in the Savoy."

He shouted a description of the Amazon passenger service that could carry you from Peru into Brazil, continuing westwards towards Manaus and ultimately the Atlantic Ocean. We then lost sight of the approaching ship as the canoe rocked violently on a sudden eddy and we pitched across a muddy spit at the end of yet another island. This time we kept close to the shore and I noticed a narrow gap in the foliage a little way ahead, a mere nick in the fringe of trees where a couple of stout trunks had been felled and a tiny platform constructed. Deftly our boatman manoeuvred alongside, cutting the engine, securing the stern and nimbly scrambling ashore to pull the dugout parallel to the landing point.

Ramirez eased his bulk out first leaving me to follow. He gave firm instructions in Spanish indicating emphatically that the driver of this primitive water taxi was to venture no further. Then he beckoned me to follow him along a path which, although narrow, was firm underfoot as narrow duckboards had been laid giving a steady passage directly into the jungle. Within a minute or two the dense green vegetation seemed to close in around us. On the river the light had been harsh; here it was soft. The forest was subdued, almost gloomy, weak flashes of illumination rippling eerily in patches where a sunbeam penetrated the leafy canopy. The sound of the river receded rapidly, the ceaseless wash replaced by disconcerting rustles from leaf or branch perhaps triggered by watchful arboreal creatures or tropical rodents scampering from our footfall. Occasionally raucous screeches from colourful macaws shattered the stillness. I had never experienced such surroundings and despite the heat shuddered with apprehension.

"Follow me, Benjamin. Not far now." Ramirez moved quickly and confidently, his words more an instruction than reassurance.

In a few moments there was light as the forest opened up in front of us revealing a small clearing containing three low wooden buildings set in a U shape. Instantly I noticed that they had been constructed out of timbers similar to those I had seen earlier in the dusty workshop. The stout red beams made substantial uprights in the corner of each building; the lighter planks provided the slatted wooden walls. Each roof was thatched, not with the neat cut thatch of English dwellings such as Field Cottage, which I had so recently admired, but layered with dry grass or reeds, their long stalks overhanging, creating deep shade over the walls. Only the construction to our left had openings resembling windows. These were merely square apertures in the wall covered with a thin metal mesh presumably serving to let in air but keep out insects.

"Raphael!" Ramirez called as we entered the clearing.

There were sounds of hurried movement, dishes being clattered, the slap of wood upon wood. Ramirez was standing with his hands on his hips surveying this unlikely establishment. I sensed that he was calculating the volume of timber, mentally reckoning up the cost of construction, probably wondering if he had parted with too many dollars.

My eyes were on the narrow portal from which came the sounds. The door, like the windows, consisted of a frame covered with mesh but it was hinged and held fast by a latch. A moment later Raphael appeared blinking in the sunlight. He was naked from the waist up, of moderate height, but obviously strong and muscular. I guessed that he was about 35 years old but in his unshaven and bleary-eyed state it was difficult to be certain. Then, just as he emerged, I thought I detected another slight but swift movement, a shadow slipping behind the wire mesh door.

He continued towards us, wiping his hands on his trousers and stretching out his right arm to greet his employer. But he said nothing.

"Raphael is a mute," muttered Ramirez." It is best that way. Silence guarantees discretion."

He then spoke in Spanish, obviously questioning the occupant of this isolated dwelling, receiving vigorous nods and strange animal grunts for a response.

Motioning to the doorway Ramirez led us inside what was obviously the most substantial of the three buildings. Directly opposite, across the compound, the timber construction was of similar size. It had a large solid double door and although the roof grasses overhung creating a shady veranda, there were no windows. The third building lay detached from the other two, sited between them at the rear of the clearing. But I could see neither door nor window because a screen of reeds ran in front of it, concealing anything behind from view.

Ramirez ducked his head and stepped inside followed by the burly frame of Raphael. As I too bent I heard a sudden strange sound, a sort of high-pitched whine followed immediately by more squawking of brightly coloured macaws. Startled, I paused. For a moment I wondered if Raphael was trying to indicate something but his guttural utterances had been deeper than this disembodied screech and I chided myself for being disconcerted by the unfamiliarity of the rainforest.

It took a few moments to become accustomed to the dullness of the interior. Subdued light crept in to the long room through the wire mesh windows shaded by the unruly roof material. There was a table in the centre on which sat a few dishes holding the remains of breakfast. In one corner were two low chairs and in another some cooking utensils. At the far end was a thin dividing wall, concealing the sleeping area, its entrance covered by a garish curtain, the only item in the room to provide any colour. From the heavy roof beams beneath the thatch two oil lamps hung on metal hooks.

"First things first, Benjamin."

Ramirez flipped open the attaché case which he had guarded so carefully as he conjured up the snapping piranha, which he had gripped so firmly as he marched down the boardwalk to this lonely encampment. The bundles of notes had now diminished considerably. No longer tightly wedged, they had spilled around the case, a few breaking loose from their thick bands, fluttering to the floor in a sudden breeze which gently rocked the doorway. This time I noticed that he counted out nuevos soles, although there were still a few bundles of $100 bills.

"Raphael will find it easier to spend these – and he will not be cheated with a poor exchange rate. You see how I look after my people Benjamin?"

Ramirez recited high numbers as he placed the grubby, torn and dog-eared notes into the outstretched palm. Raphael closed his thick fist, but with an ostentatious gesture Ramirez slapped three more high denomination nuevos soles down onto the table.

"I also pay a bonus. After all the miserable creature has been alone here for six weeks."

Raphael abased himself, his stout body visibly heaving. He was grunting incoherently, exuding gratitude.

"Now, it's time for me to show you around. You must observe how Crispin's anticipated investment has already been utilised. Then you can satisfy him that he is indeed receiving excellent value for money." Ramirez rubbed his hands, his face lighting up, his spectacles glinting in a stray shaft of sunlight.

"Firstly you must appreciate that employing Raphael is an act of great philanthropy. To have a disability anywhere is a misfortune; in Latin America it is a disaster. Where else might he get a job? So he does not mind a few weeks of loneliness for which he is amply rewarded. It goes without saying that he is illiterate and naturally he cannot speak about the work he does. Perfect for our needs!"

With that he commenced the brief tour, all the time keeping a firm grip on my attaché case.

"Very good," he said approvingly. "The last time I was here the roof was not in place. Look how stout the timber is – and all treated to repel the termites. We paid our dusty carpenter well and he has done a first rate job. Now we have an excellent base from which to satisfy future demand. From where Raphael comes this is luxury. Look he even has a bedroom."

He pulled the colourful curtain to one side and indicated a bed concealed by a heavy grey mosquito net.

"Look inside Benjamin. Go ahead!"

It seemed intrusive to enter these sleeping quarters, especially with their occupant outside, absorbed as he was with the counting and sorting of his patron's largesse. But Ramirez ushered me past, turning as he did so to look condescendingly at Raphael gibbering, scurrying to secrete his money in an earthenware pot. I stood in the doorway cursorily viewing the crude room. Then disquietingly, in the dimness I thought I perceived a strange shadow beneath the bed, barely discernible behind the skirt of the mosquito net.

Ramirez was now back in the centre of the main room standing over Raphael, still addressing him in Spanish. Intrigued, I peered more intently into the bedroom. What I had noticed was a not a shadow but a shape. As I looked it solidified and with a shock I realised that it was a person, for although the figure was still, there was a very faint aspiration. A head of dark hair was bent away from me hinting at a young slim neck and slender body cocooned in the foetal position, almost achieving invisibility behind the concealing cotton mesh. There was something unbearably tender and vulnerable about the vague figure, but it remained motionless and I said nothing.

"Now let's see across the compound." Behind me Ramirez was pushing at the wire mesh of the door, letting a sudden flood of light into the larger room, summoning me to follow.

We marched off to the blank building facing the living quarters. Ramirez lifted up a long piece of wood acting as a bar to keep the double door closed and flung it open, allowing the sunlight to illuminate the interior. Inside there were stacks of boxes, lengths of twine, bottles of water, drums of oil, gas cylinders.

"Plenty of supplies here to keep Raphael well fed," Ramirez announced, stepping inside proprietarily, his arms outstretched to indicate the hillocks of containers. "I have arranged a delivery every six weeks: water, rice, tins of meat, fruit and vegetables. But absolutely no alcohol. I insist on that. Silence has to be accompanied by sobriety. Liquor is off limits."

Beyond this disorganised jumble was a larger empty area.

"What is that for?" I asked.

"Wait and see!" answered Ramirez. "This warehouse facility will have its uses."

He closed the door and led me towards the palisade of reeds in front of the third building saying enigmatically, "I hope the Epicureans appreciate the delicacies in store for them."

Lower than the others, the back wall and short sides of the third building consisted of overlapping planks nailed solidly into the dark red upright posts, exactly as in the storeroom and dwelling. But it had no front wall. The fourth side, directly in front of us, consisted of round metal bars set firmly into solid timbers and intertwined with a stout metal mesh like strong chicken wire. At one end was a small doorway also heavy with bars, held tightly shut with a clasp secured by a padlock.

There was scurrying from within. At first I wondered if it was overrun with rats, but then my eyes adjusting to the light, I saw that the creatures were plump and furry.

"Behold your next banquet! Open up Raphael."

There was a pungent stench of animal and urine; a whimpering and chattering as around our feet about one hundred guinea pigs scurried away from unwelcome intrusion.

"Inca Enterprises no longer patronises the breeders of Lima. Henceforth your delicacy will be supplied directly," Ramirez continued. "Select the plumpest Benjamin. I will ensure it is marked and labelled to be delivered specially to your plate at your June function."

I did not respond. Instead I carefully examined another feature of this confined area now apparent in the gloom. Beyond the scampering animals I saw that there was a low wall also built of stout planks. Behind it the floor was covered in straw like a byre. There I could just perceive, crouched and cowering against the far wall, three small creatures. For a moment I wondered what they were, what genus of jungle mammal was held in this captivity. They appeared to be quadrupeds and to have dark smooth hides. One was much larger than the others. It crawled away on all fours frightened of strange intruders. The two smaller creatures lay curled into balls, but like their companion shrunk away under our scrutiny.

In a moment of shock I realised what I was seeing. They were not obscure or exotic rainforest inhabitants; they were not the unfamiliar animals of an unfamiliar continent. Trembling, naked and gibbering, they twisted in our direction revealing themselves to be wild eyed, blank faced children.

"You look startled dear boy." Ramirez was standing next to me. He flung his arm around my shoulders. "But you should not be. They are far better off here than where they have come from."

I was incapable of any response. I simply stood there gazing into that bare barred room.

The largest child was a boy. He was now turning to us, his eyes wide and staring. His mouth opened to reveal discoloured teeth and he emitted the high-pitched whine, a combination of bark and grunt, that I had heard when we entered the compound. Over rounded shoulders his hair hung lank and matted. His small crinkly scrotum and stubby penis revealed his sex, now unavoidably noticeable as a short yellow stream trickled onto the damp straw already soiled with faeces.

As if by reflex the other two infants began a low howling sound, stretching as they cried, small fists clenched, their tiny feet arched. They too uncoiled in their nakedness, their dark skin moist in the oppressive atmosphere of this crude gaol. Their mouths opened as they screamed and I noticed tiny milk teeth, pristine white protuberances, a flash of purity in their begrimed faces. As they squirmed, their legs kicking violently, I saw that they were little girls, I guessed about a year old.

"Raphael feeds them three times a day. Come, let's get him to make some coffee. Listen to what I have to say and you will understand why they are here."

I was relieved to be led out into the compound, out of sight of this distressing spectacle, away from the rising stench of urine.

Ramirez once more became garrulous.

"Don't be so squeamish dear boy. I am doing everyone a service. These are unwanted creatures, merely animals. The male was simply abandoned, at the rear of Ramirez Enterprise premises in Iquitos. No one wanted it; not even the Holy Sisters. I had it brought here. When it is big enough it can beg a living on the streets of the city. "

We were now once again entering the first building where Raphael was heating water over a burner above a small gas cylinder. In response to a curt demand for coffee he reached into a cupboard to find mugs.

We stood in a semicircle to drink the tepid brew as there was neither enough seating nor space for us all to be comfortable. But comfort was the last thing in my mind. I was perturbed, appalled by what I had just seen, tormented by the inhuman sounds still audible from the fetid cage.

Ramirez continued, warming to his theme, expanding on the short histories, the squalid brief lives of those captured children.

"In other circumstances the smaller creatures would have been aborted. However the common prostitutes of the favelas are ignorant specimens. They hope their problems will just go away. But the sister of one of my employees, a good man, has that unfortunate profession. She became pregnant and found nine months later that she had two mouths to feed. Poverty beckoned. So they turned to Raoul for help. I had the unwanted offspring brought here. It will be much easier to find a home for them back in a favela when they are old enough to scavenge or scrounge, beg or burgle.

"So you see I help my people; and then when it is necessary they help me."

The atmosphere in the room was oppressive. Ramirez was voluble, gesticulating with his left arm, clutching the mug of bitter coffee in his right. I found myself shrinking away from him, brushing against the curtain covering the entrance to the sleeping area.

"But forget about them Benjamin. Forget about Raoul's little acts of philanthropy. Do you not think that Inca Enterprises has a most useful establishment? Two weeks before your June feast your culinary supplies can be prepared in this very location. They will be stowed onto our chartered yacht moored just 100 metres away. The voyage could not be more direct – straight down the mighty river and out across the ocean to the Cape Verde rendezvous!"

I forced myself to concentrate on what he was saying, to remember that I had financial details to finalise. But I was incredulous. It was hard to believe that Collingwood had invested $1 million simply to assure one delivery of a Peruvian delicacy.

"Surely you realise that the tastes of the Epicureans will change?" I asked. "You can't have set up all this simply to cater for one event?"

"Of course not Benjamin," Ramirez responded dismissively. "My commission from Crispin became an inspiration. When I examined the logistics I realised that this secluded island would be perfect, both in the short term and the long term."

"The long term?" I queried.

"Yes. You observed how extensive are the storage facilities. You have heard my description of the transportation opportunities. This will make a useful depot from which to dispatch more of the exotic flesh which might tempt your taste buds. I can offer such delicacies as llama, alpaca, rhea or even iguana."

"Are you telling me that Collingwood invested $1 million simply to secure a few food supplies?"

"An intelligent question, Benjamin. I sincerely hope that indeed on several more occasions I might supply Epicurean delicacies, but you will realise that these warehouse facilities can also hold other commodities. Perhaps you do not understand the geography. There is a great convergence of rivers, most of them far mightier than your Thames, in this natural basin. Several of them flow south from Columbia. Do you follow me?"

Suddenly the true intention behind Inca Enterprises was becoming clear.

"It is such a pity that I suffered such severe cash flow problems. Fortunately when I explained the potential to Crispin he was an enthusiastic investor. He can anticipate a substantial return.

"To guarantee that other activities remain unnoticed the primary purpose of this establishment will of course continue. We will continue to breed cavia porcellus – our national dish – to supply the restaurants of Iquitos and the saints' feasts of neighbouring communities. Deliveries and collections will be quite normal and anything more valuable can come and go with the other supplies without attracting attention. Perfect, don't you think?"

Ramirez was beaming with amused satisfaction.

"Now Benjamin, it is nearly time to leave. But before we go, did you not notice the small path to the rear? That leads to the latest in jungle sanitary design – the Ventilated Improved Pit –the acme of Amazonian latrines. You will excuse me if I use the vernacular, but I need a pee. Here keep hold of this for me. It would be most unfortunate were it to become more intimately acquainted with the local celebrity."

He pushed his way out of the door, laughing loudly, thrusting the attaché case into my spare hand. Raphael bustled behind him grunting incomprehensibly and the door swung shut again wafted by the slight breeze, the latch clunking back into place.

For a moment I was alone, standing nonplussed, clutching my smart red case. Then behind me I heard a quiet whisper, the merest murmur of a breath.

"Senor! Shhh."

I turned and saw a girl. In that first glimpse she appeared to be no more than 18. She had an innocent, handsome face with penetrating deep brown eyes. She was scantily clothed, her arms and legs bare. Immediately I noticed, just below her left shoulder, a large livid bruise, the size of a fist. She said nothing but fixed me with a piteous gaze, her index finger held to her mouth indicating the need for silence. She was shaking visibly, trembling with fear.

"Help me," she pleaded, in clear English, followed immediately by another "shh" as we heard the heavy footfall of Raphael.

I stared at her, unsure of what to say, unwilling to become an accomplice, afraid either to accept or betray the sudden trust invested in me.

"He hits me." She gestured towards her upper arm. "Help us get away."

But now Raphael was pushing at the mesh door, lifting the latch, clumsily entering his domain once more.

"Please – save us!"

This became a desperate whisper as she slipped back into the small room. As she vanished she pressed a ball of paper into my hand.

I held it scrunched up, concealed in my palm. Raphael grinned at me, pointed to my groin, his face contorted as he tried vainly to speak, finally gesturing outside in the direction Ramirez had taken.

"No, I'm okay," I responded, shaking my head. At the same time I unobtrusively slipped my hand into my trouser pocket and released the crumpled sheet, swinging the attaché case to conceal the movement as I indicated that I did not have the same need as Ramirez.

Then he was back, standing outside.

"Come on, Benjamin, time for us to take another watery journey. I'll guard the case. I trust you have not succumbed to the greenback's lure and helped yourself in my absence."

I stepped past Raphael, recoiling at his reek of stale sweat, and lifted the door latch. Impatient, over anxious to regain possession of his dollars, Ramirez reached greedily for the case before the door was fully open. The flat side caught against the rough metal of the catch. There was a dull scraping as a deep gouge appeared in the leather, instantly marring it with a 10 centimetre brown scar.

"That was clumsy of you Benjamin. It is fortunate that our future commerce will be by way of electronic transfer. The hand luggage has become so aesthetically unpleasing."

There could be no response. Standing outside in the compound, once more I caught the waft of a foul odour from the hideous prison behind the screen of reeds; I caught the strange cries and whimpers from within. It was hard to believe that I had seen young human beings cruelly confined. I was revolted by the silent jailer and his violent tendencies, evidence of which had been plainly visible on the skin of the girl, apparently detained against her will. This was a confusing, disturbing destination; a vile place; a location of depravity.

I just wanted to get away. Although my dislike had grown beyond distaste to disgust, I was still dependent on Ramirez. I followed him down the duckboards back to our waiting dugout. Determinedly I reminded myself of the necessity of maintaining my level headedness, of keeping my focus on finance; for shortly it would be my unenviable task to enter into negotiations with him.

But as we left the hateful jungle clearing there was one other imperative that seemed to cry out to me from within. At all costs I must not betray a secret. I must remain silent about the girl. As we walked away from the compound I again closed my fist over the crumpled paper, reminding myself that what I had seen had not been an apparition.

But at the same time, and with a debilitating sense of despair, I felt helpless to go to her aid.

9

Our boatman was asleep. He lay stretched out in the bottom of the dugout rocked by the lapping of the water, warmed by the sun now well beyond its zenith. Ramirez put his foot to the prow and shook it violently. Startled and yawning, the unfortunate man scrambled up muttering apologies and helped us into his craft.

It took much longer to travel back. Not only did we have to cross almost the full width of the river but also we were now travelling upstream, battling the full force of the current rather than flowing with it. The large vessel had disappeared and was probably now unloading passengers and cargo on the city wharf.

Mercifully Ramirez remained silent on our return. Hot, tired and uncomfortable in the afternoon sun, even crouched alarmingly close to the thick brown water, I felt my eyes growing heavy as a soothing somnolence began to sweep over me. Relieved to be away from the island, in this drowsy state I travelled back to our point of departure temporarily blotting out all I had seen and heard that day.

Eventually we moored again at the crude landing stage. Several other dugouts were there idly waiting for trade which never came. As we pulled in to the wooden posts there were a few shouts of greeting and a young man reached down to grab the short rope flung by our boatman. He looked at me closely.

"You is American?"

"English," I responded without thinking.

"I speak good English. What is your name?"

This young man with dark Indian features seemed genuinely friendly. "Benjamin," I replied instinctively.

"I am Pablo," he answered

But before he could say more Ramirez waved him away, as if he were slapping at an offensive fly. Then discreetly he opened the attaché case, gently stroking the gashed leather as if consoling it, and removed one of the remaining bundles of notes.

"We don't want these undesirables to see how much we are carrying," he said in an aside.

He counted out an amount in small dollar bills into the gnarled hands of our Amazonian taxi driver who bowed obsequiously before hastily concealing the notes in his ragged clothes.

We made our way on foot back through the squalid streets. They seemed dirtier than before as if another day's accumulation of rubbish had visibly increased the griminess of the despondent area. Already the shadows were lengthening, the shops beginning to close. As we approached it the sign on Hotel Rosa crackled into life.

A taxi was waiting outside, the driver the man who had brought us from the airport the previous evening. No doubt Ramirez had accompanied his gratuity with a request for a return journey and no doubt the generous tip was sufficient to ensure compliance. Indeed the boot was open, showing our bags already installed, the leather holdall cockily sitting astride my serviceable suitcase.

"We are nearly done, Benjamin." Ramirez appeared smug. "Tonight, five star luxury in Iquitos. Then over dinner we can have our final discussion. We need to look to the future; to plan the next delivery; and of course we have to consider financial arrangements."

It was early evening when we reached the centre of Iquitos crawling through the heavy traffic impatiently clogging the Plaza de Armas, noisy with the sound of horns, hazy with the fog of diesel fumes. We drew up outside a smart modern hotel. Porters leapt to carry our bags, showing us into a large lobby, cool and refreshing, the air conditioning offering immediate relief after the humidity of the street.

Ramirez handled the arrangements with the receptionist, a smart young lady in a neatly pressed blouse, who spoke perfect English.

She looked up with a fixed smile. "Ah, Senor Ramirez I have your reservation. You have a suite and your colleague, Mr Turner, a king size room."

"Excellent," he replied. "No doubt you will wish to freshen up Benjamin. Meet me for dinner in the restaurant at 7.30."

My room was luxurious, with a large bed and adjoining bathroom with two basins, a toilet, bidet, large glass shower cubicle and deep inviting bathtub. I felt filthy; damp and soiled from the crude dugout and oppressive jungle. But more than that I felt contaminated by the day's sights and sounds. I stripped off my clothes, discarding them where I stood, turned on the bath taps, poured two small bottles of fragrant gel into the water, and immersed myself, relaxing and cleansing my body.

As I lay there I made myself think ahead, forcing myself to concentrate on the negotiation which was about to commence. Before leaving London I had carried out some initial financial planning. I knew roughly what the June vintners' account would be and what the catering and other staff would charge. The major unknown was the consideration for the venue. I was dependent on Sabrina for that. Finally there would be the payment to Inca Enterprises.

I rose from the water, wrapped myself in a thick towelling bathrobe, shaved and sprinkled myself liberally from the complimentary bottle of Eau de Cologne. Then I sat at the writing desk with pen and paper and made some calculations. The cost of the raw material – the slightly repulsive furry bundles – was insignificant. The principal expense was in transportation but, as Ramirez himself had explained, the new location made the voyage more straightforward. I considered that Collingwood's introductory fee had been generous. But I also realised that Ramirez would be even more grasping, anxious to generate a surplus so that besides his director's remuneration he could ensure a dividend for his principal shareholder. Looking at the figures I concluded that £375,000 was my bottom line.

My provisional calculations also indicated that this should yield me a handsome surplus – my 'stipend' to use Collingwood's term. It was not that I needed the money. It was simply that if there was something there to grab then you were letting yourself down if you did not grab it. You also had to get the better of someone in the process.

With these thoughts uppermost in my mind, dressed in London clothes, I went down to dinner.

Deliberately I was early. I took a seat at a table and ordered a starter followed by a light chicken dish and a bottle of Chilean chardonnay. When Ramirez joined me he was slightly disconcerted, exactly as I intended.

"Ah Benjamin. You have already ordered?" There was irritation in his voice as he noticed my glass, the droplets of water misting the exterior, masking the golden liquid beneath.

"With that choice of wine I suspect you have ordered the chicken. What a pity, as it had been my intention to introduce you to an excellent Argentinean malbec. I shall have to imbibe it by myself to wash down my choice – a steak which I shall of course take rare."

He was being deliberately contrary, trying to establish control. Before our first course arrived he took the initiative.

"You no doubt now appreciate why it was necessary to undertake this interesting voyage. You can report to Crispin that Raoul Ramirez has put in place the perfect infrastructure. But how about you Benjamin? Do you recall that, before you ruined my shirt, I offered you a shareholding equal to that of our honourable friend? You can see for yourself that Inca Enterprises offers a golden opportunity. Do you wish to take up the balance of the authorised share capital?"

I hesitated, having no desire to invest even a cent in a business operated by my odious companion. However it was imperative that the discussions commenced positively.

"I am certainly very interested," I lied. "Can you give me three weeks to think about it?"

"Of course Benjamin." Ramirez beamed but with unsubtle pressure, added, "Do not linger much longer – Crispin might persuade an American associate to participate."

Our first course arrived – three skewered prawns on an artistic bed of rice for me, a lattice of asparagus for Ramirez.

Before selecting his cutlery he reached into his wallet and handed me a card from the bank in Cusco. On the back was written: Inca Enterprises SA Account No. 18012912.

"I did not have the opportunity to hand you this before you interrupted our meal in Cusco," he explained.

I took one glance at the card and, in a moment of inspiration, ripped it into four small pieces letting them sprinkle onto the tablecloth. Ramirez was startled. A large globule of melted butter dripped from a green asparagus shoot speared on his fork, sliding over the black hairs on the back of his hand. He hesitated and I forestalled him.

"Don't you trust my memory Raoul?" I asked. "You forget my profession. I deal with large numbers all the time. This is such an easy numerical sequence that I can retain it in my head. Future electronic transfers will be to this account number consisting of the first and last two digits of the decimal scale. Now let's consider the quantum of the fee."

My apparent mathematical ability evidently disconcerted him; he would never know that my sister's birthday was 18th January and mine 29th December. He finished wiping his hand with his napkin then gulped down the remaining asparagus before fixing me with a stare, his eyes now steely, impassive behind the gold-rimmed spectacles.

"As you can see," he started, "even though we are in a remote and poor part of the world, to provide what your exclusive society requires is nevertheless a costly enterprise. There are wages to be paid, an establishment to be maintained, transportation to be arranged. But I am happy to inform you that in view of our streamlined arrangements the Inca Enterprises charge on the next occasion will be a modest £550,000."

Without replying I dissected the final prawn, dipping the flesh into the pink sauce, savouring the forkful as I finished the dish.

"Come off it Raoul," I said quietly, having swallowed the plump tail. "You don't seriously think I'm going to accept that."

Deliberately I swirled my chardonnay then sipped defiantly.

Ramirez seemed surprised. He smiled thinly.

"Very well, as it's our first contract and as I wish to maintain cordial relations, I'll offer you a discount: £500,000."

There was an enforced silence while our plates were cleared away. There would be only a couple of minutes before the main courses arrived.

"Raoul," I responded coolly and quietly, "even your so called discount leaves an excessive amount. £250,000 would be far more reasonable."

He blustered slightly but steadied himself with a sip of malbec. "Benjamin, Benjamin," he said. "Do you not appreciate the logistics of transportation?"

I remained impassive.

"Oh all right. I'll give you a 25 per cent reduction," he spluttered.

We paused as the waiter returned placing our orders in front of us. Ramirez cut into his steak, the blood spilling across his plate, dripping off the side onto the pieces of torn business card and making large red globules on the white cloth. I took a mouthful of my chicken then looked directly across at him.

"This is absurd," I said quietly. "We both know that in a remote location labour is cheap. It really is not worth interrupting this meal unless your figure moves much closer to mine. But in acknowledgment of what you say I'll go to £300,000."

Ramirez impaled another piece of flesh on his fork. I carefully sliced the soft white meat and swallowed effortlessly while he chewed.

"My, my, Benjamin; what a hard negotiator you are. Is this how you behave on the trading floor? You are forcing me to squeeze my margins; to keep my mother penniless in Jersey. Come, let's shake hands on £400,000."

I sensed he was retreating. It was tempting to request the further £25,000 and close the deal. But I hesitated.

"It's no good Raoul," I replied with an apologetic air. "What you don't know is the quantum of the other expenses. There are caterers, vintners, security staff. Besides I am expecting a considerable charge for the use of desirable premises."

I did not add that to foster my relationship I anticipated showing extreme generosity to Sabrina.

"It is exceedingly difficult for me to go beyond £325,000."

Ramirez fidgeted uncomfortably. "But you're getting a unique product, spirited in away from the prying of petty officialdom. The importation is not without risk. Naturally your society expects discretion and I have demonstrated to you that this quality pervades all my endeavours, but inevitably it comes at a price. Finally – and you will forgive my candour- you have no alternative supply."

"Quite true," I responded, "but if necessary I shall simply have to introduce club members to alternative exotic tastes."

I wiped my lips and folded my table napkin.

"You wouldn't leave me high and dry? Collingwood wouldn't allow it!" He appeared momentarily alarmed. "And those creatures are ready for culling."

He was pitifully close to sounding pathetic.

"OK," I said swiftly seizing the moment. "£350,000 and not a penny more."

"Done!" he said dully and I rose to shake him by the hand before he could change his mind.

It is always satisfying when you exceed your target. But I reflected ruefully that the amount was what he had originally required for the first consignment before Collingwood so readily agreed that his overhead expenses were legitimate.

The waiter came, deftly removing my empty plate and accepting Ramirez's indication that he desired no more of the mangled remains clinging obstinately to his T-bone.

I ordered dessert and Ramirez looked on patiently while slowly I consumed a tasteful melange of tropical fruits and ice cream.

"Let me acquaint you with our travel arrangements," he announced over coffee, his bumptiousness returning, "We are booked on the morning flight to Lima. There we must part. You go to London; I to Rio."

I attempted to conceal my relief. Within 24 hours I would be free of him. Our next contact would be electronic; I would not be required to have face-to-face discussions again for some considerable time.

As we drank the strong dark coffee and unwrapped our complimentary mints we remained civil and sober. I noticed that, like me, Ramirez had left more than a half a bottle of wine unconsumed. We said goodnight and agreed to meet after breakfast for the taxi ride back to Francisco Secada Vignetta airport.

Returning to my room, gliding effortlessly two floors upwards in the smooth interior glass lift, I felt buoyant. My negotiating skills were unaffected by this country, by the squalor I had seen, by the disconcerting experiences of the day. When it came to what I was good at, handling large sums of money, making ruthless deals, I was still master of my trade.

My clothes lay strewn around the room where I had l flung them. Feeling triumphant, not quite ready for sleep, I stooped to bundle them into my suitcase. As I folded my trousers, still slightly damp from the dugout's watery trip, I felt something in the pocket. I withdrew the forgotten crumpled paper, smoothing it out on the dressing table.

Written upon it in stubby pencil were six words.

"My name is Gilda – help us."

The flight next morning would have been uneventful had it not been late. We learnt that the low Pacific cloud covering Lima was particularly dense. By late morning we were still awaiting the incoming flight. By noon Ramirez was agitated, thumping on the enquiry desk protesting that it was imperative that he caught his onward flight to Rio which departed a few hours before mine to Madrid.

As if in response to his demands there was a flickering on the screens to announce the arrival of the plane and forty-five minutes later we were taking off. At Lima he hurried me from the luggage hall panting as we followed the walkway to the international terminal.

"Iberia is that way." He pointed at the long rows of airline desks and their impatient shuffling queues. "I must leave you. The LAN check-in to Rio is about to close. Farewell. I look forward to our next contact soon. Here – take this: just in case you forget your numerical sequence. "

He thrust a replacement business card into my hand, his stubby finger pointing to 'Inca Enterprises SA Account No. 18012912', before hurrying off, pushing his leather holdall on an airport trolley. But then I realised he was still firmly clutching my attaché case, its fresh scar, my mark of ownership, lying prominent down one side.

"My case – I want it back!" I yelled at him.

It was too late. His portly frame was disappearing behind an enormous security machine and with it went my recently violated possession.

There were still two hours before the evening Iberia flight for Madrid. I checked in, completed the fast-track through security and immigration and followed the signs to the Business Class lounge.

I was relieved to be going back to my familiar life, to handle exciting sums of money, strike lucrative international deals and enjoy my swelling status on Hazzards' trading floor. I was unquestionably on an upward trajectory. My treasurership of the Epicureans had been a double bonus. Not only did it propel me into the company of the most important players in my game, it also offered me a lucrative sideline. Although I had not enjoyed my adventure with Ramirez our association would be purely temporary. Before long my colleagues' tastes would change, perhaps to kudu or zebra, and I would arrange exotic importations from a different supplier in a different continent. While I could see the attraction of shares in Inca Enterprises I would not subscribe. It was less the potential nature of the company's activities which deterred me than the character of its creator. But after Ramirez had dictated the agenda for so long, when it came to the tough negotiation over money I had not been bested. Now I could return to London confident that the June gathering would be a success, that I had emerged superior from the deal. Raoul Ramirez had fared no better than Declan Faulkner. At the next dinner I would be the first to be toasted. I was indeed the coming man.

This demanded celebration. I made for the lengthy buffet bar offering delicate sandwiches, olives, sliced meat, morsels of spicy sausage, and a series of creative tapas dishes. Naturally the wine was Spanish, both red and white riojas. But there was also some champagne bearing a respectable label. I poured myself a flute and with a generous plate of food settled down and turned my gaze to the TV monitor in the corner.

A Spanish news channel seemed to be dominated by reports of gangland shootings in one of Lima's favelas. There were lurid pictures of bloodied bodies sprawled in foul gutters, armed policemen scowling at the scene gazing malevolently at the sullen slum dwellers. Then there were the usual interviews with police chiefs and civic representatives. It was all depressing and not terribly interesting. I began to ignore the screen, enjoying my tasty mouthfuls washed down with the creamy, nutty flavoured champagne.

Then I caught some words that were vaguely recognisable: 'Banco; financier; crisis'. I looked up and suddenly, disconcertingly, sharp on the high-definition screen there was footage of Canary

Wharf; office workers, heads down hurrying homewards; burly security guards at a building's entrance. The camera zoomed in closer for a moment and I recognised the familiar revolving door of my workplace. But it was strangely immobile, the bustling foyer deserted. The clip of film ended and I caught a few snatches of the commentary including the word 'redundante'. Then we were back to the face of the newsreader and a story about the national football team.

This was all strangely puzzling. It was unclear to me exactly what was happening in London but the people on TV seemed worried. My champagne was finished but now, slightly bewildered, I no longer desired a second celebratory flute. Eventually my gate number flashed on the monitor screen and I commenced the long trek past shops and restaurants, down escalators, along moving walkways until at last I joined the throng presenting their boarding cards, impatient to find their seats on the Airbus to Madrid.

After the meal, served once we had reached cruising altitude, it was expected that passengers would settle down to sleep. I found that impossible. The notion that something could threaten my bank had never even remotely occurred to me. The whole enterprise was rich and successful, year on year posting ever-increasing profits. I had only ever seen expansion, the trading floor becoming enlarged, new space being leased in the Docklands tower block. I wondered about the implications of the brief news item. Did it simply mean that a lucrative trade had gone spectacularly wrong or did it portend some substantial reorganisation? These thoughts frustrated relaxation, totally dispelling my transient euphoria at resisting Ramirez's excessive demands.

I suppose eventually I must have drifted off, overcome by tiredness. But if so it was a dismal drowse and I was quickly alert when the window flaps were lifted to reveal a grey morning as we descended towards the Iberian Peninsula.

There was only an hour between the arrival at Madrid and the departure for London. I hastened through the echoing airport, all marble floors and stylish wooden ceilings. This European airport contrasted markedly with those of Peru. It reminded me that I was back in familiar territory, closer to home, that London was just a couple of hours away. I reached the boarding gate, was first down the walkway, the first to be seated at the front of the aircraft and, as anticipated, the first to be asked if I would like a newspaper. I requested the Financial Times.

Hastily I unfolded the familiar pink paper. It was not the style of this newspaper to be sensationalist. The front page headline was stark and factual. It said everything I needed to know: 'Collapse of Leading Merchant Bank'.

I read quickly. During the week I had been away a crisis had been brewing. Hazzard Brothers had suddenly found itself with insufficient reserves. It had promptly ceased trading and liquidators had been called in. I turned over the long front sheet and saw in front of me a photograph on page 3. The familiar revolving door of my office building was clearly in view and there amongst a throng emerging was Justin Rhodes clutching a large black bin sack.

According to the reporter it was only five days earlier that our management had signalled there were difficulties. Frantic negotiations had taken place in the hope of a merger or a rescue package. They had been unsuccessful. When it was recognised that the situation was hopeless trading was immediately suspended. The next day accountants from one of the big four arrived to commence liquidation. All staff without exception had been made redundant.

The announcement to fasten seatbelts must have been made but I must not have heard it as I realised the stewardess was peering over the newspaper checking whether my buckle was snapped into place. She asked me if I was quite well, observing that I appeared a little pale.

I was shaken, deeply worried about what awaited me in London. As the aircraft roared down the tarmac I pressed back into my seat urging it upwards, willing us urgently to England. I simply had to find out for myself what was going on, whether I could soon return to the trading floor or whether the situation was as dire as the Financial Times so graphically indicated.

Long before we reached Heathrow I had decided I would travel straight to Canary Wharf. I took the escalator down to the Heathrow Express station and purchased a ticket to Paddington. The train was swift and comfortable, equipped with all the accoutrements of modern communication including television. There in front of me on the monitor the story was running. The revolving door was spinning, numerous people were pouring out, some of them vaguely familiar to me. The BBC economics correspondent was explaining excitedly, in very simplistic terms, what had occurred. Austere figures carrying bulky cases bearing the logo of a well-known accountancy firm were entering the building.

At Paddington I hurried across to Platform One. As the morning rush had finished the cabs were moving swiftly to the front of the rank.

"Canary Wharf," I barked when it was my turn.

"Okay guv. You're the only one going there – most are leaving!"

The last thing I wanted was a comedian for a driver. I remained silent.

Perversely the morning was pleasant. It was a clear bright spring day with a soft breeze. The new leaves on the trees in streets and parks were a fresh green. London was looking its best.

But the scene at my office was dismal. I paid off the taxi driver and approached the revolving glass doors seen so incongruously just half a day earlier on the TV screen in Lima airport. They were locked. In fact they were totally secured, held firmly in place with a shiny tough chain. A burly security guard was standing at a small side door, his back to the plate glass. I tapped hard to attract his attention.

"What do you want?"

"I work here."

"Not any more mate."

10

I was desperate for some answers. "Look," I said to the guard. "I've been away on holiday. I don't know what's been going on. I've just got back and I've come straight here."

The guard unstiffened slightly. He beckoned me in and muttered into a small walkie-talkie. "There's a guy just come in says he used to work here. Yeah, been on holiday. Okay." He clicked the 'off' button and said tersely, "Wait here a minute. Someone will be down."

I noticed that the exterior elevator was firmly grounded, its door held secure. But the lights above its interior alternative flickered and a few moments later a smart young lady, about my age, emerged. She was carrying a padded clipboard, the name of an accountancy firm clearly emblazoned on its rear.

"Hello, I'm Julia Farringdon. We are the liquidators. And you are?"

I gave my name, explaining that I had been overseas and out of contact for a few days. I needed to know what was going on.

"I can tell you very little more than you read in the newspapers." Julia was coolly professional. "It appears that there have recently been some catastrophic trades. There was a liquidity crisis and suddenly when they were required some hundreds of millions were not there. It seems that all you merchant bankers have been buying dodgy collateralised debt, or toxic assets as the press likes to call them. Your chickens, if I may use the metaphor, are coming home to roost, and they all have avian flu."

She then scanned down a list on her clipboard.

"Ah, Mr Turner. I see you are one of a handful who were not here last week. A letter will have been sent to your home address. I think your possessions must be here."

She led me over to the empty reception desk and peered behind. There were about half a dozen black bin sacks each bearing a brown label with a name thickly scrawled in felt pen. Mine, smaller than the others, was on top of the untidy collection. I undid the string and looked inside. There was my coffee mug, some pens and pencils, the three ties I kept in the office in case I need to smarten up and a couple of motoring magazines which I had never taken home. To my relief there was also my precious notebook with names and telephone numbers of contacts.

Innocently I asked if I could be permitted to enter and log onto my computer. Julia gave me a cold look of disapproval. "Your career here is over. Our job is to liquidate any assets as quickly as possible. Computers, telephones and all other equipment are entrusted to us. There can be no exceptions."

"But hang on!" I protested. "I've been away from civilisation; I've been travelling all night. Then I get here and you casually tell me I'm sacked! I want to find out about market trends, US government bonds, off market trades in New York. I need all this stuff. What do you expect me to do? And what has happened to the people I used to work with – people like Quentin Foorde, Justin Rhodes and Nick Forsyth?"

Although consummately professional, Julia did allow one small piece of information to escape. "Mr Foorde has, I understand, secured himself another position but," she looked down at her list, "Mr Rhodes and Mr Forsyth are in the same boat as you."

I stared at her blankly for a moment. Somehow I was not surprised that Quentin had got something lined up for himself.

"This has been a major trauma to you as an individual, to your bank, to the city and to the government," Julia announced, then offered the tiniest morsel of compassion. "This crisis is only just beginning. Take some time out; maybe think about a new career."

She gestured to the guard to open the glass door, shook my hand and turned back to the lift. In a moment I was outside, ignominiously excluded from the office where I had worked for the past four years.

Somehow through my shock I realised that I needed to get back home, shower, change and restock the fridge. Then I needed space to work out what to do next.

Although it was only a short distance I took a taxi back to the flat, not wishing to be seen trundling a case like a pauper. Inside it was hot and airless, the late spring sun now streaming in through the windows. Behind the door lay a small collection of mail. There were the usual catalogues offering me shirts and suits, a couple of investment magazines and a stiff white envelope bearing the now familiar logo of my company's liquidators.

Their letter was short and, although it addressed me by name, impersonal. It gave no details of what exactly had brought the bank down, saying simply that a severe and unexpected liquidity crisis had occurred. Hazzards could no longer meet its obligations and had no alternative other than to place itself in liquidation. I was dismissed with immediate effect. My salary ceased forthwith and I had no entitlement to any further bonus payment. I was reminded that any information I had acquired during my period of employment was confidential.

I recognised the style including the merest speck of soothing balm in the final paragraph:

'We regret that this course of action has been necessary and offer you our best wishes for the future.

Yours sincerely,

Julia Farringdon'

Tired and rather angry I tossed it aside. As it fluttered heavily my eye was caught by the red digits flashing on the telephone answering machine. There were five messages. I reached down and switched on.

The spooling tape whirred, clicked and then Pam was talking to me.

"Hello Ben. You're not answering your mobile so I hope you are okay. Hazel is doing fine. Get in touch when you are back."

The second message was from the garage reminding me that it was time to book a service for the Porsche. I ignored it. The car had low mileage and the dealers were too eager to inflict inflated bills on their wealthy clientele.

There was another series of clicks and then unmistakably Sabrina's seductive voice was addressing me.

"Hi Ben, darling. It's Sabrina. I've tried your mobile twice but got this number off Justin Rhodes. I'm not in London for three weeks. Ring me about the fifteenth and you can buy me dinner. Ciao!"

This was a call I had not wanted to miss. I inwardly cursed my Lima assailants and felt even more irritated with myself for succumbing to a fabled tourist trick.

The next voice was also female with an attractive French accent.

"Mr Turner. This is Gabrielle Dubois, secretary to Mr Picard-Syme. Please contact him urgently."

The final voice was that of Picard-Syme himself.

"Benjamin! Where the hell are you and why are you not answering your mobile? We must speak. Contact me immediately."

This peremptory call puzzled me. What could he possibly want? But even as I wondered it occurred to me that perhaps the key to my salvation lay in this brief message.

It was Friday lunchtime, not the best moment to make a return call. I decided to shower and change then dashed out for a sandwich. It was important to reflect before I established contact and it would not harm Picard-Syme to wait a bit longer although it could harm me if I interrupted his lunch.

It was 2.30 before I got through to him.

"At last!" was his terse greeting. "Don't you ever answer?"

"I'm sorry," I said in a matter-of-fact way. "I was away on business for the Epicureans. My mobile was stolen and I've only just picked up my messages."

"It's about the Epicureans that I wanted to speak. This Hazzards' collapse is creating waves throughout the banking world. Unfortunate questions are being asked. There is intrusive prying into private contractual arrangements between banks and their employees. Now is the time for discretion. It is certainly not the time for conspicuous consumption. I have therefore decided that until this storm blows itself out we should suspend operations. Accordingly I've cancelled our June banquet."

"But I've just spent most of the week getting arrangements in place," I protested.

Immediately I regretted the remark, regretted the momentary loss of control.

"Then unplace them," he barked.

In my tiredness I was tempted to describe the journey I had taken, the watery voyage, the unsavoury scenes on that island in the Amazon. But I realised he would be unimpressed and besides, standing in my apartment gazing over London's familiar metropolitan expanse, these recent experiences seemed unreal. But above all I reminded myself that I was dependent on him.

"Of course. I do understand," I responded, refocusing, mustering my composure. "But there is one other matter."

"Yes?"

"Like all Hazzards' traders my contract has been terminated. You know my track record. Are there any positions in Hardings?"

"The demise of our rival has indeed created opportunities. I've already recruited Quentin Foorde, who I think you know, to head up a new team. Crispin spoke highly of you. I suppose you'll fit in. Report to Quentin on Monday morning."

With considerable relief I was now able to turn to my other tasks. I telephoned Pam for an excited update about weight gain, feeding and sleeping patterns. The christening had been arranged for a Sunday morning three weeks away with a family gathering at her in-laws' house afterwards. I told her that various matters kept me in London over the next two weekends but I would certainly fulfil my role as godfather, although I still had no notion of what was expected of me.

Then, before tiredness overcame me, I went out and bought myself a new phone.

It was strange arriving on the Monday at Hardings, only a short distance away from the Hazzards building already appearing sad and shabby. Quentin was not in good humour.

"Kick Arse said I had to take you on," was his greeting.

I tried not to bridle. "You must have moved quickly. It can only have been a week since things went pear shaped."

"I have my contacts," he said with a slight sneer. "This has been in the offing for weeks. The crash merely accelerated it."

He showed me onto the Hardings trading floor, the lines of desks each with two telephones, the computer terminals, the swivel chairs, the general untidiness, all exactly as in Hazzards.

"You can park yourself here." He gestured to an empty space. "I think you know your new colleague."

Of course I did. I recognised him instantly even with his back to me, his ear to the telephone. I recognised the slightly red hair, the thick arms of his spectacles, the disguised accent in his voice. It was Declan Faulkner.

His conversation lasted half an hour, prolonged with boastful banter. Hanging up, he turned to me.

"The golden boy has lost his shine, I see." Quentin had spoken with a sneer but Declan could manage no more than a smirk. "Welcome to Hardings. Just remember we don't do dodgy derivatives here."

I was given responsibility for handling the bond portfolio of a small insurance company in run-off. Understandably it was conservative and extremely risk averse. The work was boring with little scope for adventurous deals. However I consoled myself with the thought that, as when I started at Hazzards, I simply had to accomplish the task and prove my worth.

On my third day my computer was not working. I logged on to discover a blank screen which gave no flicker when I logged off. Declan seemed to be unaffected by the malfunction.

"You'll need to call the help desk," he offered with uncharacteristic friendliness. "Here's their number."

But fortunately before dialling I noticed a rogue lead. Once I correctly inserted it into the rear of the monitor the screen came back to life.

Quentin's attendance appeared erratic. He was forever bustling in and out apparently much in demand. I did not speak to him again until the end of the week.

"How are you getting on with Declan?" he asked, late on Friday afternoon. "He's doing well here."

"Okay," I lied.

"I'm trying to get Justin and Nick taken on. But Kick Arse is being cautious. Had it been my choice I would have had them first – so count yourself lucky."

By the middle of the following week I was beginning to exploit the limited possibilities of my bond portfolio. Venturing back into dollar trades once again, Art Feinman proved a useful contact. Through him I started negotiations for some safe Midwest corporate debt. It was late in the evening and only a few of us were still on the trading floor. I was deep in a transatlantic telephone conversation hurrying to close the deal before I was outdone by a Japanese bank. Declan left with a dismissive wave as I was in the midst of a hard negotiation over basis points.

Suddenly the telephone went dead. I re-dialled but there was no sound whatsoever, not even a static hum.

Frustrated, I resorted to e-mail. I rapidly typed and pressed 'Send', but I was too late. There were no telephone problems in Japan. I lost the trade to Tokyo.

Next morning four of us had dead telephones.

"I think I know the problem," Declan announced innocently. "This has happened before. Someone must have tripped on the floor box."

Nonchalantly he bent and lifted up a panel in the carpet tiles revealing a labyrinth of power and telephone cables which then snaked their separate ways into conduits to the rear of our desks. "Look," he cried in triumph, "here's the culprit!"

In an instant, just as when my monitor was blank, communication was restored.

On the Friday Quentin was once again talkative. He returned from a lengthy lunch wearing a distinct whiff of the wine bar.

"Success!" he chortled. "Nick and Justin start in two weeks' time."

"That's good news," I responded truthfully because although neither of them was a close friend their company was preferable to that of Declan.

Then he looked at me with a slightly scornful air.

"You are a lucky sod," he slurred rather tipsily. "Crispin had me lined up for treasurer – until he took a shine to you. Just remember he is no longer your protector."

Things became worse during the following week. I had belatedly sent an e-mail to Ramirez cancelling the June delivery and anticipated a hostile response. Twice he telephoned from Rio inconveniently interrupting me in mid afternoon during the last hectic hours before the European exchanges closed. He was alternately angry and pleading. He complained that he would not be able to dispose of his growing stock and I promised to consider his request for compensation. But he still pressed me to subscribe share capital to Inca Enterprises and, to avoid upsetting him further, I continued to promise careful consideration.

I thought things were looking up on the Thursday when at last I managed to speak to Sabrina. We arranged a date for dinner the following Wednesday at The Ivy, ostensibly to discuss the venue for the next Epicurean outing. There was no need to tell her just yet that it would not take place.

My pleasure at making this arrangement was short lived. Arriving promptly at Hardings on Friday morning, I could not get my desk drawer open. It took a couple of hours for a maintenance man to come, drill out the lock and discover it had been liberally squirted with superglue. Declan claimed he knew nothing about it and blamed the cleaners. I removed my notebook of contacts; it would go home with me that evening.

Late that afternoon, as most of us were shutting down for the weekend, Quentin called me to see him.

"Not exactly a brilliant start is it?" His challenge was brusque.

"What do you mean?" I asked.

"I have here the back office figures for your first two weeks. At least they're not negative, but do you know how much profit you've generated?"

I knew that my trades had been low margin. I also knew that the telephone incident had deprived me of the most lucrative. Silence appeared to be the best response.

"I'll tell you," he barked, "£5,372.13! Not exactly a king's ransom. Declan is knocking spots off you. You'll be in trouble if Justin and Nick overtake you."

It was useless protesting.

"Thanks for letting me know, Quentin. Have a nice weekend," I said stifling my irritation.

"You too," he responded out of habit rather than sincerity.

I had every intention of enjoying my weekend.

Early on the Sunday morning, warm bright and clear, I drove down to Eastleigh. Pam and Gary were ready for the christening early. Hazel, a pink smudge in a cascade of white, was asleep, oblivious to the preparations. We left in convoy for the church a few miles away, my Porsche absurdly out of place behind the Vauxhall Vectra driven by Gary's father and the Ford Focus of their next-door neighbour.

As the simple ceremony was to take place at the very end of the morning service we found the parking spaces at the church occupied. With some reluctance I left my vehicle on a broad grass verge further down the road and walked back past Field Cottage to rejoin the party. It was curious, I thought, how its image had come to me 6,000 miles away in the unreality of a jungle clearing. Today it looked sad, the garden borders having succumbed to a spring riot, a 'For Sale' sign now standing beside the gate.

The christening went smoothly. I felt happy for Pam, pleased that despite the anxiety of prematurity she had a fine healthy baby. She obviously revelled in being a mother and was proud to hand her child to the clergyman who had married her to Gary. As godfather I was required to do nothing more than make a few empty promises. Of course I would also make a suitable financial contribution to my niece.

We filed out of the church into the morning sunshine and paused for photographs. I had brought my Leica, purchased a couple of years earlier but rarely used. I fiddled with the lenses, took photographs of the group and close-ups of Hazel now alert and gazing with wide-eyed astonishment at the fuss around her.

Again I drove the Porsche at the rear of a short cavalcade, this time to the home of Gary's parents. We gathered on their patio for champagne: Moët et Chandon rather than Crispin's Dom Perignon. Then we wandered in the garden admiring the rhododendrons in fresh flower and the views across the rolling hills of southern Hampshire, before helping ourselves to cold salmon or chicken.

At one quiet moment Pam approached me.

"Here you hold her – you've not yet had a chance."

She was right; I had seen only photographs of my niece until that day and in the church my formulaic responses required no physical contact. Gingerly I accepted the light bundle and gazed down at an exquisitely pretty, innocent face. Hazel's expression remained calm, one of infant trust and acceptance, but her tiny fist closed tightly on my little finger.

Pam smiled and said wistfully, "I can see mum in her face."

I was surprised at how moved I felt by the brief experience, but not wanting to betray my emotions, I returned the child to her mother and went in search of a drink.

The party drifted on into the afternoon. I could not leave early as it was imperative that the alcohol wore off before I drove back to London. Pam and Gary were staying overnight and for the first time the new granddaughter would sleep in the house of her only grandparents.

At some point tea and cake were produced and then Pam announced she would settle Hazel to sleep for the evening after bathing her.

"Come on Ben," she said, "you can help."

This was taking me far outside my comfort zone. But somehow I sensed that, although smothered in kindness from her in-laws, Pam needed the support, admiration and approval of her own kin. Accordingly I acquiesced.

We went up to the bathroom with its pink pedestal mats and a plump doll disguising the spare toilet roll. Pam filled a plastic baby bath and then carefully removed her daughter's baptismal gown, now no longer pristine, slightly milk stained. Gently she lowered her into the tepid water.

Softly she caressed the delicate skin, wiping each miniature finger and toe, sliding the soapy sponge over chubby cuffs and plump legs. Lifting the limbs slightly she swished the water over the secret crevice then over the navel, still slightly birth red.

Pam turned to me. "A penny for your thoughts Ben – you seem miles away."

"I was just thinking that you were right – she does look like mum."

But in truth I was miles away; 6,000 miles away. The only other time I had seen a naked female child was four weeks earlier. Then I had noticed bare skin glistening not with soothing baby soap but with rank perspiration in the semi darkness of a foul confinement.

That image brought another; an image of a cowering girl, an ugly bruise on her arm, desperately seeking my help.

I still felt troubled when an hour later I said farewell and set off for London. Deliberately I drove slowly, pondering on the re-awakened memories, recalling what I had seen in the Amazon. I had forgotten the unsavoury aspect of my adventure, smugly satisfied that wherever in the world I might find myself I could be confident that my negotiating skills were consummately successful. I had suppressed those mental images; I had persuaded myself that arrangements made by Ramirez, however distasteful, were none of my business.

But they were my business. I had just seen what childhood should be; I had just seen what womanhood should be.

As, abstracted, I hugged the slow lane of the M3, a daunting, heavy notion gained purchase within me. I could not do nothing.

Then south of Basingstoke I was stopped by the police.

"Have you been drinking today, sir?"

"Yes officer."

"Ah ha! Thought as much. Porsche drivers always speed except when they've been drinking. Then they keep to the speed limit thinking they won't be caught!"

I was required to take a breathalyser test. A small amount of alcohol registered but Mr Brown's champagne had almost worn off. The policeman was crestfallen. He checked my tyres and lights then hurried me on my way. He could not understand that this Porsche driver was simply preoccupied.

Back in my apartment I went straight to a drawer in the bedroom and retrieved the crumpled piece of paper discovered in my trouser pocket and instantly put away on my return. Once again I smoothed out the folds and studied the hurriedly pencilled words.

"My name is Gilda – help us."

I had resolved to say nothing to Ramirez to betray the presence of this other captive. There was something in her vulnerability, in the pleading clandestine nature of her emergence and in the brief moment of trust and hope, which compelled me to silence.

I realised now that amidst the horror of that island encampment she had reminded me of my sister.

My mind was made up. I was compelled to return.

The next morning at Hardings, once my computer was booted up, my coffee ready but still too hot to drink, I ignored Declan's arrival and sought out Quentin. He was puffy cheeked and bleary-eyed, subdued and surly.

"Good morning, Quentin," I said. "Did you have a nice weekend?"

Ignoring his grunted response I continued. "I'd like to have two weeks' holiday starting as soon as possible please."

He shook off his torpor. "What?" he snapped.

I repeated my request. "Something urgent has cropped up. Obviously I won't have any holiday later in the year."

"What is it – your mother's funeral?"

I suspected he knew my personal background and the hurt was deliberate.

"Nothing like that." I endeavoured to remain unemotional. "It's just that I have to settle something that can't wait."

"Were you listening on Friday?" He was sneering now. "You've only just started here, you're lucky not to be in negative territory and you have the temerity to come and ask for time off!"

He paused then said abruptly, "The answer is no! Now get out there and make some money!"

My guard almost slipped, but struggling to retain a veneer of professional detachment, I managed to suppress my feelings. I simply stared at him, swivelled on my heel and walked away.

But after a few paces I turned and faced him once more. It was a turn that was to change my life – and the lives of several others.

11

I have often asked myself if I would have reacted differently had it been anyone other than Quentin.

His attitude and disdainful haughtiness angered me intensely but, initially at least, my cool head silenced my heart.

A number of thoughts had been in my mind on the cautious drive back to London. The three weeks at Hardings had been difficult and unhappy and I was not sure that I could avoid being marginalised. I had been the coming man at Hazzards; at Hardings there seemed to be a conspiracy to frustrate my progress. Neither could I depend on Collingwood who seemed to be maintaining a trans-Atlantic silence, no doubt absorbed with his new responsibilities. The suspended Epicureans had lost their allure for although I held a degree of residual responsibility I was denied any activity or money making opportunity. Instead I simply suffered the whining calls and e-mails from Ramirez.

Those thoughts were with me still as I broached the possibility of some time off.

I had anticipated grudging agreement, even perhaps a fortnight's holiday without pay. Despite my outward appearance of sang-froid Quentin's blunt refusal shocked me.

In those moments, with my back to him, I clenched my fists and bit my lower lip to contain my rage. Even in my fury I was focused on the jungle compound, the stinking naked children, the frightened imploring girl. The strength of my conviction that I had to return, that I had to do something to achieve their liberation, was undiminished.

There was only one course open to me.

After I turned I stared at Quentin for a moment. Then I spoke slowly, calmly and briefly.

"I resign – with immediate effect."

Swiftly I strode away, down the ranks of traders, past my smirking neighbour absorbed in a telephone discussion. I swept my few belongings off my desk, in the process managing to spill my coffee over Declan's keyboard. That gave me a disproportionate sense of satisfaction as resolutely I stepped out of the building.

Two mornings later I was on a flight to Madrid with an onward connection to Lima.

It is surprising how much you can achieve in a short time when your mind is made up. Back at the flat I called the agency and cancelled my cleaning contract. Then I made an appointment for the following morning at Coutts. I discovered that the London Travel Centre could provide me with antimalarial tablets that day. Determined this time to be properly protected, I took a couple of hours to attend the clinic and obtain my prophylactics.

Before that I spent some time on the internet booking my ticket and finding somewhere suitable to stay.

I did not know then that my banking career was over. I simply recognised that there was unfinished business to resolve. Once this had been accomplished then I would seek a new position, perhaps with the investment arm of a high street bank or even with an insurance company. I had certainly made a significant amount of money which was still sitting untouched in my account at Coutts. That would sustain me for some considerable time and remove the urgency of fresh employment. Before then perhaps I could do a small amount of good.

Experiencing both the shock and euphoria of freedom I resolved to be cautious. I was not sure how much money my vague South American plans would cost me. I anticipated that I might have significant expenditure on travel. Thereafter, should I be successful in releasing the children, I might need funding to obtain medical treatment and place them in an orphanage. On my return I might have to draw on my capital until I again found a permanent position. It was therefore imperative to be financially prudent.

In my travels I would avoid luxury; but I was no longer a student. Accordingly I flew economy class and booked a mid-range hotel.

On Monday evening I telephoned Pam. There was no need to tell her that I had walked away from the world of merchant banking. That would complicate matters; make the reason for my impending absence difficult to explain. Instead I simply informed her that I was urgently required to go on another business trip to Peru and I was not sure when I would be back.

I was also feeling guilty. While I had muttered my responses around the font I had done nothing tangible for my niece. I promised that a little something would arrive in the post very shortly. Then I sat down to write a cheque and found myself confronted with a dilemma. What does one give to a child a few weeks old? Above all what would be proportionate when I could easily purchase everything that my sister and brother-in-law possessed and still be a millionaire twice over? I withdrew the first slip from my personal Coutts cheque-book and wrote down £1,000.

The following morning the Coutts official listened attentively to my requests. Although I had a prestigious credit card I had seen the power of cash on my previous trip. I had no desire again to carry a case stuffed with notes but a supply of dollar bills would be useful. I also decided to take $300,000 in large denomination travellers' cheques. These were no problem and were prepared while I waited. The cash would be sent to me by courier that afternoon as I had particularly requested a mix of high and low value notes.

I also decided that I would travel light. I returned to Selfridges, this time not to purchase an attaché case but to acquire a serviceable holdall.

My preparations were completed remarkably quickly. That evening I telephoned for a pizza, drank the remaining two bottles of Peroni from my fridge and went to bed early.

I was out of the flat at 5.30 the following morning carrying my holdall down to Canary Wharf station. It was strange to see it deserted, cavernous and echoing, not yet invaded by the thousands who pour in daily to the office towers above. I changed at Green Park and took the Piccadilly line to Heathrow.

The underground system was operating efficiently. I arrived early, found no queue for the bag drop and was soon in the departure hall with plenty of time to spare.

Wandering around the airport shops already open, busy with browsing morning travellers, I had two moments of inspiration. If I successfully returned to the Amazonian island I was determined to have a photographic record of the conditions Ramirez had created. I had decided against bringing the bulky Leica thinking that my new mobile phone would be adequate apparatus. However I noticed a better alternative. For just over £100 I purchased a neat little digital camera that fitted into my trouser pocket. Then browsing in a bookshop my eyes lit on something else that would be useful – a small Spanish dictionary.

As I boarded the plane I felt a sense of accomplishment. In less than 48 hours I had walked away from an uncongenial bank and uncongenial colleagues; I had rapidly reorganised my domestic affairs; I had booked myself tickets and accommodation; I had taken medical precautions. Above all, although a little nervous, uncertain of how I would accomplish my mission, I felt a curious inner conviction that I had resolved to do something which was right.

It was not until the Spanish coast slid away 35,000 feet below us that I remembered my table at The Ivy. With a pang of regret I realised that probably for the first time in her life Sabrina would find herself stood up.

Although cautious about excessive expenditure, I took a taxi from Lima airport, not wishing to risk robbery on the unreliable city bus service. This time I did not patronise the Gran Hotel Bolivar. Instead I had the driver take me to a modestly priced establishment in Miraflores discovered during my internet search. By now it was late in the evening – the early hours of the following day in European time. Exhaustion swept over me and I crashed into bed, fortunately remembering to swallow my anti-malaria tablet.

As I drifted off to sleep I recalled how fortuitous it was that I had been pulled over onto the hard shoulder of the M3. In those minutes, while the police officer was inspecting my tyres and checking my lights, I realised that the assistance of his Peruvian counterpart would be essential if I were to accomplish what was taking shape in my mind. However I could not simply stroll into a Peruvian police station, describe the squalid encampment with its criminal potential and expect immediate assistance. Besides the language difficulty, it was unlikely that sceptical officers would believe that I had ventured a month earlier to a location so remote and inaccessible; still less that they would readily embark on a journey of inspection and liberation.

No, my approach to the authorities had to come by way of an institution which would both command attention and secure a positive response; an institution which I intended to visit the following day when I would request urgent assistance. This was an added reason for the choice of accommodation in Miraflores. Not only was it reasonably priced, it was also close to the British Embassy.

After breakfast I found my way down the bustling boulevards to Avienda Jose Larco. I entered an imposing tall building of dark glass and, certain that I was embarking on the correct course of action, took the lift up to the ambassadorial floor.

My request for an appointment about a confidential matter was met with an air of dismissive impatience. When I become more persistent I found that my guarded explanations seemed to make matters worse. Eventually the irritated receptionist, becoming terse, forced a thin smile and said, "If there is a matter in Iquitos that is troubling you it's obviously about internal travel. You need the consular desk."

I was directed to the end of the slow, straggling consular queue. There were Peruvians seeking visas; four young backpackers, all highly agitated, one of them with his leg in plaster and a voluble middle-aged British couple complaining loudly about how they had been held up by their taxi driver and robbed of $4,000. I surreptitiously checked my bulging wallet and hoped that my room safe was secure. It was after 11.45 by the time I reached the head of the queue only to be told that someone could see me at 9.45 the following morning.

The delay was frustrating. Back outside in the humid midday, taking a light lunch in a pleasant café with tables spilling outside and cluttering the pavement, I again unfolded the small sheet of paper. I had placed it into my pocket before I left my apartment and in the heavy atmosphere it was limp, the edges soft and furry. But still the message stared back at me.

"My name is Gilda – help us."

I consulted my Spanish dictionary. 'Un billete de ida y vuelta' – a return ticket – was what I required. Finishing my toasted sandwich and strong dark coffee, I retraced my steps towards a travel agency passed on my way to the embassy. My hasty Spanish lesson proved superfluous. The smiling young assistant spoke perfect English. She explained that there were several flights to Iquitos daily and even checked availability. If I required it there would be no problem in making a booking with a flexible return.

The following day I was back at the British Embassy, waiting as the doors opened. But it was precisely at 9.45 that my meeting in the consular section commenced.

I was seen by a pleasant official named Jonathan Edwards who appeared to be a little younger than me and had none of the gravitas that I imagined was necessary for a diplomatic appointment. He seemed to be quite nervous and confessed that he had been in the country only three weeks and that this was his first overseas posting.

"What exactly is the assistance you require Mr Turner?" he asked.

I decided that I would give a simplified account. I had toyed with the idea of going back to the beginning, explaining about the dinner in Knightsbridge, my treasurership of the Epicureans, my meeting with Ramirez which had brought me to Peru and finally what I had discovered on that island in the Amazon. But I realised that I had to be careful not to incriminate myself. After all I had colluded to circumvent stringent UK regulations governing food importation and food hygiene and no doubt adherence to government requirements would be a major concern of the embassy. Accordingly I gave a more straightforward version.

"Until recently I worked as an investment banker. In that capacity I came here a month ago and was invited to subscribe share capital to a company founded by a contact, a certain Senor Ramirez, who I first met in London. Part of his venture consists of what I suppose you might call a warehouse, located on an isolated island in the Amazon off Iquitos. I want you help to me expose him. Firstly I suspect that this depot is a staging post on a cocaine route from Columbia. Secondly he is holding some children captive, keeping them in appalling conditions. I would like you to help me with an approach to the Peruvian authorities – and I am sure you will know who exactly these might be – to secure their release."

Jonathan appeared slightly nonplussed. I imagined he was mentally searching for the appropriate page of his briefing manual.

"Is this Ramirez a British National?" he asked.

"Not to my knowledge," I replied.

"What is the name of his company? Is it a société anonym registered here in Peru?"

"It's called Inca Enterprises," I responded, adding, "It has a registered office in Cusco."

"How do you know this?"

"I've been there."

Jonathan seemed suddenly to take more interest. "You've been to Cusco?" he enquired.

"Yes, but only for a brief visit."

"What did you think of it?" He was becoming enthusiastic.

"I didn't enjoy the altitude."

"As soon as I get some leave I'm going to fly to Cusco. If I get the chance I want to trek the Inca Trail. I've always wanted to see Machu Pichu. They tell me this time of year is best."

The tourist circuit obviously intrigued him more than my unusual concerns. He paused and returned to our discussion. "You said that you suspect this warehouse, as you term it, is used for drug smuggling. What makes you think that?"

He might have been inexperienced but this question was pertinent. I hesitated. Ramirez had given a nod and a wink – nothing more – but his intentions had been obvious.

"Let me just say that Ramirez has had a substantial storage facility constructed in a remote location. He pointed out that it was convenient for river traffic from Columbia."

"You suspect. But you have no firm proof?" Jonathan was beginning to probe. He obviously had sufficient acumen not to accept things at face value.

"No. But to my mind it was obvious. You do not store something innocent on an island miles from anywhere in the Amazonian jungle."

"And did you invest in this enterprise?"

"I told Ramirez I would think about it," I answered truthfully.

"So you declined investment and now want to make trouble to demonstrate that your prudence was warranted?"

He spoke with a cynicism that I had not anticipated.

"No, it's not that. It's simply that having discovered what he is up to I thought I should draw someone's attention to it. Besides there are the children. He is keeping them in conditions that are surely not permitted."

"Tell me exactly what you mean."

I described as best I could the long low shed, the teeming menagerie, the stench of animal, the boarded barrier in the fetid cage and finally the patch of soiled straw, home to feral infants. I explained what Ramirez had said about their background and their likely future.

"What are you trying to achieve?" he asked.

"We can't just turn a blind eye. No child should exist like that," I said passionately.

Jonathan considered for a moment.

"You say you saw all this a month ago. Why has it taken until now for you to come to us?"

This was impossible to explain. He would not want to hear about my change of career, my unhappiness at Hardings, my struggling relationship with Quentin Foorde. Still less would he be interested in my niece's baptism. I also judged it unwise to mention the girl and the slip of paper which had travelled with me, safely tucked inside my pocket.

"I had to return to London immediately," I replied lamely. "This was the first opportunity."

He sat back and despite his junior status tried to look and sound magisterial.

"I really do not think that you require consular assistance. The person about whom you have spoken is apparently not a British national, you have no direct evidence of involvement in the narcotics trade and frankly the conditions in which people choose to raise their children are not of diplomatic concern."

This was emphatic. Nevertheless I tried one more tactic.

"I can understand why you do not wish to get involved. But at the very least is there someone who can come with me to the Peruvian police?" I asked, trying to convince him that my quest was not simply to be abandoned.

His polite refusal having failed to move me, he now appeared a little unsure. He stood up and with an expression of resigned irritation said, "Just wait here a minute – I'd like to request a little advice."

I sat in the claustrophobic interview room wondering if on his return, he would be more accommodating but inwardly fearing that my dismissal would be more emphatic. My fears were well founded. When Jonathan walked briskly back in on my solitude he was businesslike, not even bothering to sit down.

"I've had a word with the second Secretary." He paused before pointedly putting a question obviously suggested by his superior. "Tell me, when you were in Cusco did you take coca?"

"Yes – I told you I had problems with the altitude."

"Ah!" His expression indicated his conclusion. "You have to be careful with that stuff. It's pure cocaine. It wouldn't be allowed in the UK. Have you any idea what it can do to your brain?

It can make what is normal seemed distorted. You can imagine all sorts of things that you would otherwise never dream of!

As I have advised you, the Embassy view is that there is no basis for any consular involvement."

Clearly I had exhausted both personal and institutional patience.

"Thanks for your time anyway," I muttered.

"There really is nothing we can do for you Mr Turner." Jonathan was indicating the door. "Just remember," he said in parting, "if you go travelling take care and don't do anything foolish."

I took the lift back down to the ground floor and emerged into the pale light of Avienda Jose Larco, shrouded with heavy grey cloud spreading in from the south Pacific, trapping both my worries and the day's humidity beneath.

I wandered slowly back towards my hotel, weighed down both with the atmospheric density and a sense of foreboding. But firstly I called again at the travel agency. Although I did not relish undertaking the journey without official involvement, I would nevertheless set out the following day to travel south. Thereafter I was uncertain about how I would go about my task; uncertain about what I would find; uncertain about when I would return.

In fact there was only one certainty. What I had to do I had to do alone.

12

Well before noon the next day I was once again landing at Francisco Secada Vignetta airport in Iquitos. Wishing to travel onward in the relative security of full daylight I had decided on an early flight. Besides, I wanted time to locate the rudimentary wharf and consider the practicalities of my river journey.

Much as I had disliked his company it was strange to arrive without Ramirez to steer me through the teeming concourse. Even in mid morning the airport held a degree of menace and as I cleared the baggage area I clutched my holdall as firmly as he had clutched my purloined attaché case. I was jostled and importuned by dubious tour operators, touts and drivers, but having previously experienced this reception, elbowed my way through and, avoiding the motokars, made for the official taxi rank.

"Hotel Rosa," I demanded of the first driver. He looked at me blankly then spoke to another in Spanish. Quickly I was surrounded by about half a dozen, all questioning in various tongues. Eventually a younger man with a smattering of English interrupted, "Hotel Rosa? Is a long way, yes?"

I replied, "Yes, a long way." Then remembering the previous journey and the power of the greenback, added, "$70."

That was sufficient spur. We set off towards the city then after about 15 minutes veered from the main arterial road. I relaxed a little as I noticed the crumbling neon lights, last seen dimly illuminated, gradually petering out into dismal squalor, relieved that we were apparently on the correct route. Soon once more we were on less satisfactory roads, their edges crumbling into stony indistinct verges, potholes jolting us when we swerved too late to avoid them. Fortunately my driver knew the way. Eventually I caught a glimpse of the broad brown river then, shortly afterwards two old and filthy petrol pumps, some rundown shops and finally the beaded doorway of Hotel Rosa, its crackling sign now extinguished and silent, a discoloured skein of veined plastic in the midday light.

I had evidently paid generously. My young driver obligingly carried my case through the doorway into the tiled reception area and gratefully accepted the agreed fare. I pressed a button on the small deserted counter and heard in the background a faint electric buzz. Moments later Rosa came bustling from the back room. She recognised me.

"Senor. You have come with Senor Ramirez?" she asked with a look of puzzlement on her face.

"No, this time I am alone. Do you have a room free?"

There was a row of keys hanging on a rack behind her, all of them in place. Business was evidently slow.

"Yes Senor. How many nights?" she asked.

"I don't know yet," I answered truthfully. "Maybe two or three, maybe more. Is that okay?"

"Of course Senor. You would like dinner this evening?"

After I had confirmed that I would she led me upstairs. This time I had a different room. It was adjacent to where I had slept previously and slightly bigger. I quickly realised that last time it had been occupied by Ramirez. But the linen was fresh, the room was tidy and I trusted that any lingering malign miasma had been expelled when it was cleaned.

It was still only very early afternoon. I asked Rosa to open the small safe behind the reception desk and, trusting her not to interfere with my possessions, left in it a bundle containing some of my remaining cash together with my travellers' cheques. Then I ventured out into the heat to seek some transportation downriver.

It was hard to believe it was just a month since I had last been here with Ramirez. On that occasion, as we had driven off, I was anticipating a comfortable room and an uncomfortable discussion. I had left, anxious to get away, never consciously contemplating the possibility of a return.

Although having been suspicious of where he was leading me, and having watched him closely, I had not attempted to memorise the route Ramirez had taken to the river. But it was not far and, returning unexpectedly, I found that I recalled details originally noticed but instantly forgotten. The grimy ironmongers stood unchanged in a midday sleep, its detritus still piled against the wall outside. The small food store appeared no more inviting. I was sure that I even recognised the dog rooting outside. My instinct seemed to take me correctly in the direction of the river, past the workshop where Ramirez had dispensed bundles of dollars, down towards the clumsy sloping planks serving as moorings for the outsize dugout canoes, the water taxis of the Amazon.

There were several such boats idle at this landing spot, their owners sleeping in them or else joining in a game of cards outside a nearby shack. I knew I would have to employ one of them; I also knew that it was necessary to find someone I could trust. Additionally I required someone who might be able to follow my hand and arm directions as, knowing neither the name of the island nor the exact distance of travel, this was the only way I could set a course for my distasteful destination.

Then I had a moment of luck. One of the card players looked up.

"Senor Benjamin," he shouted with a triumphal note of recognition.

For the moment I was nonplussed, surprised by the sound of my name.

"You come here before. Remember me – Pablo. I speak good English."

Another detail from the previous trip came back to me. I recalled the discomfort of the long voyage back then, as we clumsily disembarked, Ramirez flapping his hand as if swatting an irritating insect when one of the wharfside boatmen tried to be friendly.

"Pablo. Now I remember you," I answered, relieved that perhaps here was someone who could take my instructions orally. "Are you a good boatman?"

Pablo confirmed that he was. He could indeed take me on the river the following morning and would be guided by my directions. We agreed on a 7 o'clock start. Uncertain of what was a reasonable fare I offered $100. Pablo accepted instantly and I promised a bonus if we carried additional passengers for the return journey. Finally I gave him strict instructions that once we were moored at our destination he was not to leave the boat, not to set one foot on the island. Instead he simply had to wait, and then bring me back together with anyone else who might accompany me.

Despite the strange requirements Pablo seemed friendly, eager to please. I decided to take a risk.

"Here, you can have $20 now. The rest when we come back tomorrow."

We had strolled away from his colleagues who evidently did not understand our discussion. Pablo discreetly put the notes into his pocket.

"Thank you Senor Benjamin. I will be here. 7 o'clock."

I felt reassured by this display of cooperation. The first part of the journey was arranged.

As I turned to walk back to Hotel Rosa I began to think carefully about what I would do having alighted from the rudimentary craft, walked back along the duckboards and for a second time entered the clearing with its three crude buildings.

I anticipated that Raphael would not necessarily be hostile towards me. After all Ramirez was his employer and in his eyes clearly I was an associate. I would tell him that Ramirez had sent me and try to win his confidence. However it was unrealistic to expect him to be other than suspicious if I simply demanded the release of the caged children. Furthermore the girl, Gilda, was also apparently a captive. He was unlikely to permit her departure in response to a simple request.

But I was also beginning to realise that I might have to use force. The notion disturbed me. I had never been in a fist fight and certainly had never handled weapons of any sort. Although reasonably fit I had no idea how to fell a man. Possibly with Gilda's help Raphael could be restrained; but I wondered how we would manage if he needed to be secured.

All of this was on my mind as I made my return through the streets, avoiding discarded plastic bottles, filthy wrappers, decaying fruit and the rusty pipework scattered outside the hardware store. As I passed I glanced through the dirty window and noticed several items on display coiled on cardboard drums. There was some wire, chain linking, plastic cord and next to that something which could be very useful: a roll of blue nylon rope. I went inside and by pointing and holding up three fingers I managed to purchase 3 metres, which I decided was probably enough to bind a person to a chair or a post. Furthermore the coil, twisted into a figure of eight, was neat enough to be concealed within my holdall. Then I went back to my room to rest, think further about the next day and wait until it was time for my lonely meal.

That evening Rosa produced a hot stew with thick chunks of meat mixed with vegetables and potatoes. While she served, as tactfully as possible, I enquired what was in the dish. Relieved to learn that it was pork, I ate as much as I could washing it down with a beer. However, my preoccupation with the challenges of the coming day was greater than my appetite. Eventually, after toying with the ample portion for some time, I placed my cutlery upon the congealing mess and looked up. As when I had been here with Ramirez I was facing the small bar at the rear of the room. I remembered the dark movement that had drawn my eyes to the bottles of spirits and I shuddered at the recollection, thankful that the scurrying shapes did not reappear. Perhaps since my last visit Hotel Rosa had engaged pest control, if such existed in this part of the world, or perhaps, I grimly fantasised, the rats had departed with the larger vermin.

But as I peered at the optics, the shots of whisky, rum and brandy ready to be dispensed, an idea came into my head. Possibly I was subconsciously recalling the fateful evening in that penthouse flat 6,000 miles away when Collingwood had persuaded me to accept the treasurership.

I rose and approached the bar. There were four upturned bottles of spirits. Evidently whisky sold well as there was one variety labelled 'Johnny Walker', showing the long legged Scotsman striding gaily towards inebriation even here at the edges of civilisation; there was another named 'Black and White' with two beguiling terriers encouraging the deception that the contents were charmingly benign. There was a half full bottle of 'Captain Morgan' rum, the eponymous skipper inviting piratical pleasures and finally a bottle of 'Martell' brandy, its nobly restrained decoration suggesting more refined debauchery.

I asked Rosa for the 'Johnny Walker' which was almost full. She reached for a small dusty wine glass and quickly placed it under the optic.

"No," I said, "I want the whole bottle."

She looked startled but did as she was asked, finding the cap and temporarily leaving a gap in the rack. Then I asked her for the 'Black and White' which had only a couple of shots remaining and finally, for good measure, the 'Captain Morgan' rum.

She did not normally sell this quantity of spirits and in broken English urged me to be careful. With gestures and simple sentences I tried to assured her of my moderation. Her expression became doubtful, the doubt turning to surprise when I made my next request.

"Please," I asked, "can you make me a pot of tea?"

"Tea, Senor?"

"Yes please. Tea – in a teapot."

She shrugged and disappeared into the kitchen, obviously troubled that this strange guest was acting so bizarrely. There was a light sound of metal clashing before she emerged with a small stainless steel pot, the tag and tail of a tea bag dangling from it. I waited for it to cool then poured the weak brew into the 'Black and White' bottle. By now she had probably concluded either that I was an eccentric Englishman, or else that I was completely mad.

The bottle was still only half full. I requested another pot of tea and repeated my actions. Rosa then handed me the cork and could observe that to the unsuspecting eye the two terriers were guarding seventy centilitres of whisky.

Satisfied with my proposed subterfuge I requested a 6.15 breakfast and wished my hostess goodnight. She appeared slightly unhappy at having to rise early but, apparently remembering the previous dawn start and the generous payment she received, confirmed that something would be ready for me.

I felt a growing confidence that I could outwit Raphael. I was pleased with my flash of inspiration having recalled that Ramirez had been quite adamant that on the island no alcohol was permitted. A second flash of inspiration came to me the following morning. Pablo was waiting as promised, standing outside one of the shacks which served as an office, a tarnished clock within showing the time as a few minutes past seven. As I stepped into his long dugout canoe I remembered that the previous day, just outside the rickety construction, I had seen him in a card game.

"Do you have your playing cards?" I asked.

"Playing cards Senor?"

"Yes – Ace, King, Queen, Jack. Or do you say Knave?"

He reached into a wooden box beneath the outboard motor and fanned open a filthy pack of greasy cards, the royal pictures gaudily coloured, the ace of spades large and sinister.

"Good," I replied. "May I borrow them?"

Pablo shrugged his shoulders. Like Rosa at the hotel he must have regarded me as strange, but like her he too was in thrall to reliable American dollars.

I placed my holdall at my feet. In it I had carefully packed the length of blue nylon rope, my three bottles from the hotel bar, my digital camera, my dictionary and $5,000 in bills of various denominations. At the last minute I had stuffed in some of my clothes, realising that if I were to bring anyone back it might be necessary to conceal nakedness.

As we pushed off from the jetty I immediately felt vulnerable. I was on the largest river in the world, swiftly and inexorably flowing westwards, vigorously coursing towards the Atlantic. It contained innumerable hidden terrors as I had witnessed on my previous voyage. It was disconcerting, frightening, that all that protected me from the rushing water and everything beneath it, was a narrow hollowed out tree trunk.

But I had to concentrate, to banish these thoughts and direct Pablo downstream to a small island difficult to locate, hazardous to approach.

I gazed across the river, shielding my eyes from the low sun, trying to discern features through the dark undergrowth of the jungle shore. Then I realised that we were passing the large island which I had previously mistaken for the far bank. We were quickly beyond it and a few minutes later I noticed smaller outcrops ahead of us, their branches and creepers reaching out and furtively trailing in the water.

Pablo yelled something from the rear of the boat. I glanced round wondering if I was to be treated to the sight of more sinister reptiles or bloodthirsty fish. Instead he pointed to a column of smoke, at first thin and insignificant but quickly billowing upwards, aspiring to become a cumulus cloud.

"They chop down trees. Then burn," he shouted. "Not good men."

We sailed onwards, spray flying from the outboard motor, my eyes still fixed on the banks, hoping I could recall the gap in the foliage and direct us to the point of disembarkation. Noticing that my watch showed the time as almost 7.30 a.m. I remembered that our previous outward journey had taken about half an hour. Unless I was badly mistaken we should be approaching the island, nondescript and apparently uninhabited when seen from the water, but in reality an outpost of depravity.

Suddenly, without warning, our little craft pitched and bucked on a swirling convergence of currents. For a moment I was afraid of being tipped overboard into the angry water but I remembered that this was exactly what had occurred previously just before our arrival. I yelled at Pablo to follow the line of the bank. He understood, promptly steering the craft parallel to the muddy shore, deftly avoiding the low branches threatening to ensnare us. Then with an enormous sense of relief I discerned a small gap, the slight parting in the jungle wall. I turned, pointing ahead, and shouted to Pablo.

"There – there! See – a landing stage. Turn off the motor!"

Reaching down, he seized a wooden paddle and slowly, silently and skilfully steered us in to the wooden landing stage.

With accustomed agility he clambered out of the craft and swiftly tied it to the small platform lest the racing current swept it away irretrievably. Then he helped me out, lifting my holdall and expressing surprise at the weight. Finally, but slowly and deliberately, I repeated my instructions to him.

"Listen closely to what I want you to do. You are to wait here and not move from this platform. You are not to come onto the island, not even a short way. Do you understand?"

There was a pained and puzzled look on his face. My behaviour must already have appeared odd; now in this remote location I was acting even more strangely. Then it crossed my mind that were something to frustrate my plans or should I meet insurmountable intransigence, I might need assistance.

"But if I am not back by four o'clock," I added glancing at my watch, "then, and only then, can you come and find me."

"Okay," he answered slowly, "but Mr Benjamin I do not have a watch."

I glanced at the sky and saw that already the sun was rising above the level of the tree canopy and that it would be well into the afternoon before the landing stage was in shade.

"All right. You may come to find me when the sun is there," I explained, indicating with an outstretched arm the nearest of the numerous tall trees fringing the small island.

"And remember too," I said looking very seriously at him, "we may have some passengers to take back and I will need your help to get them into the boat."

Pablo adopted a grave demeanour. He was clearly worried but also intrigued. Perhaps also he could sense my nervousness. I had to trust him and trust my own judgement that the lure of the dollar would hold him faithful.

I picked up the holdall and tapped it. "I have your money in here, Pablo. I will pay you well."

With that I stepped from the platform onto the damp and slippery planks of the board walk and commenced my cautious progress through the clinging jungle towards the compound.

I had already decided that before I was in sight of the low buildings I would call out so as not to alarm Raphael. Although the sun was climbing, the day becoming warm, it was still fairly early and I anticipated that he might be in bed or at least only just risen. A call might disconcert him but this was preferable to a defensive reaction if I caught him unawares. He would not be expecting me, but surely he would remember me and with the aid of my dictionary I would tell him that I came on behalf of Ramirez.

Pablo and the small landing stage quickly disappeared from view as the path meandered into dense foliage. I noticed a number of large exquisite spiders' webs glistening with dew, their makers, plump and expectant, poised at the centre of their handiwork. Then passing a large tree, the point of no return, I took a deep breath and yelled out, "Hola!"

This was a strange sensation. The word disappeared into the jungle. A couple of macaws screamed; two small monkeys were swinging rapidly away shaking the branches above me. Then once again stillness returned and with it the soft sigh of the jungle and the ceaseless susurration of river and leaf.

For a sickening moment I wondered if I had made a terrible mistake. Had I perhaps arrived on a different island? Was this path leading me not to a lonely prison but into a fresh clearing fiercely guarded by an unwelcoming tribe of native Amazonians? But the walkway appeared substantial and familiar. I breathed deeply to calm my nerves and continued onwards as the path skirted thick tree trunks, their huge bases splayed out in broad buttresses damp with moss.

I paused, took another deep inhalation and again cried out, "Hola!"

As before there were some startled squawks, the rapid flapping of wings and the flutter of cascading leaves. Then again all was still. I was certain now that this was indeed the correct location, but this certainty encouraged foreboding. Perhaps I was embarking on something consummately ill fated and foolish; perhaps I was blundering into a colossal disaster.

Of course Raphael could not shout back in reply. But I half expected some sound in acknowledgement, perhaps the beating of a stick on wood or a clap of the hands. At the very least I anticipated that he would emerge down the pathway and would have time to see me and recognise me so that I could smile at him, extend a handshake and start gaining his confidence.

I had now come almost the full distance from the river. I could see the end of the pathway, the sunlight pouring into the narrow cleft of the clearing. For a third time I filled my lungs and called, "Hola!"

Convinced that I must have been heard, I was certain that Raphael would now appear before me at the entrance to his domain. But after a minute or two I was still alone, staring down the walkway, the jungle sinister and oppressive around me.

Slowly I walked onwards until I stepped out of the dense foliage and once more into the small prison compound. To my left was the thatched dwelling, its doorway held closed by the latch that had gouged my attaché case. To my right was the blank wall of the storage shed. Ahead of me was the reed screen concealing the fetid cell in which I knew I would find a multiplying mass of creatures and next to them, shivering and cowering in their corner, those small bundles of humanity condemned to a childhood of captivity and squalor.

The stillness and silence were disconcerting. I wondered if the place was deserted, the delicacies despatched elsewhere, the children transported to a different gaol. Perhaps Gilda had managed to escape or perhaps Raphael had done her some serious injury.

I crept towards the first of the meshed windows and peered inside. It was difficult to discern anything through the gauze, the interior appearing dark and indistinct after the brightness of the compound. I continued carefully along on the veranda, crouching beneath the overhanging thatch, until I reached the door.

I placed my holdall down onto the wooden floor planks and stretched out to raise the latch.

Suddenly I was grabbed from behind and jerked violently backwards. I could not cry out as a stout arm, matted with black hair, closed round me, crushing hard against my windpipe. I sensed my legs slipping from under me on the damp boards, but I was grasped even more tightly, held firmly in a choking grip.

Then I saw Raphael's contorted face inches from mine. I felt something cold and firm against the soft skin of my neck.

He was thrusting a knife to my throat.

13

"No," I gasped. "Ramirez ..."

But no more words would come. The pain across my throat was intense, suffocating, unlike anything I had ever experienced before. Only the terror of impending death had jerked from me, in a desperate choking cry, the name which my assailant might recognise – and might fear.

What in reality must have lasted a few seconds seemed to be prolonged interminably. As if in slow motion the blade was inched away from my throat, the pressure relieved from my neck and a gulp of air rasped into my lungs.

Raphael brought his stubby hand around to my chin and stared closely at my face. I thought I detected a glimmer of recognition, perhaps a realisation that he may have attacked the agent of his employer. After a moment, coughing and gagging, I managed to splutter, "It's me, Benjamin. Ramirez sent me."

Only then did he finally back away, the waft of his foul breath receding with him. His arms dropped to his side, one hand clutching the black handle of a long kitchen knife. Finally he lowered his head and struggled to utter some soft guttural sounds as if in apology for his behaviour.

I crumpled to the floor, grasping my throat, the bones and muscles in my neck intolerably painful. I was shaking and retching, still gasping, incapable of movement.

Raphael stood there idiotically, unsure about my presence, slightly less defensive but apparently disinclined to more violence. The onslaught had shocked and sickened me. For a few minutes, quaking and shivering, all rational plans deserted me.

Collecting himself, Raphael reached down with his free hand, hooked it under my armpit and lifted me upwards, guiding me through the mesh door into the clammy dim interior of his dwelling. He sat me down on one of the hard chairs, placed the vicious knife on the table, poured some water into a kettle and began heating it on the cooking stove.

Gradually I felt the life returning to my body. My breathing slowed; the trembling subsided. The hot coffee handed to me in a tin mug was soothing and invigorating. As I swallowed the final dregs I began to recollect myself, to regain control, to remember what I needed to do.

The holdall was still outside where I had placed it before being forcibly seized. I glanced at Raphael and made a gesture of lifting something by its handles. He understood, rose in his lumbering fashion and stumbled outside to fetch the bag. Momentarily I glanced at the brightly patterned curtain concealing the sleeping area. I wondered if I detected movement. But then Raphael was back, placing the suspiciously heavy item of luggage down in front of me and again uttering his disconcerting grunts.

"Ramirez wanted me to pay you."

I said the words slowly and clearly, pointing firstly at myself and then at him. Discreetly I undid the zip and slid my hand into the holdall, concealing most of the contents. I withdrew a wad of $20 bills and began counting them out onto the table. Raphael looked on, at first apparently surprised but then with a greedy grin spreading across his face as I reached the twenty-fifth.

I pushed the splayed fan of notes across to him. "For you. Ramirez is pleased with the work you do."

I did not know whether he understood every word, but he appeared to grasp my meaning. Then with momentary alarm I remembered that Ramirez had paid him in nuevos soles and I eyed him cautiously for a moment, concerned that his suspicions would be aroused. But I had nothing to fear. Once again the greenback demonstrated its lure and Raphael grabbed at the notes, gathering them into a disordered bundle which he thrust hastily into the cupboard containing the mugs.

Meanwhile I delved again and found my Spanish dictionary. "Ramirez requerir inspección," I said as clearly as I could, painfully conscious that I was using the infinitive and probably sounding like the universal parody of a foreigner.

But once again he seemed to understand, nodding his head gravely. Slowly, apparently reluctantly, he led me outside across the bare quadrangle.

As before we went firstly to the store room. It was open, presumably having just provided Raphael with his breakfast requirements. However I noticed that now there were metal clamps on each end of the sturdy beam which secured the closed door with round holes for padlocks. Inside it was evident that the supplies had been replenished. In the area previously empty there were several bundles, about the size of my holdall, tightly wrapped in hessian. Raphael evidently thought that these were the object of my inspection for he pointed, nodded his head vigorously and made a thumbs up sign. I said a brief word of approval as we stepped back outside and moved towards the reed screen.

As we turned past the concealing lattice the first thing I noticed was the stench. Evidently the cage had not been cleaned that day and I had to cover my nose and mouth to quell a wave of nausea. As Raphael unlocked it the teeming animals panicked at our approach, squealing and screeching, scurrying into corners, becoming aggressive towards each other in their flight. There appeared to be more furry bodies than previously and I noticed a number of babies and some heavily pregnant sows.

I lingered for a moment as if assessing the quantity of scurrying livestock, then moved to the far end of the enclosure. Raphael hung back and, although a bear-like man, seemed to shrink in embarrassment.

I peered into the foul prison. There at the back I could see the appalling sight I expected, the feral boy, crouched like a dog, his eyes staring. He noticed us and started a chilling, frightened whine, shrinking further back against the rear wall, paroxysms shaking his immature frame. Just along from him I perceived the curled ball of a small girl. She had apparently been asleep but now her tiny limbs began to stretch and she too commenced an animal whimpering. I advanced further looking for the third child. I wondered if she lay cowering behind the howling boy and peered over his shaking limbs. But it was soon evident that this vile cell contained only two captives.

Holding up my hand to Raphael I counted out, "Uno, dos" striking a finger as I did so. "Where is the third?" I demanded in English, my demeanour and gestures clearly communicating my meaning.

Appearing more awkward and timid, he beckoned me away, out of the stinking enclosure, locking it behind him, and onto the small pathway leading to the latrine. He pointed to the edge of the jungle where I spotted the small fresh mound of a recently dug grave.

"What happened? When did she die? What did you do to her?" I was shocked and angry.

Raphael simply hovered there shrugging his shoulders staring down at his feet. But he knew exactly what I was asking. This brute of a man would be cruel to a dog if he kept one. I could imagine how he had behaved towards those caged children.

The sight of the lonely mound unsettled me. I reproached myself for delay; had I returned a few days earlier I might have prevented this.

"I will tell Ramirez," I snapped.

At this Raphael began gibbering once more, forcing constricted choking sounds from his mute throat. He held his hands imploringly in front of him as if begging me not to tell what I had seen.

I regretted now that I had prematurely rewarded him with dollars. Could I trust him not to escape from this benighted island, commandeering my dugout and leaving me stranded while he disappeared into the grubby alleys of Iquitos? If he was so minded could I be sure he would not once again wield the ugly knife still lying on the table in the long dim cabin? Still suffering the lingering effects, I was only too aware of his capacity for violence. I decided to watch him closely and to implement my plan immediately.

We made our way back into the compound, Raphael still uttering constricted sounds in animated despair as he followed behind me. I pushed open the door and sat myself down behind the table in the living area, making sure I was facing the rear curtain. I reached into my holdall and grasped the bottle of 'Black and White' whisky, placing it down firmly in front of me. The knife was still lying there. I considered it prudent to ignore it and made to pour a slug of liquid into my empty coffee mug.

Raphael was standing looking at me. His expression firstly indicated incomprehension, then envy. "You like a drink?" I asked gruffly, gesturing towards him and pointing to the bottle.

He reached into the cupboard for a mug, momentarily disturbing the wad of dollar notes, then lumbered into the chair opposite me. I picked up the bottle. Then deliberately, as if reflecting carefully, I put it back down again and looked at him closely. I shook my head and moved my two hands swiftly in a lateral motion indicating that I had changed my mind.

"No. I have something better."

I stretched to one side and groped in the holdall until I felt 'Johnny Walker's' smooth glass neck. Seizing it firmly, I unscrewed the cap and poured a liberal measure, glugging invitingly into the ungainly mug. Then I pushed the bottle across the table.

"For you. Keep it."

Raphael grinned his thanks. I shot an equally large 'Black and White' measure into my mug then took a large gulp, flinging my head back, grimacing at the strange combined taste of whisky and cold tea. Raphael followed my example, although I suspect his grimace was provoked by the searing sting of liquor on a throat unexpectedly relieved of abstinence.

Now it was essential to keep him engaged. I had to force myself into distracting conversation, to steer my listener down the road to insensibility, knowing throughout that he would fail to understand most of what I managed to say.

"A man needs a drink from time to time," I started.

Raphael looked at me blankly. I pointed deliberately at the bottles, then at the liquid in our mugs and made the thumbs up sign. Hesitant nodding signalled some degree of comprehension.

Encouraged I said, "Cheers," and topped up our mugs before taking another swig. Again Raphael studied me with a quizzical gaze, but he was not to be left behind and he too picked up his tin mug and swallowed another mouthful of 'Johnny Walker'.

Frantically trying to recall Spanish salutations, I tried "Santé." There was perhaps a flicker of recognition and thankfully the desired effect was obtained. More whisky sank into the throat opposite me; more cold tea sank into mine.

Encouraged I reached for my dictionary and flicked through the English words beginning with 'h'. There opposite 'health' was the word I was seeking. I seized the mug again and toasted Raphael with "Salud."

At last I had achieved understanding. Up rose his mug and out splashed the contents, dribbling from the corner of his mouth into the thick stubble over his chin.

I looked down at my wristwatch. It was still mid morning. I pointed to the dial and moved my finger around to the 3, saying as I did so, "My boat will come at three o'clock."

Raphael furrowed his brow. Again flicking rapidly through the dictionary I found the appropriate words: "Barco, venir, tres horas."

I was ignorant of tenses but my meaning was clear. A vigorous head movement confirmed his understanding. He knew he was in for a long wait and, importantly, he did not realise that a means of escape was moored nearby.

We drank some more and again I reached into the holdall. This time I extracted the pack of playing cards. Raphael's swarthy countenance scowled in surprise as I slid the well thumbed cards from their stained pack and began shuffling. Carefully I counted out a row of seven in front of me trying to recall exactly how to play patience, realising that my only other games had occurred in moments of distraction on the computer.

It took me a minute to lay out six neat piles, a singleton face up and a dealer's stack. This was long enough for Raphael to take a further gulp, not matching one of mine. I also noticed that unbidden he had dispensed more of 'Johnny Walker's' contents into his mug. Now the bottle showed clear glass above the diagonal sash of the red label.

The cards were contrary. I hardly got beyond the first deal of my patience before reaching impasse. Reassembling the pack I offered it across the table, raised my mug to my lips and sipped more of my tannic concoction. Pulling his chair forward, a look of intense determination on his face, Raphael took a swig of his more malign distillation and topped up his mug. Then with his course thick fingers, dark lines of grime under the nails and black hairs in bushes behind the bare knuckles, he started to deal.

As he bent preoccupied over the cards, I looked towards the garish curtain. I thought I detected the slightest movement; the outline of someone standing behind. I lowered my eyes to floor level and there, unmistakably, beneath the soiled curtain hem where it touched the bare boards, peeping innocently into this extemporised drinking den, were five brown toes. Even as I noticed this confirmatory sign it was withdrawn. I glanced directly at eye level, placing my finger firmly across my mouth in a gesture indicating silence to my unseen observer but concentration to the card player.

The first game was unsuccessful. It was apparently some form of gin rummy but Raphael had to demonstrate by example exactly how to play it. After a few mistakes, a degree of confusion and the consumption of more whisky we started afresh, this time in earnest.

Raphael clumsily shared out the cards, sticky on his thick fingers damp with sweat, allowing me first selection from the undealt stock. Soon I was forming sets as we commenced the steady process of select and discard. But before I was remotely ready to declare, Raphael opened his hand to reveal an array of twos and threes, spreading them wide to indicate his victory. We drank some more and the dealership passed to me.

The cards fell luckily for me with three aces already in the hand. It did not take me long to win emphatically. Raphael took another drink then with a gesture pushed his chair back and groped across to the cupboard where he kept his money. He returned with a bundle of Peruvian currency. Slowly peeling off the top note from the dirty bundle he held it up to me. It was 10 nuevos soles. He dealt the cards and, indicating with gestures that it was stake money, placed the note in the centre of the table holding it down with the knife still menacingly lying there. I reached into my holdall and groped under the tightly coiled rope for more American dollars. Fortunately I had some single bills. I counted out three and placed them next to Raphael's stake. But he shook his head pointing at the remaining notes, insisting that I gave a far better exchange rate. I placed down a fourth note and once again, with a drink to our health, we started to play.

He won. He snatched at my dollars almost lustfully but left the nuevos soles for the next game and encouraged me to deal. I gave a cursory shuffle, counted out the necessary cards and placed another four dollars on the table. Raphael won again. For a second time his grimy fist closed over the money and he drank greedily to his success. Then he pushed back his chair, grunted something, pointed in the direction of the latrine and staggered noisily to the door, fumbling with the troublesome latch before his footfall receded as he took the short path out of the compound.

The curtain moved. Hesitantly, almost guiltily, Gilda emerged. She was wearing a thin dress, slightly ragged but sufficient to cover her nakedness. I noticed another bruise on her arm and an ugly mark on her cheek. But through her bedraggled appearance I sensed a feisty spirit and noticed again, as I remembered, that she was an attractive woman. We eyed each other quickly and cautiously.

"You came," she said, softly, breaking the silence. She spoke clearly in English, her voice a mixture of fear and relief.

"I have a boat waiting – for you and the children," I whispered.

"We must be careful," she responded. "He becomes angry." She winced pointing to her injury.

"Don't worry." I tried to sound reassuring. "The whisky is strong. Mine is not alcohol. When he sleeps will you help me?"

"I will wait quietly until you are ready," she said seriously. Then with a muffled sob, "Thank you. Thank you for coming back."

The sound of irregular footsteps reached us, followed by a loud clomping noise as Raphael stumbled onto the veranda and negotiated the mesh door. Silently Gilda disappeared behind the curtain. I poured more liquid from the whisky bottles, noticing with some satisfaction that Johnny Walker was now stepping jauntily along on plain glass with only a couple of centimetres of liquor below his booted feet.

Raphael slumped into the seat opposite me, his breath now heavy with the smell of drink, sweat pouring from his forehead, his bodily odour oppressive. But he seemed to have lowered his guard, to be enjoying his gambling success and to be steadily succumbing to the effects of alcohol. He picked up his bottle giving it a rueful look.

"Don't worry," I said delving once more into the holdall. "We can drink this when it's finished."

I placed the bottle of rum down on the table, the action illustrating my meaning. In response he beamed pathetically then once again picked up the playing cards, left his stake underneath the knife, and dealt.

Now it should have been easy for me to win. His hands were unsteady; from time to time they trembled, momentarily exposing the faces of his cards indicating which suits and numbers he was assembling. But I deliberately made perverse collections from the pile or, if I was in danger of having to declare, discarded recklessly: Spades if he was collecting Spades, the Jack of Diamonds when I noticed the King and Queen in the untidy fan jerking before him.

Still we quaffed from our mugs and still he greedily snatched four dollars from the table after each round. I became worried that he would sense the deception or become suspicious of my willingness to participate in such a one-sided affair. But I did not want to provoke his anger, the evidence of which I had again witnessed on Gilda's slender figure during his brief departure. Instead, to make our results appear closer, I held back so that sometimes his declaration occurred only just before I was apparently home and dry. At this Raphael would grin, make more of his grunting noises then eagerly commence the next hand.

It was well over three hours before he succumbed. By now Johnny Walker was striding on clear air and the Captain's rum swirling round the base of his tin mug. As we played another hand Raphael's head nodded to his chest, his mouth curiously twisted, saliva trailing from one corner. He had been about to win but instead of reaching for the money his hand flopped limply onto the table as he exhaled with an ugly snore. But this jerked him back to consciousness. He regarded me blearily through glazed and heavy eyes but was alert enough to gather the four dollars, although they dropped to the floor as his growing bundle had long since drifted out of control and was now littered around his feet.

It was my deal next. I took my time to shuffle the pack, mixing and remixing the cards, sticky with the spills of alcohol, furry from the damp heat of our jungle encampment. Then once more I counted out seven to each of us. Raphael let his lie on the table. He stared at them for a moment, then his eyes closed, his hand drooped into his lap and he slumped half in his chair, half across the table. His mouth gaped open, revealing an ugly, flaccid, furry tongue. A thin brown drool oozed through a gap in his irregular yellow teeth. His rank breath came in shallow snorts. At last he appeared to have slipped into oblivion.

I pushed back my chair and stood up. The time had come for swift and decisive action.

I called out, clearly but softly, "Gilda!"

It was the first time I used her name.

"He's asleep," I added hurriedly.

She emerged once more from behind the curtain. She had combed her hair and carried herself proudly in her thin floral dress. Despite the desperate situation my eyes were irresistibly drawn to the curve of her breasts and the tiny hummocks of her nipples.

"The children," she said. "Those poor children."

"There is room in the boat. You, me and the two little ones. But they are wild. I will need your help."

"I will try," she said. "But they are afraid of people – especially men."

"What happened to the girl?" I enquired as gently as I could.

"Two days ago. She would not stop crying. Raphael struck her. Then her breathing stopped. He was angry. He hit me." Gilda pointed to her arm and the mark on her face. "Then he made me dig ..."

But she stifled her sobs. I sensed her summoning up courage, focussing, concentrating all her attention on the coldly practical.

"The key," she said. "We need the key to unlock the door. In his pocket."

Raphael's bulk was still slumped at the table, his bulging stomach pressing forward over his stained trousers. He sprawled there, slowly rising and falling in an alcoholic stench. The thought of touching him was abhorrent but I had no choice. I approached and, pressing back the damp flesh of his large belly, slipped my hand into his left pocket.

It was not easy to remove the key, deeply buried, half covered by a spreading left thigh; but slowly it emerged attached to a short length of tight chain. As I gingerly extracted the metal links Raphael stirred and grunted, his eyelids momentarily fluttering open, his arms reaching outwards, causing us both to shrink back and pause for a moment. Then, noticing the kitchen knife still lying on the table, still holding down a stake of 10 nuevos soles, Gilda seized it, snatching it to safety away from the grasp of her assailant.

"The chain is attached. There is a button inside the waistband." Gilda pointed at Raphael's midriff.

He appeared to sink into a deep sleep once more. Again I approached and eased him back in the chair. I stood over him, passing my hand over his swelling stomach down to the button at the top of his trousers. With a struggle I managed to get it undone, peeling back the cotton material around his waist. Immediately I realised that he was not wearing underpants and I cringed as my hand brushed a moist forest of black pubic hair. But I groped around the flabby flesh until I found the button holding the short chain which passed through a slit in his pocket to the security of its anchor within the waistband.

Then I faltered. The attachment was tight. Struggling against the weight of a slumped comatose body, despite my exertions, I could not release it.

Gilda approached, still holding the kitchen knife, and urged me to grasp the waistband in both hands. I did so pulling it forward as far as I could. Working quickly and carefully she brought the knife down, sawing through the yielding band, cutting round the point of resistance so that suddenly, after one final stroke, key, chain and button flew away onto the wooden floor.

What happened next was swift, sudden and sickening.

I crouched down to retrieve the key which had come to rest, the chain coiled next to it, almost under the table, just behind Gilda's bare feet. As I groped for it Raphael's chair shifted. He let out a loud incoherent grunting sound and staggered heavily and clumsily to his feet. I leapt up, grasping Gilda from behind, pulling her towards me, away from him. He gave another primeval roar.

"Get back! Don't touch me!" Gilda yelled, the knife outstretched in front of her.

But he was angry, disorientated, out of control. I tugged Gilda backwards, away from danger, towards the entrance behind us. But it was firmly shut, blocking our escape. Raphael advanced on us like an enraged bear.

Then he lunged, flailing his arms, seeking a soft target to punch and pummel. He rushed forward on to us roaring, stumbling, over-balancing, tipping forward in a long slow heavy fall. We were pressed hard against the insect proof door shrinking away from him. But still he came, his bulk and weight accelerating his inevitable descent; his final gasping, guttering descent, as his chest collapsed onto the knife still firmly clutched within his victim's defensive grasp. At the last moment, in the confused melee of three tumbling bodies, I managed frantically to haul Gilda sideways so that as we crashed onto the bare floor Raphael's broad torso smashed heavily into the mosquito mesh of the doorway.

I was winded; shaken but unhurt. Gilda was gasping, sobbing and shivering. Raphael lay motionless across the wreckage of the entrance.

Slowly I dragged myself into a crouching position, then upright. Now, trembling, shocked and still cautious, I peered at our attacker. He was face down, crushing the shattered door, the latch embedded in his right arm. I bent down and felt his neck. There was no trace of a pulse.

Then I saw that from underneath him a river of deep red blood was trickling over the veranda.

14

I crouched down and clutched Gilda to me. She was still shaking, her slender body heaving and shuddering involuntarily. We were both stunned, shocked by the raw animal violence of Raphael as he had lunged towards us. Roaring in his hot blind fury, his senses hopelessly dulled, he had stumbled onto the same knife which hours earlier he would unhesitatingly have used on me.

"Don't look. He's dead," I said gently.

She shivered as I lifted her away from the wreckage of wood, mesh, metal and the twisted sprawled body. Again we clung to each other for comfort as she allowed herself a few deep sobs, her face buried into my shirt. Then once again she stifled her cries. Summoning her resolve she looked down at the pool of red now slowly seeping across the bare planks around the cabin.

"I am not sorry," she hissed softly. "I would have killed him before now if I could, after what he did to me."

She indicated the ugly bruise on her arm then, nodding in the direction of the reed screen, added bitterly, "And he was cruel to them too."

It had never been my intention that Raphael should come to any permanent harm. I thought that after his alcoholic coma he would eventually awaken to a raging thirst and debilitating headache from which, over twenty-four hours, he would slowly recover. He might then be marooned in anxiety and frustration until his supplies arrived and he was able to return with the boatman and alert Ramirez to my trickery.

Now, however, the situation was desperate. I forced myself to keep calm, to maintain a steely focus on the essentials as I had trained myself to react at crisis time on the trading floor when the screens were flashing red, the telephones were ringing incessantly and the braying excitement encouraged rash decisions. I took long slow breaths, summoning the discipline to think analytically.

No one would believe that I had not travelled with malign intent towards Raphael. Were I to report the sudden short horrific incident I could not be confident that the local police would understand the situation in which Gilda and I had found ourselves. To a hostile sceptic, a desperate kidnapper might well become a callous murderer. Furthermore it was distinctly possible that Raphael had relatives who, in frenzied justification, would respond to misadventure with vengeance.

There was only one course of action.

Determined to complete what I had come for and to escape this grim location, I said quietly, "We can't leave him here. Can you help me move him?"

We grabbed him by his burly arms, already cold and clammy, and pulled. He bumped down the wooden step into the compound, the handle of the kitchen knife appearing to sink more deeply into his chest as it caught on the tread. I thought of simply hiding him in the jungle, then had a far better idea. But now, limp and prone on the ground, we could move him no further. Clearly we needed help.

I hesitated. There was a strong young man nearby who could undoubtedly assist. But I had required his services only as ferryman, not as undertaker.

But instantly I decided that there was no option.

"Unlock the children," I instructed Gilda. Then indicating the holdall, "There are some clothes in there. They may be too big but they will have to do."

I set off running to the small jetty, slipping on the damp duckboards, hastening now to finish the business.

Pablo was dutifully waiting, squatting near the water, chipping with an old penknife at a piece of dark wood, painstakingly creating a miniature dugout canoe. He leapt up as I approached, clearly surprised at this dishevelled apparition emerging from the jungle.

"Come quickly," I ordered. "There has been a terrible accident."

We set off rapidly along the walkway. But after several paces I stopped sharply. Pablo almost collided with me as I turned to him in the hot damp pathway and gave a concise explanation.

"Pablo, you need to trust me. Listen. A man has died. It was an accident. But no one is to know. I want you to help me with the body. Then we go back. There will be three new passengers. Do you understand?"

Anxiety etched his face. He paused before hesitantly answering, "Yes."

"Good," I responded. "When we are back you will say nothing."

Again a drawn look darkened his countenance.

"I will pay you well. There will be an extra thousand dollars."

That was ten times our agreed fare. Despite his concern once again the lure of the greenback prevailed. His faced lightened and with less reluctance he replied, "OK. Show me."

Moments later we were back in the compound. Hearing our hurried approach Gilda emerged from behind the reeds.

"This is Pablo, our boatman. He will help us," I explained.

I could tell that Pablo was trying to make sense of what he was seeing; struggling to understand the purpose of the compound; recoiling at the swarthy body sprawled on the veranda; bemused at the presence of an attractive girl; disturbed by the strange wailing now coming from the hidden cage.

Raphael was still lying face down. Pablo and I each seized an arm to drag him away but he bumped over the ground, resisting our efforts. The impediment was obvious. I had perhaps naïvely thought that Pablo would regard the accident as a heavy fall, a stumble after being taken ill. But now if we were to make any progress we had to turn the body over.

"Gilda, go back to the children," I shouted in an attempt to distract her.

"But they are frightened. They are crying. They will not come. And the clothes are too big," she replied despairingly.

"Do your best, but go back." I was insistent, not wanting her to witness what we had to do next.

Then I turned to Pablo. "Help me turn him over."

Seizing the cold heavy limbs we tugged at the fallen monster, rolling him clumsily on his side and then further still in the same direction until with a final jerk he dropped flat on his back. The front of his shirt was a soggy sponge of blood, the handle of the kitchen knife flattened against him, the blade angled upwards towards his heart.

Pablo gasped, recoiling, a look of profound shock on his face.

"It was an accident. I swear it was an accident." I was desperate to make him understand; desperate to convince him of what had occurred; desperate to dispel his evident belief that I was a murderer.

But he stood there shaking his head.

"Look I will show you."

I stepped over the shattered mesh door and seized the empty bottle of whisky together with the rum.

"He was drunk. Look at these bottles. He was crazy. He attacked us. He fell on the knife!"

Pablo was cautious. He stood still, regarding me with disbelief.

"This is bad," he muttered.

We remained still gazing at each other in silence. Then with a gesture to Pablo to wait, to suspend judgement, I went back inside. Thinking quickly I retrieved the $500 from Raphael's small wooden cupboard and the loose bills of his easy winnings. Somehow it did not seem immoral to recycle these bank notes, but I balked at stealing the dead man's nuevos soles. Then, after removing my camera and the coiled nylon rope, I flung the money into my holdall.

This now contained both the dollar bills with which I had deceived Raphael and the neat bundles, reserved for emergency use. Reappearing I tossed the holdall to Pablo. "Here," I said. "Take it. There is $5,000. But then you say nothing."

He looked inside at what to him was an enormous a quantity of cash. After a brief hesitation, perhaps a brief debate with himself, he looked up and said, "Okay."

I bent over Raphael's body and, wincing, wrapped my fingers around the handle of the knife, prising it up and away from the torn shirt, cold, wet and heavy. With a tug I withdrew it and laid it by the dark stain on the veranda. Then we each grabbed a heavy lifeless leg and dragged Raphael out of the clearing.

There was an obvious place to leave him; a hole already dug. We followed the narrow path up to the latrine. Inside, the pit was covered by a wooden box in the top of which was a circular hole covered by a circular lid. We kicked at this construction which moved easily from its anchoring points. Then we tipped it upwards and over onto its side. Seizing the body again by the legs we dragged it to the edge of the shaft. After a final strenuous heave Raphael dropped swiftly, landing several feet below with a soft thud.

There were large drums of dry soil and wood shavings nearby, evidently to be scattered after defecation. We heaved their entire contents down into the blackness. Then we replaced the crude toilet seat and shut the swaying wooden door. Despite the tension, despite my anxiety and desperate desire to be away from this island prison, I could not suppress the thought that there was no more fitting place for this brutal animal than upon a mound of his own excrement.

Although she had succeeded in opening the caged enclosure Gilda had not been able to bring out the children. We discovered her struggling with the wild boy. He cowered in a corner making horrible animal noises, pressing his back against the wooden wall when Gilda approached, kicking at her with his feet. She was trying to clothe him in one of my shirts of blue cotton, draping it over his head like a nightdress. But he was lashing out, screeching agonisingly, her gentle persuasion merely provoking his distress. The little girl was whimpering in imitation but being younger and smaller could not offer the same degree of resistance.

"Leave the boy – take the girl," I shouted above the awful wails.

Gilda picked up the struggling child and with a firm but tender grip gradually restrained her as she stepped over the whimpering guinea pigs scurrying from her footfall. The crying seemed to subside as the infant was brought into the compound, emerging for the first time beyond the confines of the reed screen into the heat of the afternoon sun.

While Pablo stood disconcerted, trying to make sense of this distressing scene, I retrieved my rope intended for a different purpose, and with the knife, still sticky with blood, cut two short lengths from it. Then I went back into the cage and approached the boy. Once more he retreated, cowering in a corner, uttering distressful shrieking sounds, flailing his limbs violently. But with my weight I pinned him to the floor, gagging at the smell of stale urine, and wound one length of rope around his legs. I tied the second around his arms so that although he squirmed and shuddered it was possible to cover his nakedness. Now he tried to bite me but I pulled the buttoned blue shirt quickly over his head and dragged him into the light.

"Gilda, take her to the boat," I directed firmly. "Pablo get ready. I will come with the boy in two minutes."

Pablo made sure he grabbed the holdall but I was relieved that he was not so mercenary as to neglect his passengers. He lingered with Gilda, helping her to carry the girl, making sure she did not slip on the duckboards.

I had remembered my camera. Now I would have evidence, proof of the immoral, criminal activities of Ramirez. I opened the storeroom door and hurried inside, making straight for the hessian bundles. Stabbing the topmost with the knife I created a deep gash out of which, as I expected, came a cascade of white powder. I lifted the camera and took a few shots from different angles. Outside once more I photographed the compound, the storeroom and the reed screen. Next I focused on the cage concealed behind it, the scurrying animals still panicking at my feet as I chased them out into the jungle, and took close-up shots of the open lock and key with its tail of linked chains. Finally, as carefully as possible, I captured images of the boy's face, his sunken cheeks and staring eyes still giving him the appearance of a nocturnal jungle creature rather than a human child.

Then I carried him to the edge of the compound and placed him on the ground at the start of the walkway.

Quickly I returned to the living quarters. Looking round I grabbed the garish curtain concealing the bedroom and hauled it from its pole, crumpling it into a loose bundle. I seized the fallen bottle of rum and tipped the remaining dark dregs onto the material before striking a match to ignite the burner on Raphael's cooking stove which excitedly burst into life with a hissing blue jet. I flung the curtain onto the flame. There was a sudden whoosh as the liquor was greedily consumed and then, almost instantly, hungry tongues of fire sprang upwards, eager for more substantial gratification.

I raced outside to see the first glow of red appear in the roof thatch and a spiral of smoke swirl upwards through the tree canopy.

The boy had fallen silent, his eyes now tightly shut. I gathered him up, turned my back on the developing inferno and made for the boat.

Pablo was sitting in the rear of the dugout with Gilda in front of him tightly clutching the small girl. I clambered in towards the prow and set the boy between my legs. Then we pushed off, the engine complaining noisily as we met the inexorable flow of the Amazon determinedly pushing us eastwards while we struggled to turn west, back towards Iquitos.

The little craft bucked and protested as it fought against the strong current. Already the sun was sinking in the sky, blinding us on our slow progress upriver. Trussed at my feet the boy was secure. However it seemed cruel, a denial of the very freedom I wished to deliver, to keep him bound like an animal. I reached down and loosened the ropes noticing that already his thin limbs had been chafed by the nylon twine. As gently as possible I eased his arms into the sleeves of my requisitioned shirt, rolling them upwards so that his hands were free. Thankfully he remained still, his eyes now wide and staring, his tongue lolling out of his thin mouth.

Gradually the island receded into the distance and looking back I observed with satisfaction, that rising above it was a thick plume of dirty smoke. There appeared to be little river traffic but anyone venturing here and noticing the billowing column would simply assume that some native tribes were creating a new settlement or that another gang of speculators was clearing the rainforest.

Conversation was impossible above the loud throbbing of the outboard motor but in any case, emerging from the shock and trauma of the last few hours, we were all numbed. The girl seemed to have fallen asleep nuzzling against Gilda. When I glanced round Gilda pointed at her, a half smile indicating both exhaustion and relief.

It was difficult to know what was preoccupying Pablo. He would return to his base on the river bank below the town, a rich man. But would he remain discreet or would his sudden wealth loosen his tongue? Had I perhaps offered him far too much and would I now be a victim of blackmail or extortion?

These reflections led to an inevitable conclusion. I had to leave the area as quickly as possible. Gilda would presumably travel home or to some suitable accommodation, but until we were off the river and alone, intelligent discussion was impossible. I would take her and the children back to Hotel Rosa but once there it was essential that we made some quick decisions.

By now we had travelled much further. The evidence of my conflagration was diminishing into misty wisps, pink in the setting sun. Ahead of us I could dimly see, like miniature matchboxes in the hazy twilight, the cluster of shacks at the distant moorings.

It was as I was peering that I became conscious of a deep throbbing sound behind us. At first I thought the outboard motor was straining even harder against the tug of the swirling water. But steadily the noise grew even more insistent, a pounding more rapid and rhythmic than the spluttering diesel protests from our stern. Simultaneously we all turned. Behind us, churning the water as it overhauled our creeping progress, the large white river boat came, racing the dying sun, determined to reach Iquitos before the last glimmers of fading dusk.

In a few moments the boat was parallel to us. Lights were blinking on its decks, a few passengers leaning over the rails, itinerant workers returning home, small time river traders, the sick coming to hospital or relatives returning from weddings or funerals. The decks were piled with cargo: a miscellany of boxes; crates; nets retaining bags and battered suitcases; barrels and tools. The sides of the boat were streaked with rust. The choking smell of exhaust drifted over the water towards us.

Even the boy, subdued until now, turned his head, his sunken eyes widening at the sight of the vast craft towering above us. He started to make an inhuman sound, softly at first but then rising to a piercing crescendo. Witnessing a phenomenon totally unknown to his young brain, he appeared both alarmed and intrigued. His small hands gripped the rough edges of the canoe as he hauled himself to a kneeling position and howled like an animal. Then he started gesticulating, raising his thin arms above his head. The shirt ballooned around him, momentarily transforming him into a wailing blue banshee.

Very quickly the boat moved beyond us churning the water behind it. Someone on deck emptied a rubbish bin and a fleeting cascade of food waste, bottles and cans spilled into the water. There was a brief commotion as hundreds of unseen snapping jaws tore into the scraps instantly dragged under the surface in a seething frenzy.

Then almost immediately we hit the wake. A series of creamy brown waves rolled towards us. Pablo shouted instructions to hold on tightly as the first pounded the prow, splashing into our canoe tossing violently in this sudden agitation. The boy squirmed and yelled at the shock of the water hitting him, already the blue shirt drenched, sticking to his puny body. I turned around and saw Gilda clutching the little girl, firmly gripping the edge of the craft with her free hand. Pablo was grappling with the motor, squeezing the throttle to full power to counter the force of the filthy wash engulfing us.

The boy had now hauled himself up into a half standing position with his arms, ludicrously blue from the clinging shirt, reaching out over the side. He had flung his head back and was screaming, yelling with sounds barely recognisable as human. Then the little boat bucked sharply as the remainder of the wake rolled against us, lifting the prow clear of the water before it crashed back down and another cascade came pouring into the swirling pool already up to our ankles.

The flat bottom of the canoe slapped the surface of the river. Turning again to reassure Gilda I twisted awkwardly, lost balance and tipped backwards, my head hitting her knees. She screamed and for a moment I feared that I might have hurt her. But she was not screaming at me. As I scrabbled upright I glimpsed a splash and what appeared for a split second like a sodden blue pillow transported by the swirling current. The jolt that had shaken my equilibrium had flung the boy, hopelessly disorientated, clear of our struggling craft and into the merciless waters of the Amazon.

I leant out as far as I could desperately stretching for the blue bundle. The canoe tipped dangerously to one side and both Pablo and Gilda cried out in panic. Everything seemed to be happening so swiftly. In a second the current had carried the boy past the end of the boat. Pablo let go of the motor and reached out in a last futile attempt to snatch at the wet cotton of my shirt. Then in one awful final moment I saw the boy's head tip back as his face was swamped with the last of the waves, the brown river water swirling into his astonished, gasping, twisted jaw.

He disappeared beneath the surface. There was a sudden furious commotion, the water angrily boiling, violently disturbed by whatever was lurking just inches below us. Gilda cried out again, enfolding the girl into her body, turning away from the sudden maelstrom. Pablo cut the motor but instantly the current caught us, spinning us around, rocking on the troubled surface. We swept the area with our eyes but in the fading light no signs of survival were visible.

The motor jerked into life again, wrenched to one side as Pablo desperately steered back onto our course. I thought I detected some scraps of blue in the brown flood, but in truth everything had been swept away; the drinks containers tipped over the side of the ferry, discarded cigarette stubs, jettisoned scraps of food and now, cruelly, this wild, abandoned, unloved child.

I doubt whether anyone on the large boat, steaming steadily away, its stern lights cheerfully twinkling, had witnessed our fateful encounter with the vicious furrow of its wake. It continued ignorant and impassive, sailing into the bronze disc of the sun sinking into the brutal Amazon. More in frustration than in expectation of assistance, I raised my arm and shouted. Our little craft rocked unsteadily once more and Pablo urged me to be still, tossing me a small tin can to clear the water from our feet.

Thankfully the little girl had seen nothing. She still lay, her head buried in the cotton of Gilda's dress, in merciful oblivion. Gilda herself was trembling, but her face was set in determination as she grasped more firmly upon the thick chiselled side of the boat.

In this manner we continued slowly back to the tiny wharf. With relief I ceased the awkward bailing as the shacks at the waterside loomed closer. Silence fell as finally the motor was shut down and we slipped alongside the moorings.

Pablo helped Gilda and the child out onto the small unsteady jetty. I followed, steeling myself to manage this changed situation, determined that, despite the horrors of the day, deliverance should await my two surviving refugees.

I took Pablo by the arm. "Remember," I said. "You say nothing of this to anyone."

"Yes Mr Benjamin." He was subdued and inscrutable.

"And take care of that – use it wisely," I added, glancing at the holdall held firmly in his strong hands.

Then I turned to Gilda. "We will stay tonight in Hotel Rosa. It's not very far to walk."

I took the child and we set off slowly. We were both cold and numb. It had been a day of two deaths: two unanticipated, violent deaths. But we could not discuss our ordeal, could not explain these awful events and could not, through explanation, achieve absolution. Instead I concentrated on keeping control, on taking the necessary practical decisions and on rehearsing how I would ask Rosa if she would be kind enough to find a suitable orphanage for the child.

She was expecting me. Indeed, plump and matronly, she was standing anxiously in the doorway, the crackling neon sign casting a livid glow across her face, creased with concern as to whether the strange Englishman was irretrievably lost or whether he would return to claim his room and his property. She was startled to see Gilda and the child.

"Do you have a room for one night for the girl and the baby?" I asked as if this were an everyday requirement.

To her credit Rosa, although relieved by my return, betrayed no emotions. She simply lifted a key from the rack and led us upstairs.

The aroma of cooking followed us and I suddenly realised that I was desperately hungry.

"I would like a meal for myself and my guest, please," I said simply, adding, "Can you also prepare something for the child?"

Gilda was given the room next to mine. Tactfully our hostess retreated downstairs and left us alone as the infant stirred, emerging from her drowsiness.

Before I could speak Gilda grasped me by the hands. "Thank you. Thank you for coming back. You are a good man," she said with obvious sincerity.

I did not know how to respond. My mind was racing ahead trying to catalogue everything that needed to be done.

"Gilda," I said earnestly. "I do not think it is safe for me to stay here. I must leave tomorrow and fly back to Lima. Do you understand?"

She looked crestfallen. "And what should we do, senor?" she asked.

"Do you have somewhere here – or in town, in Iquitos?" I enquired.

"I used to, senor. But if it is not safe for you, it is not safe for me."

Then I realised the truth of what she was saying. If I did not trust Pablo and if I felt that Raphael's relatives might arrive seeking retribution, then indeed Gilda was not safe. If I were to escape to the anonymity of the city it was only right that I gave her the chance to do likewise.

I made an instant decision. "If you like you can come with me back to Lima."

"Yes please, senor," she answered.

"But what do we do about the girl?" I asked.

I had assumed that we would find somewhere for the children in Iquitos. Having delivered them from captivity I had anticipated that there would be a mission or charitable establishment that would take them. Now tragically there was just one helpless infant but of course I would be willing to pay for food, clothing and shelter until perhaps a foster family could be arranged.

Gilda looked me straight in the eye with a visage set in stubborn determination.

"The child comes with us. Now she is mine."

15

We arrived in Lima in the early afternoon, just another young couple, nondescript among the hurly burly of the airport's domestic terminal.

In contrast to the preceding day everything went surprisingly smoothly. The child seemed to sense safety, clinging to Gilda and thankfully, in the comfort of contact, no longer shrieking like an injured beast.

Those cries had ceased after we washed her hair the previous evening, gently combing it, untangling the twists and knots, restoring lustre to the sleek dark tresses.

Rosa had been both discreet and maternal. Once an early departure for Lima had been decided, I told her that I had come from Gilda's family in the city, sent to rescue her, as it was known that her husband beat her. After all, the mark on her cheek proclaimed the veracity of this statement and the strangeness of the child was consistent with an abusive environment.

With only a little prompting some baby clothes had appeared, as well as a pair of jeans and a blouse, red and plain but with feminine buttons, for Gilda. She wore these for our flight, with a pair of flip-flops on her feet. Still she appeared to have little underwear and I noticed the animated stare of the security guard upon her chest as we passed through the airport scanner.

A taxi had been summoned for 8 a.m. It was a battered ancient vehicle but it survived the crush of the early traffic around Iquitos and delivered us to the correct entrance for an internal flight from Francisco Secada Vignetta airport. A rather grubby money exchange offered me a poor rate for a large traveller's cheque but this was no time for locating more favourable currency conversion as I needed to purchase a second ticket. Fortunately there was still space on one of the morning departures and there was no difficulty in securing a seat for Gilda Alvarez. No one doubted that the child was hers nor that she was under two years old and did not require a separate seat.

Gilda had obviously flown before. She instinctively reached for the seat belt and I noticed her intently studying the diagram about emergency procedures, lingering on the instructions about securing her own oxygen mask before the child's. When we landed she was among the first to unclip and stand prematurely to create an instant queue impatient to disembark.

We travelled back to the hotel in Miraflores, slipping anonymously into the official taxi queue and thence into the general dispersal of traffic heading into the city. At the reception desk I booked two rooms for a week, in the expectation that during this time we could settle on more permanent arrangements.

It took us three days to recover. I ventured out briefly to purchase disposable nappies and baby food, taking instruction from Gilda as to what was required. But apart from this we remained in the hotel, taking room service meals, caring for the child, avoiding contact with other people, escaping from the evils outside.

During this time, as the mark on her cheek diminished and the bruise on her arm faded, so Gilda's confidence returned. Gradually as the raw shock faded, she told me more about herself, about her family and, despite the pain, the tawdry deception that had led to her island confinement.

She was 20 years old, the youngest of three sisters. Her father had been a successful lawyer in Lima, specialising in transactions connected with shipping, air transport and international trade. Her mother had run a dance school. Childhood for the Alvarez children had been happy and eventful. For two blissful years before Gilda was 10, her sisters already teenagers, the family lived in San Francisco. She remembered crossing the Golden Gate Bridge, visiting Alcatraz, seeing the rustic Californian Spanish missions, the vineyards of the Napa Valley and the majestic Yosemite.

At the International Preparatory School Gilda had done well, becoming totally fluent in English. Her sisters had attended high school where their handsome features and lithe figures attracted hosts of eligible young admirers. Indeed the two teenagers were inconsolable when the family returned to Lima. They were reluctant to

177

settle back to Peruvian life and eventually their father agreed to a university education at Berkeley. There they met their future husbands. The elder sister, Carmen, specialised in languages. Married to an accountant she now lived in Tokyo, busy with translation work while her husband managed the finances of an electronics company. The other sister, Isabel, just eighteen months younger than Carmen, had her mother's artistic temperament. She taught dance in Seattle where her spouse, an engineer, was part of a discrete team developing new aircraft for Boeing.

Back in Lima, Gilda was enrolled into the prestigious Franklin D. Roosevelt American School. She was a bright pupil and had plans to study languages at university and then to become a teacher, perhaps emigrating and seeking a suitable school near one of her sisters. But over two years earlier, just after she was 17, her comfortable existence was suddenly and violently extinguished.

One of Senor Alvarez's clients was a major international air freight carrier involved in a dispute concerning a consignment of office equipment flown into Lima from the USA. The construction company, which had ordered state of the art photocopiers for its new headquarters, claimed that major malfunctioning was due to negligence either during transportation or storage prior to Customs clearance in the secure warehouse at the international airport. The freight company argued that it had exercised appropriate care. The goods had been properly secured in robust air freight crates; a senior official had personally overseen their loading and unloading. Customs clearance was severely delayed but if during this period damage occurred, then the responsibility had to a lie with officialdom.

The dispute dragged on for three years of claim and counterclaim, the matter becoming more sinister with allegations of corruption at the lower levels of administration. Eventually a case was commenced in the courts where Senor Alvarez found himself handling the extremely tortuous litigation. He was outstandingly successful. Not only was his client company exonerated, but he also exposed the construction company as opportunist and even duplicitous. Furthermore, huge suspicions were cast over the Customs operation at Lima airport. But while Gilda's father became a hero to his client, he also made some powerful enemies.

Exactly 2 weeks after the verdict and exactly 2 days before his 50th birthday, Senor Alvarez left his office just after 5 p.m. and drove his Mercedes to his wife's dance studio. He parked his car and watched while a group of girls came out, waving as they clambered onto buses or waiting vehicles. Apparently he did not notice the sporty BMW which had drawn up behind him.

Senora Alvarez then emerged, locking the studio behind her. Her husband, always the gentleman, held open the car door, then returned to the driver's side and drove off. The BMW roared past. As it did so three shots were fired. The Mercedes bounced from the kerb, coming to rest embedded horrendously and bizarrely in the window display of a bridal wear shop.

Senor Alvarez was declared dead at the scene with two bullet wounds to the head. His wife died in hospital two days later.

Gilda told me all this with remarkable composure. But as she reached the climax of her narrative there was a bitter edge to her voice and tears in her eyes.

"The police said there was nothing they could do." She spat the words. "It was a violent robbery that went wrong. But everyone knows that someone was paid to do this. It might have been the company; it might have been the government. We will never know the truth."

In the immediate aftermath one of the partners in her father's law firm took care of all the practical arrangements. He purchased plane tickets for Carmen and Isabel and booked them rooms in the Simon Bolívar Hotel; he organised the funeral; he located the will written by Gilda's father. This had been signed years earlier before the family's sojourn in San Francisco. It named Gilda's aunt, her mother's sister, as guardian should the parents die before the children reached the age of majority.

The sisters had very little time together when they met for the funeral. There was some inconclusive discussion about Gilda going to stay with one of them. A trip to Seattle would have been feasible but Isabel's apartment was tiny and in any event it was preferable for Gilda to remain to complete her education in Peru. For similar reasons an extended stay with Carmen in Tokyo was out of the question. It was therefore concluded that in the short term Gilda should take up residence with her aunt.

When he had drawn up the will Senor Alvarez had no doubt acted with the best of intentions. His sister-in-law, Senora Martinez, was then in her early 50s and living in Lima. However, three years before the shootings, she had been widowed and had left the capital to live with her son, Jorge, in Iquitos.

Senora Martinez had become depressed and reclusive. Gilda had not seen her since she had left Lima and it was even longer since she had met Jorge who she remembered as an unpleasant young man, crude and domineering. Her aunt did not even return for the funeral and, to the relief of Carmen and Isabel, their cousin also stayed away. Nevertheless, still grieving, Gilda undertook the journey north to Iquitos in expectation of sympathy and a comfortable home until she could return to Lima to complete her studies.

The lawyer had arranged the flight and dispatched Gilda with a small amount of nuevos soles saying that it would take time to settle her parents' estate. There were some complications as all of her father's capital was tied up in the firm. Gilda had not realised it but the family apartment was rented. Her father although not poor had no easily realisable assets. However once things were unravelled then her share of the inheritance would be available to her. In the meantime, until she became eighteen, she was the responsibility of the named guardian who was obliged to provide food, shelter and guidance.

Gilda quickly found that the Iquitos household was unhappy. Jorge, now in his early 40s, was frequently away from home leaving his wife Teresa to care for his mother and their two teenage sons. Almost from the very first day the atmosphere was heavy with restrained resentment. Gradually Gilda perceived that the Alvarez family, successful and cosmopolitan, had been envied by the Martinez family who were reluctant to support this young relative forced upon them in such horrendous circumstances.

Within a few days a letter arrived addressed to Senora Martinez. It was actually meant for Gilda's aunt but, having few scruples, Teresa regarded it as being for her attention. She read it with great interest, knotting her harassed brow, broadly appreciating the content but puzzled by the legal terminology. Eventually she had no choice but to ask Gilda to confirm her understanding of exactly what this unexpected communication meant.

The sender was the lawyer. He thought it helpful to explain that indeed the Alvarez daughters would eventually receive a sizeable inheritance. However there were legal complexities. It would take time to reconstitute the Law Practice, to release funds from it without jeopardising the interests of the remaining partners and thereafter to distribute the residual estate. The process would inevitably be protracted, taking a year or more. In the meantime he trusted that Senora Martinez would take responsibility for her niece and doubtless, on the occasion of the final distribution, suitable financial recompense for her care and the additional household expense would be appropriate.

For a short time thereafter Teresa became more pleasant and conciliatory. She made Gilda's room a little more comfortable; she spoke in complimentary terms about the Alvarez family. But the veneer soon wore off, revealing her mercenary motivation. She would make the occasional oblique remark, heavy with inference, as to what a good wife Gilda would make and how she was sure that there was nothing to prohibit marriage between second cousins.

One thing she resolutely failed to do was to give Gilda any allowance. The nuevos soles which had accompanied her arrival were soon appropriated. She was left with nothing of her own. There was certainly no question of school fees being paid or the purchase of an air fare back to Lima.

Gilda anticipated that somehow, once she had reached her 18th birthday, she would be able to gain her independence, leave Iquitos and start to rebuild her life. However although the occasion brought best wishes from Tokyo and Seattle, it brought nothing from the lawyer in Lima. Without any means of support Gilda remained totally dependent on the Martinez family. They in turn were now reluctant to encourage her departure anticipating that shortly she might be a moderately wealthy young woman.

After a period of soul destroying idleness Gilda was set to work. Jorge was often absent, travelling extensively to inspect crop production throughout a vast network of rubber plantations. At home in Iquitos Theresa had developed a number of sidelines. One of these was a small, rather seedy liquor store in a shabby street two blocks from where they lived. She would often spend the afternoons here but, diverted by other tasks, it became convenient to delegate to Gilda. After all she was literate, numerate and competent to handle goods and money. Very rapidly she became familiar with the varieties of beer and the spirits that could bring temporary elation or oblivion to her dissolute or desperate customers.

Gilda paused when she was telling this to me and for the first time a flicker of a smile played upon her lips.

"So you see, I knew exactly what you were up to with Raphael."

But the time dragged heavily as her teenage years slipped away. There were letters to and from Tokyo and Seattle and the odd surreptitious international telephone call, although the time difference frustrated meaningful dialogue with Carmen in Japan. Her sisters implored her to have patience; they were certain that the lawyer would resolve matters as quickly as possible.

At first Gilda kept in contact with her school friends from Lima. There was a flurry of cards and even some presents when Christmas came around. But she was unable to reciprocate and one by one her acquaintances fell silent.

From time to time she would write to the lawyer. She did not always receive an answer and those replies that did come were generally brief and noncommittal. She was repeatedly told that she had to understand that these things took time and until matters were resolved she should be grateful that her aunt was providing her with a home.

She hated serving in the liquor store. The older men leered at her when they came for whisky or rum. Younger men came in for a beer and made suggestive remarks. As some became persistent she refused to stay at the shop after dark, much to the irritation of Teresa.

One of her customers was the man simply known as 'the mute'. He would come in from time to time, place a bundle of torn and filthy nuevos soles on the counter and point to the can of beer he required. She felt sorry for him and, despite the numbness of her soul, tried to smile and speak pleasantly to him.

She wondered if that encouraged him; if that was why she became his victim.

One afternoon, a few weeks before our first almost silent encounter in that remote jungle clearing, a middle-aged lady walked into the shop. Teresa was also there at the time, checking stock and ensuring that the till records were accurate as, despite the family association, she kept a sharp eye on the business to ensure her reluctant assistant did not fund an escape by diverting takings. On reflection Gilda wondered if the encounter had been prearranged. The shop's customers were invariably men and it was surely more than a coincidence that the visit should occur when the proprietress was present. She also noticed that outside the grubby glass window, obscured by a metal burglar grille and the garish advertisements for gin, whisky and rum, the mute was standing sheepishly, anxiously twisting his hands together.

The unexpected visitor evidently knew Teresa. She had come, she said, to communicate on behalf of her brother who was himself unable to speak. Through an acquaintance he had secured a position at a new establishment which was shortly to open several kilometres away from Iquitos. One of its purposes was to house maladjusted children who were best kept isolated from the local community. A care assistant was required on a temporary basis. Gilda's competence had been remarked upon by others in the neighbourhood. She would be ideal for the position.

Teresa immediately welcomed the suggestion. This shocked Gilda who suspected that the Martinez finances were under pressure which would be relieved slightly by her temporary departure. She herself was ambivalent. While the thought of getting away from her stultifying existence was attractive, she balked at the idea of working in the vicinity of Raphael. Though she had tried to be pleasant out of sympathy for his disability, she found him physically repulsive. She doubted she could tolerate his guttural grunting, his dumb directional pointing with outstretched swarthy arm. Above all she feared his wordless sinister gaze.

But Teresa became insistent. It was the chance for Gilda to do something different, to give her a change of scene. After all that had been done for her, her refusal would indicate a lack of gratitude. The work was only temporary. She would not be away long. It could only be a matter of weeks before the legal matters in Lima were resolved and Gilda came into her inheritance. It would be admirable, what her parents would have wanted, for her to do something socially useful in the meantime.

She ceded to the pressure. Two days later she set off to travel downriver.

Gilda found the rest more difficult to relate. She was angry and tearful when she described what she encountered at the conclusion of her voyage. Although she had anticipated a remote location she had been given no indication that she was being taken to an island accessible only by boat. She was shocked and horrified at the realisation that she was virtually a captive.

It was evident that construction of the encampment had only just been completed. The compound was littered with piles of wood shavings, sawdust and remnants of roofing material. The deranged boy was already secure in his cage where, the cavies as she termed them, were fattening. Like me she had been shaken by his inhuman cries, by his sunken haunted face, by his confinement like an animal next to animals.

The following afternoon a boat had arrived. It carried a burly man apparently acquainted with Raphael. He stamped heavily into the clearing clutching the two small girls both screaming loudly. Gilda was forbidden to leave the living quarters and was too scared to cry out. She watched helplessly, peering through the mesh of the window, as the two infants were bundled behind the reed screen. Then the visitor hastened away back to the river, anxious to complete his task and leave the stench and sounds of the remote compound.

She had seen no one else until a few days later Ramirez and I arrived.

"That other man looked as evil as Raphael, but I knew I could trust you," she said sincerely.

Reaching into my pocket I produced the crumpled scrap of a note. "My name is Gilda – help us."

"That went with me back to London," I said. "While I had this piece of paper I could not forget you."

It felt true. At that moment, holding her, it seemed to me that from the first I had been compelled to return, haunted, drawn back by her handsome pleading face. I struggled to explain the upheavals in my life and to rationalise the month's delay.

It was her turn to be consoling. Touching my face she whispered, "But you came. That is all that is important."

On the fourth day we went out. I found a bank offering a reasonable exchange rate and encashed six of my travellers' cheques. Then, with ample funds at our disposal, we found a shop selling baby equipment and purchased a buggy and other supplies for the child. An hour later we were seated in McDonalds. To any casual passers-by we were just another young couple enjoying a burger and Coca-Cola while their child slumbered nearby.

After lunch we went to the hairdressers. I chose an upmarket cosmopolitan establishment where as much English as Spanish was spoken. I left instructions that Gilda was to have the attention of the best stylist and, pre-empting her protestations, paid in advance including a generous tip.

I wheeled the child back to the hotel and awaited her return. Some two hours later I heard her light tap on my door. She looked stunning. Her long unkempt locks had been carefully trimmed, shortened but not cropped, tidily shaped in contemporary style around her face, now revealed as striking but with a charm and softness. She smiled broadly and kissed me on the lips. That night she moved into my room.

The next day I sent her shopping.

Gilda had fled with only the jeans and blouse hurriedly collected in Hotel Rosa. She needed clothes, shoes, toiletries and make up. Of course she knew the centre of Lima well and suggested that she could acquire everything under one roof at the large Falabelle store. I called a taxi. We were cautious, anxious not to be seen, aware that Raphael's disappearance would be noticed by someone. We were still unsure as to how far we could trust Pablo, whether already he would have spoken of what he had seen and whether someone would be on the lookout for us. It would be unwise for either of us to be remarked upon or for Gilda to be spotted by a previous acquaintance.

She returned wearing a light cotton dress which clung seductively to her slim waist, carrying numerous smart carrier bags. She had purchased jackets, light trousers, blouses, footwear and a bag full of underwear and other female requirements which she playfully but defiantly whisked from my gaze. She sat down and tried on a smart pair of shoes, light grey in colour with delicate straps and daring heels, stretching out her bare light brown legs, smiling as if rediscovering her femininity. Then she apologised for spending over $3,000 and thrust the unspent cash into my hand.

Before I could react she stood up, reached into her concealed bag, produced a small package and kissed me.

"That is for you. You are a good man. Thank you for saving my life."

I unwrapped the packaging to discover a bottle of expensive aftershave. But before I could thank her she was again fishing another item from her treasure trove.

"And this is for you," she said handing a small plastic toy on a bright string to the little girl who she plucked from my arms.

The infant grasped the bauble with soft chubby fingers. Throughout the day she had been quiet, staring vacantly through many of her waking hours. Now there was a flicker of something in her eyes and a slight pursing of the lips as if she were learning to smile.

Gilda caressed the child's face. "But what should we call you? We must give you a name. Ben, what do you suggest?"

"You choose," I answered.

"No, both she and I owe everything to you. I would like you to name her."

I thought for a moment, pondering on everything that had happened since my return to the Amazon. The encounter with Raphael had gone horribly, fatally wrong. The liberation was fumbled and frightening. The return voyage had been hazardous, the demented boy horribly swept from our sight. Our only good fortune was in finding sanctuary in Hotel Rosa. From Rosa we had risen; we had literally taken flight.

I also realised with a jolt that what had become paramount in my life was the welfare of others: Gilda and the child, Pam and Hazel. They were all female. Then I reflected there had once been someone female who had loved me, cared for me and who unhesitatingly would have faced unimaginable danger had I required rescue.

The name for the child was obvious. There was a conjunction of circumstance and sentiment. I looked up and smiled.

"We will call her after my mother. Her name will be Rose."

Gilda's eyes moistened. Then, insistently and intrusively, my phone rang. It was Gabrielle Dubois on behalf of Picard-Syme.

16

During the second morning in Miraflores I had switched on my phone, silenced during the fateful trip to the interior. Although she had been unaware of my destination and ignorant of the hazards to be faced, I nevertheless wanted to speak to my sister. I needed to have some contact with the outside world, to have the assurance that I was indeed coming back to the reality of normal existence.

I also discovered numerous missed calls and three voicemail messages. Bizarrely the first was from the garage reminding me that the Porsche had still not been serviced. The second was from Pam herself thanking me for my cheque which had been slightly delayed in the post. The third had been a curt demand to contact Picard-Syme's secretary.

This time Gabrielle Dubois did not need to leave a message.

"Mr Turner," she said. "I have been trying to contact you. Please phone Mr Picard-Syme as soon as possible."

"It's inconvenient," I replied harshly, irritated by this interruption. "What is this about?"

"You really do need to speak to Mr Picard-Syme," she said haughtily. But then faced with my defiance added, "Your resignation also terminates your treasurership of the Epicureans. Please return the cheque book."

I burst out laughing. The notion that having survived a violent ordeal, having rescued two captives, having important practical matters to resolve, returning a few slips of paper was my highest priority was hilariously absurd.

Gabrielle seemed affronted.

"Don't worry I'll attend to it as soon as I can," I answered collecting myself and ending the call.

The next day we went to the real estate office.

We took one further decision after agreeing a name. We would rent an apartment. There was nothing requiring my immediate return to England and, although I had dispensed dollars liberally, my capital would guarantee our existence indefinitely. At that point neither of us knew what the future held but wonderfully and inexplicably I was surprised at my pleasure on becoming part of a new, suddenly intimate family.

There were several furnished apartments ideally suited to our needs. All were in Miraflores and all of contemporary design in residential blocks. For a rental of US$3,000 per month, with three months paid in advance, I took on the lease of a small flat only two streets away from our hotel. My travellers' cheques were as good as cash and there was no question of my reliability as a tenant. As our selected property was empty we were free to take up occupation a week later once the agency had ensured that all services were functioning correctly.

We gave notice to the hotel and busied ourselves over the next few days with various expeditions. I required a Lima wardrobe. Gilda helped me select soft leather shoes, light jackets and linen trousers, all chosen to assist the transformation from tourist to resident. I began to revel in Gilda's delight as we selected other essentials for our apartment such as towels and bed linen.

We noticed now that Rose was beginning to respond to us. She was starting to push herself up on elbows and knees as if, belatedly, she might soon crawl. But of course the dust and dirt would cling to her clothes and quickly she would lose her pristine appearance. She too required clothes. On one shopping expedition we purchased a whole week's worth of different small garments taking a taxi back to Miraflores crammed with bulging bags full of dungarees, dresses and dainty socks.

We had become more relaxed about venturing out and about. Gilda's appearance was now transformed. To any casual observer she must have appeared as an affluent young mother accompanied by a presentable husband. But nevertheless we still maintained a degree of caution, invariably preserving anonymity behind sunglasses.

It had become pleasurable to take leisurely strolls, wheeling a wide-eyed Rose in her new buggy. Though not as lively as other toddlers and still prone to the occasional piercing cry, she nevertheless presented a very appealing picture, particularly when clad in her new cotton dress, white with a design of red strawberries, set off by a matching baby mob cap.

She was dressed in this combination on our final afternoon before leaving the hotel. We were enjoying a meandering walk on our favourite route along the seafront in Miraflores, admiring the huge sculpture of two lovers in a passionate embrace in the Parque del Amour, when we noticed an elderly couple smiling at us. No doubt they were thinking to themselves that Rose was the product of a similar embrace.

Blushing slightly, as we strolled past, Gilda smiled and said, "Ben, Rose does look cute. Can we buy a camera and take some shots of her – and of us?"

"No need," I replied, "wait until we get back."

My camera was with the rest of my things in the hotel, still at the back of a drawer where I had stowed it after our arrival. Returning to the room, I retrieved it while Gilda propped Rose against some pillows on the bed, positioning her to advantage for a photograph. I pointed and clicked maybe five or six times. Gilda then clambered onto the bed and sat with Rose on her lap while I clicked again. Remembering there was a time delay button I fiddled with the settings and positioned the camera on a dressing table before leaping onto the bed myself just in time to grin at the brief white flash.

This seemed to amuse Rose because, for the first time, she emitted a soft sound like a gurgle of delight. Gilda clasped her gently, encouraging her with murmurs of approval. Then I took another photograph, this time executing an exaggerated leap so that the bed bounced, Gilda laughed and Rose brought her hands together in delight. For several minutes we skylarked, now pulling faces at the camera, now striking ridiculous poses. Finally we lay together, all three of us on the bed laughing and giggling, at last forgetting the terrible events which had led to our flight.

The mood did not last.

I flicked the black switch on the rear of the camera, permitting us to view the shots, pressing the small dial to move back from our clownish grimaces, back from our hurried poses, back from the innocent child propped against pillows, her mob cap flopping down her face. The photographs slid past almost with their own momentum, until replacing Rose, like a ghost onto the screen came the hollow haunted face of the boy.

Over my shoulder Gilda glimpsed the spectre. I felt her shudder and promptly switched off the camera. There was silence between us for several minutes. Neither of us wished to relive those events but neither could we ignore them. We simply could not speak. Eventually, as if the bleak change of mood were dragging her back, dragging her down again into foul confinement, Rose cried out. Instantly we both turned to her, relieved to focus on a child's physical needs.

I could not sleep that night. In the small hours I crept out of bed and looked again at the camera, scrolling beyond the frightened creature with sunken eyes, back to the barred cage and the scurrying creatures, back to the storeroom, the spilling white powder, the hessian bundles.

There in my hand I held photographic proof of the schemes of Ramirez. I had been dismissed by the British Embassy as someone deluded, but now I could demonstrate the veracity of what I was saying. I suppose I wanted to be vindicated.

In the morning I telephoned the Embassy and made an appointment to see Jonathan Edwards.

The meeting took place a week after we occupied our apartment. I left Gilda feeding baby cereal to Rose, sitting in her new high chair wielding a pink plastic spoon, and stepped outside into the clinging humid air. After a twenty minute walk once again I entered the tall building on the Avienda Jose Larco.

Jonathan immediately took the initiative, greeting me in a manner businesslike rather than friendly.

"I shouldn't really be seeing you," he said. "But I remembered your name and what you said on the last occasion intrigued me. I trust you have done nothing foolish?"

I chose my words carefully. I had decided to be what he would call 'economical with the truth'.

"You perhaps thought that I was mistaken, even perhaps deluded. But I assure you that everything I told you before was true."

I gave him details of my journey back to Iquitos, my fortuitous encounter with Pablo and the hazardous voyage to the island about which I had spoken at our previous meeting. He had been sceptical when I described the appalling conditions in which the children had been kept, doubtful about the likely link with a Columbian drug route. But now I had incontrovertible evidence.

I reached across the desk revealing the display on the back of my camera already set at the first of the shots taken before my destruction of that remote encampment. There in front of us were the hessian bundles in the warehouse building; then the spilling powdery cascade. I moved on to the hurried shots of the compound and the innocuous reed screen. Then we were behind, looking at the bars of the cage, the scurrying animals visible at their base. I showed the close-up of the open lock and key. Last of all sliding onto the miniature screen came the boy's face, emaciated but distressed and alive.

"Now perhaps you can understand what I was saying," I said forcefully. "I told you about Ramirez. You can see what trade Inca Enterprises is involved in. You can see that what conditions those children were kept in."

I could tell that Jonathan was both fascinated and horrified. He was also sharp.

"You said 'were kept in'. What has changed?"

"I released them."

Then his questions came rapidly as he subjected me to an intense interrogation. I told him that I had bribed the guard, considering it preferable not to mention my subterfuge, the stupefaction of Raphael and the final terrible lunge onto that knife which hours before he would unhesitatingly have plunged into my throat. As expected, a quantity of cocaine had been delivered to the secret warehouse and there was space for considerably more. I recounted our cramped journey from the island squatting in the long narrow craft, recalling how it was necessary to restrain the children. Finally I described the monstrous riverboat bearing down on us, pitching and tossing us over its filthy wake, the lifting of the bow, the plunge and the sudden flailing of the agitated howling child, unbalanced, tumbling headlong into the impenetrable brown waters.

It shocked me to relive that awful afternoon. I could not remain unemotional. To his credit Jonathan acknowledged my distress.

"And what happened to the little girl?" he asked softly after a few moments' silence.

"She's safe here in Lima," I answered enigmatically.

"At least for the moment I have stopped Ramirez in his tracks," I added. "It will be some time before he gets his act together again."

"What exactly do you mean by that?" Jonathan enquired.

"Before I left, I torched the place, burnt it to the ground."

"I'm not sure I can condone that," he murmured. "But if what you say is right what is your purpose in telling me this? What exactly are you expecting from the British Embassy?"

I thought this was obvious but I spelt it out.

"Surely I have given you enough information for you to contact the Peruvian authorities and have Ramirez and Inca Enterprises investigated."

Jonathan hesitated before he replied. "These things are not as easy as you might think. You have a few photographs but these could have been taken anywhere. Did you keep a sample of what you say was cocaine?"

"How could I?" I responded tetchily. "If I had been stopped in the airport at Iquitos carrying cocaine I would have been in a Peruvian prison now rather than the British Embassy!"

Once more I could see we were straying into territory beyond the instruction manual. Jonathan's everyday world revolved around replacement passports, repatriation of tourists and stranded backpackers. He leaned back slowly tapping his pen on a writing pad.

Finally he spoke. "You have clearly had a harrowing experience. I take seriously what you are telling me but potentially there are widespread ramifications. I need to think about this and consider it with others in the Embassy."

I felt I had made an impression on him. "Can I telephone you to come for a further meeting when we can discuss these matters again?"

"Yes of course. I have plenty of spare time at the moment." I wrote down my number on the proffered Embassy pad.

"Also it would help if I could have copies of these photographs. Can you download and print them off?"

I hesitated. "Here in Lima I don't have a computer," I said, then added, "I suppose I could go to a print shop. But I'm afraid my Spanish is not up to explaining what I would need and in any case I'm not sure that we should let others see these images."

"Yes it would be preferable to keep this discreet," Jonathan responded, pausing for a moment then making a tentative suggestion. "If you don't mind perhaps you could let me keep the camera, or at least the memory card, for a day or two. I'll have to get it virus checked but then our resident geek can download onto one of our computers."

I did not want him to view the other photographs more recently taken. But they were simply of a young lady and a child with my own image in a few. There was nothing compromising and I had been careful to avoid any mention of Gilda. I flipped open the casing and slid out the small plastic square.

"Okay," I said, handing it to him. "But there are also some shots of my girlfriend. Promise me you will just download those that I've shown you."

"Ah, you have a girlfriend in Lima! Now I understand why you are so attracted to Peru!" Jonathan smiled, perhaps out of envy, but perhaps out of relief that he had me pigeonholed. "Be assured, I will print out only what I need. This afternoon I will prepare a summary of what you have told me and request some advice. I'll telephone you again when I have a response."

The meeting ended rather more amicably than our last. I took the lift back down to the ground floor and feeling reasonably satisfied, walked more confidently back through the avenues of Miraflores to my new home.

Gilda and I spent much of the next few days debating whether we should arrange for Rose to be examined by a paediatrician. With a proper varied diet she was now appearing healthier although we could not be certain as to her expected weight and height. Indeed we could only guess at her exact age. Psychologically she appeared to be settling down, from time to time showing us enormous affection despite occasionally waking in the night and screaming with sudden harrowing shrieks, her eyes wide, her tiny fists clenched.

I still had substantial funds remaining and with a little research we were able to locate some exclusive clinics with well qualified practitioners. However we would have enormous problems explaining the background. We had no idea of Rose's exact parentage and had no desire to explain to incredulous medical staff what had occurred on that island in the Amazon. We feared that if we so much as alluded to an escape, unwelcome questions would follow, an investigation might commence. Gilda was adamant she would do nothing to jeopardise the safety of her unofficially adopted daughter.

We therefore decided that the best we could do was to continue a regime of regular and nutritious meals; to clothe Rose properly; to allow her to experience stable and comfortable surroundings and above all to give her love and attention.

This was not a decision taken in an instant, rather we drifted towards what we considered was the only possible conclusion. But I remember that at some point towards the end of an afternoon I screwed up our draft list of paediatric clinics and tossed it into the waste bin. As I did so the ring tone sounded on the phone. I answered to find my caller was Jonathan. He sounded guarded, rather abstracted. Quite tersely he suggested I returned to see him first thing the following day.

Yet again on the next morning I took the now familiar walk to Avienda Jose Larco. I arrived at 9.30 as the consular section was opening and, as before, met Jonathan in one of the small meeting rooms.

He was ill at ease, not hostile but certainly not comfortable.

"Good morning Ben – you don't mind my using your first name do you?" he started.

"No. Not at all."

"I've received a response to my memo and I've been wondering how to put things to you."

We were still standing. He was tapping his fingers together anxiously, hovering before sitting down.

"What's the matter?" I asked. "Have you asked me here simply to tell me that you are going to do nothing?"

"No, not exactly," he replied cagily. "Look, Ben, I feel I've got to know you as a result of our meetings. You've been through a tough time; you've seen some pretty harrowing things. Actually, speaking personally, I think you've been incredibly brave and ingenious. I must stress – and again please understand that I'm simply speaking for myself – that I don't want to see you in any trouble."

"What's going on?" I demanded rather angrily.

"Just let me finish," he replied, quietly and not unkindly. "There really should be no need for me to see you today, but I've decided what I'm going to do."

Then he gestured to the desk on which lay a sheet of British Embassy A4 paper bearing a few typed lines.

"I have here a reply to my note. You will appreciate that I have to follow the advice I have been given, whether I like it or not. Sometimes it can happen that indeed one dislikes what one has to do."

"What on earth …?" I blurted out.

But again he held up his hand in a gesture of silence and continued.

"Now obviously this is an internal document, the property of the British Embassy and not to be seen by persons outside the Embassy. The contents are effectively my instructions. I don't want to read them out as in such circumstances the listener may nevertheless seek an assurance that the text is not the invention of the speaker. But if, let's say, I was summoned out of the room urgently and neglected to take this with me … obviously there would be no means of knowing whether or not my visitor stole a surreptitious glance. Vous comprenez?"

I looked at him with incredulity, muttering something to indicate my perplexed understanding.

"Ah!" he uttered in deadpan fashion. "I've just remembered something."

Then he swiftly rose and left the room.

With a degree of hesitation I reached across the desk and picked up the memorandum. It read:

To Jonathan Edwards:

Your memorandum asks for consular advice regarding matters reported by a British citizen Mr Benjamin Turner.

It misses the point. Not only does Mr Turner have no authority to engage in private investigations he has also indicated that whilst in

Peru he has apparently engaged in illegal activity. He admits both to arson and kidnapping. These are serious matters which should properly be referred to the Peruvian National Police. Naturally were he to be arrested we would provide consular assistance but if verified his admissions warrant a significant term of imprisonment.

While it is the responsibility of others to contact the Peruvian authorities we should not be perceived to be hindering their legitimate enquiries. Accordingly if requested they should be afforded suitable assistance to locate and apprehend Mr Turner.

I could scarcely believe what I was seeing. I felt betrayed, angry and bewildered.

Then my eyes travelled down to the name at the foot of the page. There was a florid scrawled signature and beneath that, neatly typed:

Tristram Collingwood, Second Secretary

I stood gazing at the name for a moment, shocked but beginning to grasp the implications. Silently Jonathan slipped back into the room.

"I'm very sorry," he said. "But you see how it is?"

I realised that it would be disastrous to raise my voice, to create a scene. I clenched my jaw to contain my anger.

"Je comprends," I managed to say quietly, aping diplomatic sophistication.

"Now one formality," Jonathan added, passing a pad of paper across the desk. "Perhaps you can just leave your address for us here in the Embassy."

My mind raced. No doubt there were 'unofficial channels'; whispered words at ambassadorial gatherings; cultivated contacts who could perform favours and expect favours in return. It would not take very much for someone to suggest quietly at a suitable moment in a diplomatic cocktail party that the Peruvian authorities might like to request assistance in locating a particular individual.

However a truculent refusal to comply would create an unpleasant confrontation.

'Gran Hotel Bolivar' I wrote down on the pristine sheet. Then I looked up and said, "Of course you already have my phone number."

Jonathan reached into his pocket and handed me a small envelope.

"Your memory card," he said. Then gesturing to the door, "I'm sorry things have turned out like this. Take care of yourself."

I had the lift to myself as, worried and frustrated, I descended into the humidity of Lima, the impenetrable bank of cloud still obscuring the tropical sun. Needing time to think before I returned to the apartment I dawdled, reflecting on the unsatisfactory encounter. As I walked I visualised the glimpsed memorandum, its patrician tone, the words both written and unwritten, portents of impending danger. I pictured the scrawled signature, belonging to a man I had never met, but a man I seemed to know: the man in cricket whites who had grinned at me from the framed photograph on the wall of a Thameside apartment half a world away.

Eventually I wandered into a coffee bar, relieved to be hit by the cold blast from the air conditioner and grateful for the opportunity to collect my thoughts. I took my cappuccino to a seat at a free table in a corner. As my camera fitted easily into my pocket I had brought it with me instantly to be restored to life. I opened Jonathan's envelope, slipped out the small plastic square and inserted it, closing the casing with a satisfying click. I switched on and watched the lens adjust itself until the display appeared showing the surface of the cappuccino like miniature mole hills in a snowy field. I moved the rear switch to reveal the stored images. Nothing happened. I examined the camera and reset it. I pressed the small arrow forwards and backwards. Again no images appeared.

Then the truth dawned on me. I had no means of knowing whether it had been deliberate or inadvertent, but the memory card had been wiped clean. My evidence was gone.

17

Forty-eight hours later I was in London.

It had been a tough decision, but ultimately both Gilda and I concluded it was necessary. We wondered if already there had been a visit to the Gran Hotel Bolivar. Gilda was convinced, from bitter personal experience, that the National Police did not act independently and that if someone had malign intentions towards me it would require only a subtle inducement or a few words in the right ear for them to cooperate.

We had no means of knowing if in reality we were in danger or whether the words which I had been encouraged to read clandestinely were simply a veiled threat designed to silence me. Perhaps by now Pablo, who in his terms had been made fabulously wealthy by my desperation, would have been unable to conceal the origin of his good fortune and would have ferried others to that charred compound, explaining what he had witnessed. Gilda was certain that Teresa Martinez would not be expecting her return for a few weeks. However it was highly likely that supplies would be taken to the island or that Ramirez would pay another inspection visit. When one of these occasions occurred, if indeed one had not already occurred, then the general devastation as well as Raphael's disappearance would be apparent.

Fortunately Gilda and Rose would be difficult to track down. The apartment was in my name and in any case no one would suspect Gilda of having the wherewithal to live comfortably in a desirable suburb of Lima. I took the precaution of discarding the SIM card in my phone making me untraceable and instead purchased an anonymous pay-as-you-go card for Gilda, careful to reveal no residential details.

Our discussion had been hurried, tearful and intense. We had to focus on practicalities. A quick telephone call established that there were indeed seats available on the next day's flight to Madrid. Before it closed we walked into the nearest branch of Banco Continental BBVA and opened an account in Gilda's name, funding it immediately and substantially with all of my remaining travellers' cheques. This would ensure she possessed ample funds to live comfortably for several months.

Then we went back home to enjoy our last evening together.

In those first few hours after my belated return from the Embassy, already fearful of an encounter with the police, we had thought only of the short term. Now was the time, over our last meal and a bottle of Chilean wine, to consider the longer term. There was one thing about which Gilda was adamant – she would always be a mother to the child.

She was vaguely aware of the correct civil procedures and very conscious that we held no papers for Rose. In all likelihood she did not exist as a recognised individual and accordingly there was nothing to prevent Gilda registering her birth, claiming to be her natural mother. We estimated that Rose was now about 15 months old and any delay in registration could be explained by the fact that she had been born in a remote area and that only recently, once her mother had returned to Lima, was it possible to complete the formalities. Once this task was accomplished then there could be no doubt about Gilda's rights as parent.

Inwardly I was certain of what I most wanted but I was wary about yielding too readily to my emotions and reluctant to place Gilda under any duress. That day when had I walked out on Hardings it had never been in my mind, even remotely, that I would find myself captivated by those I had journeyed to free.

We approached the options cautiously.

"You could go to stay with one of your sisters," I suggested.

"But I have been careful not to contact them since we came here," she replied. "Remember we decided that we would not draw attention to ourselves. I cannot explain things over the phone to Carmen and Isabel and I can't risk anyone knowing that I am living in Miraflores. Besides," she added ruefully, "if they could not take me when I was on my own, they will not provide a home for me and Rose."

"Tell me then," I asked, "what would you really like to do?"

"Can we come to England?" she asked, the gratitude, commitment and trust eloquent in her eyes.

"Is that what you would really like?" I gently asked.

One word followed. "Yes."

I held her hands in mine. "You possess far nobler values than a world of Quentins and Crispins. Since meeting you, respecting you, admiring you, loving you, I have no desire to return to the world of merchant banking. I have enough money to live comfortably for a year or two but I have no idea what I will do next. If you come, can you accept that?"

Gilda smiled broadly and happily. "I also do not know the future. But I know you are a good man; you are a good father. When I am with you I feel as if I am waking from a terrible night. I am ready to walk into the daylight."

I was touched by her fluency and sincerity. I recognised in her all the qualities that the girls in the bank jettisoned when they put on their tight skirts and mascara. Faced with this simple pure goodness I felt humbled.

"You will need to apply for a visa," I said, the mundane practicalities, a useful cover to mask the painful moment.

"Yes I know. Sometimes when I have been out I have been checking what I need to do. I must fill in a form from your Embassy – and when I do can I say that you are my fiancé?" she asked, unnecessarily hesitant.

We both had tears in our eyes as I nodded my agreement. Then Rose shouted, Gilda leapt to pick her up and I went off to pack my things.

All of these fresh memories were buzzing in my head while the connecting plane from Madrid decelerated along the runway flashing past the hotels of the Old Bath Road and taxied to a halt at Terminal 3, London Heathrow airport.

Back in my flat, hot stale and airless on this late June morning, I ignored the flashing light on the answering machine and immediately dialled the Eastleigh number. My sister answered. She welcomed me back but after a few cursory questions about my travels was keen to describe Hazel's first smiles, weight gain and general progress. Eventually I was able to steer the conversation around to my principal objective.

"Pam," I said, "I'm not sure if you remember, but the day Hazel was christened, the thatched house, 'Field Cottage', near the church had a For Sale notice outside. Can you find out for me whether it is still on the market and if so ask the agents to send me the particulars?"

Then I checked my messages. There were two from a tetchy Gabrielle Dubois asking me to telephone Picard-Syme urgently. There were a further two from the garage insisting that it really was highly desirable that the Porsche received its service. The tape whirred for the final time and I heard a newly familiar voice.

"Hi," it said. "Hope you have got home safely. We are missing you already."

It was strangely incongruous, but deeply moving, to be welcomed back by Gilda.

Deciding to ignore Gabrielle but to respond to the other messages, I again picked up the phone.

"Ben Turner here. You left me two messages saying my Porsche requires service. I'll bring it round tomorrow. But I don't want you to service it; I want you to sell it."

The garage was the first of my calls the following day. I saw a young Cockney car dealer more interested in tempting me with the latest model than disposing of my two-year-old vehicle. He was insistent that the superiority of the new design would immediately appeal to me. Of course if I upgraded he would be able to offer me a far better price. It was beyond his comprehension that I was no longer interested solely in speed. After a rather fractious discussion bedevilled with frustration on my part and incredulity on his, we settled on a price of £37,500.

He was even more incredulous when he saw me march next door to the BMW dealership. I promptly purchased a one year old 5 Series estate, providing plenty of room to carry a child and baby buggy.

By the time I returned to the flat the postman had called leaving a plump envelope from a firm of Winchester estate agents. While I was slitting it open, noticing not only that Field Cottage was still on the market but that it had been subject to a price reduction, the telephone rang. This time Gabrielle Dubois did not hesitate.

"I have Mr Picard-Syme for you."

In the next instant a caustic voice scorched my ears.

"At last; the man who deserts his post; who never answers his phone; who never returns his calls; who never returns property no longer his."

"I can explain all of this," I began. But Picard-Syme was dripping acid.

"Since you walked out on Hardings and the Epicureans I have been reviewing the club's finances. You settled the accounts for our March dinner but would you kindly explain to me why you drew yourself something over half a million pounds in cash in mid April?"

I was not sure how much he knew about Inca Enterprises SA and Collingwood's investment. I decided to be accurate but brief.

"That was not for myself. It was on behalf of Collingwood – an advance on his treasurer's remuneration."

"Really? 'It wasn't me – it was him' has been the plea of the pusillanimous for generations."

"But he told me that this was payment due to him and that you knew. I trusted him."

"As a Sorbonne man I never trust an Oxford man. Besides a corollary of the suspension of activities is a suspension of remuneration."

"Then you must speak to Collingwood about it," I answered curtly.

"I shall do no such thing. You can if you wish. This was an unauthorised withdrawal undertaken by B. Turner. I expect B. Turner to reimburse the full amount within a week. If you don't, you will hear from our solicitors."

Picard-Syme ended the call without a goodbye, doing nothing to encourage the suggestion that his nickname was undeserved.

Already disillusioned with life in Docklands, this corrosive conversation was pivotal to my next decision. I requested a couple of nights in Gary and Pam's spare room, made an appointment to view Field Cottage and put my flat on the market.

Although cramped, slightly uncomfortable and intermittently disturbed by my niece, the following weekend in Eastleigh was useful. The three of us viewed Field Cottage on a bright summer's day. The garden was becoming overgrown. Untended, several attractive pink roses trailed mischievously over the porch. The interior required some modernisation and redecoration but held an instant appeal, friendly and welcoming. Gary assured me that the thatched roof was perfectly safe. He had done work in several such houses and was adamant that the fire risk was no greater than under a conventional roof. A favourable report a few days later from an acquaintance thatcher, a former Cambridge dropout named Diggory Dickens, established that the existing material was sound and that replacement should be unnecessary for at least 20 years. Further research revealed that the property came with the adjoining field and that the sale was on behalf of executors who were anxious to complete and realise funds for distribution.

During my stay I was also able to explain about Gilda and our adopted child. Already I had learnt in one of our daily phone conversations at bedtime for me, early evening for Gilda, that she had obtained a visa application from the British Embassy. She was required to name a sponsor who could demonstrate the wherewithal to give financial support. It was hard for my brother-in-law to understand why it was prudent for my name not to appear but to his credit he was willing to allow his to be used. I arranged a transfer of £25,000 to his bank account as ample demonstration of his liquidity and capacity to support a foreign visitor.

Once I had returned to London, unable to dismiss Picard-Syme's threat, I tried to make contact with Collingwood. His UK phone number was no longer recognised and it proved impossible to get beyond a secretary when I called Grossmans in New York. Neither could I obtain a personal e-mail address.

But I was too preoccupied with other matters to persevere. I received daily progress reports on the visa application and tried to support and encourage Gilda during this long lonely period when she had only Rose for company. Thankfully no one appeared to be searching for her. On her regular walks along the Pacific seafront she noticed the occasional sinister character regarding her with a fixed stare but concluded that any male attention was carnal rather than criminal.

Having received the report portentously entitled 'Field Cottage – a survey by Diggory Dickens Master Thatcher' I travelled to Winchester to make an offer. I opened £35,000 short of the asking price. The young estate agent demurred. He would have to discuss the matter with the executors. In the meantime he insisted on driving me around the lanes of South Hampshire to view three similar properties in different locations. Apparently the market was sluggish. Those requiring picturesque properties also required modern electrics, bathrooms and central heating. Everything on the market would benefit from improvement.

A few days later I sold my flat. It was purchased by a Russian who wanted it lock stock and barrel and immediately. I agreed to the lock, stock and timescale. The keg of ale had long since been consumed.

When, a few days after that, an envelope bearing the name of a firm of solicitors arrived I assumed that it was in connection with the conveyance. Instead on opening it I found a demand for payment on behalf of the Epicureans of £512,820. I replied directing my correspondents to Crispin Collingwood at Grossmans in New York and sent the letter on to him by airmail at his office address marked 'personal' with my sender's name clearly showing on the back of the envelope.

My offer on Field Cottage was not accepted but I was given an indication that a slight improvement would secure the purchase. I increased the figure by £10,000 with a request that the alpacas be included with the adjacent land. By the third week in July the entire property was mine, subject to contract. I did not need a mortgage and instructed my solicitors to make haste. In the event I had to lodge with Pam and Gary for three weeks in August as the Russian raced to completion while land registry problems delayed occupation of my rural dwelling.

During the conveyance I took the opportunity to change the dwelling's uninspiring name. Mindful of its potential young occupant and of the summer blooms around the porch, Field Cottage became Rose Cottage.

The enforced hiatus between sale and purchase was fortuitous. With time on my hands, and with the growing conviction that I sensed a lucrative business venture, I again visited the three unsold thatched houses still looking forlorn in the estate agent's window amongst the neo Georgian residences preferred by the citizens of Winchester. I returned on a third occasion with Gary and Diggory Dickens. They decided that one needed to be re-thatched ("I'll finish off with a couple of proud pheasants straddling the ridge," Diggory added almost poetically) and that all would benefit from improvements such as electrical rewiring, the installation of alarms and security gates. Completion of these works together with rapid garden makeovers would transform each of them from attractive anachronisms into modernised marketable properties. Studying the market, we concluded that we could make an average profit of £200,000 on a resale.

My funds had already been depleted by my expenses in South America and it would have been imprudent to invest every remaining penny into this venture. Instead I made an appointment with Coutts to discuss a business loan to a new company to which I would subscribe £1 million share capital and in which Gary and Diggory would become directors.

Hardly had the discussion been arranged when I received an unwelcome, worrying communication. It arrived by courier on a unseasonably wet day in the last week of August, the leather-clad bike rider unnerving Pam as, clutching Hazel, she took the stiff brown envelope from him and signed the receipt.

The senders were the solicitors representing the Epicureans. They reminded me that they had not received a satisfactory response to earlier communications. They stated quite simply and starkly that my withdrawal of US$1 million or £512,820 in sterling was unauthorised. I was offered one final opportunity to reimburse the amount or a legal action would be taken. Indeed there was even an implication that I could be subject not to civil but to criminal proceedings.

Yet again I tried to contact Collingwood. As before I could speak to no one other than a secretary who tartly insisted that my calls would not be taken. I was trapped. If I did not make the payment I faced at best a lawsuit, at worst a criminal investigation. Moreover I could forget any hope of registering a company and commencing an attractive business venture. After a couple of sleepless nights I telephoned Coutts and authorised a transfer from my account to that of the Epicureans.

At least this removed the immediate threat and cleared the obstacles to incorporation; I would track down Collingwood as soon as I could. Indeed already I was considering a stratagem to be deployed when the time was ripe and over the next few weeks developed it further, but for now I was fully engaged with forming my company and acquiring its initial stock.

As happened so frequently over that schizophrenic summer, my temporary gloom was dispelled by a ray of good news. On the very day that I contacted Coutts, Gilda telephoned excitedly. At last she had a date for the next stage of the visa application process, an interview at the British Embassy scheduled for mid October.

This welcome progress buoyed me as I took up residence in Rose Cottage. Rapidly I learned how to operate the Aga, cope with the idiosyncrasies of irregular windows and, most importantly, how to care for the alpacas. Fortunately their field was lush and they needed no supplementary feeding although it was necessary to have an expert visit to shear their fine coats.

Throughout the early autumn my nascent business venture kept me wholly occupied. By the end of September offers had been accepted on the three properties. By the time contracts were exchanged I had registered my company.

Naming the new enterprise proved to be infinitely more difficult than naming the house. Eventually Pam made a kind and sensible suggestion.

"I don't know all you have been through, Ben, but I can see you have walked away from a world which has left you scarred and changed," she said carefully. "Soon you will welcome a partner and a child. You have come back to us and truly have a new beginning. There is only one possible name: 'Renaissance'."

From mid October to the end of November Renaissance Restorations Ltd absorbed all my time. Besides the work commissioned from Gary and Diggory Dickens I required the services of reliable plumbers and painters and decorators. One of the gardens lent itself to a complete redesign involving the removal of a huge cupressus hedge to offer a stupendous view across the countryside near the site of the Civil War Battle of Cheriton. It was necessary to order materials and supplies such as gravel to improve driveways and heavy security gates. I realised that should the business be successful there was ample scope for it to employ Gilda.

She reported that her interview at the Embassy had been satisfactory. Fortunately she had seen a young female officer and was able to tell her simply that we had met while I was on business in Peru. Within a few weeks she would have the necessary endorsement in her passport and would at last be able to leave her lonely existence. Rose offered some companionship and was now responding well to stimulation even acquiring a rudimentary vocabulary. But sensibly Gilda continued to wear dark glasses and struck up no more than a nodding acquaintance with the uniformed nannies who daily paraded their charges along the Pacific seafront.

There was indeed plenty to keep my mind diverted from Collingwood and the Epicureans. It angered me that with patrician disdain he should ignore all attempts to make contact. Furthermore having committed most of my capital to Renaissance Restorations Ltd I could not lightly disregard the US$1 million which he had in effect appropriated. I stuck to my resolve that as soon as an opportune moment arrived I would fly to New York and beard the lion in his den.

That moment came at the beginning of December. The weather changed, winter descending with penetrating frosts and short cold depressing days of wind and rain. Outdoor work on the company's properties ceased and temporarily there was little organising to be done.

But what impelled me was the good news from Peru. Gilda had obtained her visa. It was necessary only to give notice on the Miraflores apartment, make travel arrangements and then bring her and Rose to the safety of a new life. If I were to confront Collingwood, early December would be my only opportunity.

We booked a flight for Gilda and Rose from Lima in the third week of the month. There would be time for us both to enjoy the anticipation of Christmas and then the day itself, the first for all of us as parents, as Pam reminded me. Their journey settled, I searched

Expedia and booked myself a seat from Heathrow to New York JFK on a British Airways service leaving on 9th December at 13.35.

It was difficult to explain exactly what was taking me across the Atlantic. I simply insisted that it was necessary for me to travel: to conclude some unfinished business. Although not wholly satisfied by this, a slightly mystified Pam offered to run me to the airport.

We left Eastleigh at 10 a.m. on a dull day, the entire country covered with low grey cloud; the M3 motorway drizzle damp; car windscreens flecked filthy with tyre spray. Progress was good despite some heavy traffic near Basingstoke. It was not until we were just beyond junction 3 with no prospect of an alternative route that we hit trouble. Cars and lorries slid to a halt, tail lights blinking alarmingly in the murk. A few minutes later police cars and ambulances raced up the hard shoulder. Being in good time we were initially relaxed, but by 11.30 gnawing anxiety began to grip us. I tuned into the traffic news to discover there had been an accident at the junction of the M3 and M25. Wreckage was being cleared but delays were inevitable.

Thankfully by noon we were edging forwards and ten minutes later were part of a crawling line of cars perceptibly sidling onto the M25, winding past a rather mangled Vauxhall Vectra being extracted from the rear axle of a huge Norbert Dentressangle articulated truck. Thirty minutes later we were pulling into the drop off bay at the bright new Terminal 5.

With a necessarily cursory goodbye, clutching my computer printed boarding card, I raced through the wide concourse to the baggage drop. There was the usual hurried examination of my passport, the usual questions about personal packing before I could run up the escalator two steps at a time to join the snaking queue anxious to complete security screening.

By the time I had re-laced my shoes and buckled my belt not only was the display screen showing my flight number at the head of the list, it was also flashing a warning that boarding was about to close. I hurried past the duty free shops and down the long corridor to the departure gate. Two smartly uniformed members of BA staff were closing down their computer screens, positioning a barrier across the departure gate. With no-one behind me I was hurried down the long ramp, through the extendable walkway and into the aircraft where a crew member was standing impatiently, ready to dismiss the gantry operator and close the door.

I was urged onwards through the first cabin where a stewardess was snatching at the final empty glasses of champagne and discarded face towels. I continued forward, out of breath, making for the rear of the aircraft, no longer envious of these privileged travellers. But then someone caught my eye. Sitting there in the last row of Business Class, idly flicking through the Financial Times, was a person I had not seen since my last working day with Hazzard Brothers. It was Justin Rhodes.

Then next to him in the window seat I recognised someone else. It was the stunningly beautiful Sabrina.

18

I spent part of the flight wondering what I would say if I met Justin and Sabrina at the luggage carousel. A prior encounter was unlikely as I was seated in the very last row of the plane and in any case the spacious front cabins were hidden by a heavy grey curtain.

Sabrina was no doubt still smarting. I could imagine her waiting for me at The Ivy's table, a glass of champagne already ordered and charged to my account. She must have been furious when I did not appear and even more furious at having to purchase her own aperitif.

But I need not have worried. I was one of the last to leave when we landed at JFK New York. The queue for immigration was slow and by the time I reached the baggage hall the suitcases from my flight were already repeating their bumpy circuit. The absence of any tell-tale 'priority' labels indicated that business class passengers had long since departed for their onward journeys.

Besides finding me a suitable flight Expedia had also found me a reasonably priced hotel room. I took the airport bus to Times Square, checked in to the Westin, and as it was past 8 p.m. ordered a room service sandwich. Then I took the first step towards my planned confrontation with the person who was so studiously avoiding me.

Irritated by the stubborn refusal of secretaries to permit dialogue with a director and annoyed by the total lack of response to all communication, I had decided on a back door approach through an old contact. I still possessed my notebook containing within it the home number of my former mentor Art Feinman. Once I had booked my flight I called him and arranged to meet him on my arrival in New York. He knew of course about the collapse of Hazzards and he had also heard of my departure from Hardings. But he was happy to see me especially as I might be able to supply inside information about his new director, the Englishman with the curious name of the honourable Crispin Collingwood.

I picked up the telephone.

"Ben, how are you doing?" Art Feinman answered, his voice immediately distinctive.

"Hi Art. I'm here safe and sound in the Big Apple," I said. "You still on for lunch?"

"Yeah. Tomorrow is best. How about one o'clock. Luigi's deli?"

"Great. See you then."

I remembered Luigi's very well. Art and I had enjoyed pastrami on rye there on a few occasions during my stay at Grossmans in those distant days of my early employment with Hazzards. It was fortunate that almost immediately I could begin to implement my strategy. Despite my tiredness I sat down and committed to Westin notepaper the message, brief but hopefully irresistible, which for several days I had been composing.

Adding my extension number to the hotel's, I wrote:

Dear Crispin,

DI Hunter of the Drugs Unit, Metropolitan Police is very interested in Inca Enterprises SA and its principal shareholder.

Regards,

Ben Turner.

Having placed the note in a blank envelope, I telephoned Gilda. For the first time since our hurried separation we were able to talk late into her evening, temporarily contending with a time difference of only one hour.

Next day as I left for my rendezvous with Art I asked the puzzled hotel receptionist if she would kindly write 'The Hon. Crispin Collingwood' on my envelope. The recipient might be unfamiliar with my handwriting but I dared not risk recognition and immediate consignment of the unopened note to his wastepaper bin.

I arrived early at Luigi's, among the first of the lunchtime customers. I was drinking my second cup of coffee when Art Feinman stepped inside, rather hesitantly, clutching a flat brown business case.

I could tell immediately from his downbeat greeting that something was wrong. He gave the impression of being distracted, having little time.

"Hi Art," I greeted him. "Good to see you again."

"Hi, Ben," he replied noncommittally.

"What are you having?" I asked. "I owe you one from the Chicago deal."

I ordered some sandwiches and a couple of Coca Colas. Art started to gobble his down hurriedly. Our conversation was tense and I sensed that he was holding something back.

"What's up?" I asked, desperate to establish rapport and hand him the note for Collingwood.

"Look, Ben," he answered, glancing around furtively. "Two hours ago I am afraid I let slip to Collingwood that I was meeting you. He went ballistic. I'm not sure what you are supposed to have done but he instructed me to keep away from you. "

I was upset but not really surprised. Collingwood had been avoiding contact for months and was now ensuring that my exclusion from former circles was total. I shrugged in resignation.

"There is so much you don't know, Art." I said.

I could not even begin to tell him everything that had a happened. This was no time to mention Collingwood's creation, the elite club known as the Epicureans, or to explain about Ramirez and the doubtful activities of Inca Enterprises. He could not envisage my journeys to that remote Amazon island nor imagine the ordeal of Gilda and the children and the horrors accompanying their release. Picard-Syme was a pivotal figure in London, but not even his nickname was known in New York. Above all I could not expect Art Feinman to believe in the duplicity of his boss.

I simply added, "Please do not think badly of me – and do not believe everything Collingwood says."

"I can't afford to make an enemy of Collingwood," he said ruefully. "It's been good knowing you Ben, but this is where our ways must part."

Our lunch was coming to a premature and unsatisfactory conclusion.

"I'm very sorry," I replied, the regret in my voice sincere. "But can you do one last favour for me? Just give this to Collingwood's secretary – or if you like, leave it in her in tray so she will never know that it was you who brought it …"

My words were competing for attention with the muffled but rising sound of a ringtone. Art seemed distracted and I realised that the tinny melody, louder and insistent, was coming from his case.

"Excuse me a moment," he said. "I'm expecting an important call."

He picked up the slim case and quickly flipped it open on the table. Inside were a few papers, an envelope and a couple of business cards tucked in to a bright red elastic strap tight across the interior of the calfskin lid. Almost unthinking he dropped my envelope inside then extracted his phone.

"Hi, Art Feinman. Sorry, I didn't catch a word of that." He sounded irritated. "I'm in a deli; losing the signal. I'll just move outside."

He dashed to the doorway of Luigi's to continue his animated conversation, his back to me, the phone pressed hard to his ear. The case still lay open on the table where he had left it.

There was something about the envelope lying inside, now partly covered by mine, which was curiously familiar. It was fashioned from high quality paper, deep cream in colour with a tasteful gilt edging. On the back, in the centre of the triangular flap, was an embossed monogram. I stretched across and eased it towards me.

Now I recognised what I was seeing. Gingerly I lifted the flap and slid out a gilt edged card. Here was the monogram again, quite elaborate in design with far more scroll and whorls than the monogram I so vividly remembered. As I glanced down the reason for the excess ornamentation of the lettering, a flourishing E entwined with a sinuous N and Y, became obvious. Neatly printed in an elegant script I read: 'This certifies that Arthur Feinman, having met the qualifying conditions, has been admitted to membership of the Epicureans, New York.'

There was something else shockingly familiar in that case. Carefully I replaced the monogrammed certificate; equally carefully I extracted a business card from the red retaining strip.

Immediately I knew what I was holding. It was from Ramirez's bank in Cusco. With a sickening sensation I spun it around in my fingers certain of what I would see. There were a few words in recognisable handwriting and a number: 'Inca Enterprises SA Account No. 18012912.'

There was only one conclusion. Collingwood had established the Epicureans in New York and Feinman was treasurer.

He was still talking into the telephone. Quickly I replaced the card then folded down the lid of the case, stood up and walked to the restrooms.

A few minutes later, when I returned, Feinman had gone.

But my stratagem worked. When I returned to my hotel room the small red message light was flashing on the telephone. I picked up the receiver and heard Collingwood's voice. "I leave for Tokyo tomorrow afternoon. Come to Grossmans at 11 a.m. Say you are Nick Forsyth."

The following morning was dull, grey and cold. As I left the Westin I pulled my leather jacket tight to keep out the penetrating damp before descending to the subway. The tower which housed Grossman brothers was very near Luigi's. I left the subway at Wall Street then walked up William Street and into Pine Street, soon recognising the imposing glass doors at the foot of a frighteningly tall skyscraper.

I pushed at the revolving door closely watched by the burly security guard standing by an adjacent door opened only for important visitors. Under his suspicious gaze I walked across the echoing marble floored hall to the reception desk which served the various establishments renting the offices above.

"I have an 11 o'clock appointment with Mr Collingwood of Grossman Brothers. Nick Forsyth," I remembered to say. There was a quick tapping on a computer and I was promptly directed to the elevator and the Grossman reception on the third floor.

I emerged into a very different environment. Just as I recalled it the Grossman third floor lobby was spacious and deeply carpeted. It had an atmosphere of subdued confidence. There were two low reception desks of polished rosewood and behind them two well groomed young ladies wearing tailored blouses, their only overt affiliation to the bank the discrete gold 'Grossman' brooches pinned with geometric precision above each left breast.

I repeated my identification and was offered a seat while a call was put through to Collingwood's office. About two minutes later there was a restrained ping as the lift doors opened and the man himself appeared.

He was curt and aloof, not deigning to offer a greeting.

"We can't talk here, come with me. I'll give you 15 minutes, then I leave for JFK. "

Without a further word he led the way back to the elevator. The doors closed silently and we were alone, unavoidably scrutinising each other as the enclosed lift compartment had full-length mirrors on each wall. The motion upwards was imperceptible, only the numerical display indicating that we were rapidly rising, flashing past the 10th, 20th and 30th floors.

Collingwood had changed noticeably since I had last seen him in London some eight months earlier. The traces of athleticism had disappeared. His waist had broadened and his face was slightly florid. He was uncharacteristically taciturn.

"Why the subterfuge?" I asked, breaking the silence.

He looked at me stonily. "My staff have been informed that Grossman Brothers are to have no contact whatsoever with Benjamin Turner. I could hardly break my own rule."

"So that's why my calls were never taken, my e-mails never answered and my letter not even acknowledged," I responded instinctively.

Still the elevator was speeding upwards. We had passed floors 40, 50 and 60 with no indication that it was slowing.

"You don't get it do you?" Collingwood said with patrician sarcasm. "You have been extremely foolish, an enormous disappointment to me. Your career takes off, you become one of the trading elite, you are propelled into a lucrative and desirable situation thanks to the patronage of one who discerned some talent in you. Then what happens? You simply walk out!

"I heard all about it from Quentin. Not only did you desert the Epicureans, you also deserted Picard-Syme. I commended to him the coming man who unhesitatingly took advantage of the most valuable introduction in London during his hour of need. Then he deserted. Kick Arse is powerful; he is also vengeful. His epithet was not acquired by accident. He has completely cut me off, refuses to take my calls. My stock in London is worthless!"

At that there was a sudden deceleration. The numbers on the panel flashed more slowly – 72, 73, 74. Then as the number 75 illuminated there was another ping from the door and while I was still composing a response we emerged into light.

We stepped into an open plan area with a number of seats interspersed with monstrous brass ashtrays set on marble plinths at the right height for sedentary smokers. The strange room was drab and dusty, its air stale as if it were unused.

It seemed to me that the towering building was narrower at this elevation, this floor noticeably smaller than its lower neighbours. The windows on all sides ran from floor-to-ceiling slanted steeply inwards with the sloping line of the building, flooding the room with soft light although the clouds were low and grey. Immediately I felt uncomfortable, nervous about moving from a fixed spot. My legs weakened; I found it hard to concentrate. Even though I stared at Collingwood I could not help noticing the roofs of lower buildings, the traffic on the Hudson River, the green streak of the Statue of Liberty.

I suspected he had chosen this elevated location deliberately. He smirked as he spoke. "I heard you had no head for heights – neither physical nor financial it appears."

"Where are we? What is this place?" I asked, groping for one of the seats.

"The Grossman Airport Lounge of course," he replied. "We are directly beneath the helipad. Sadly executive hospitality has fallen into desuetude; we demigods of finance can no longer hover over Harlem. Since 9/11 all flights have been grounded."

Cautiously I looked around. I could see that a metal spiral staircase led up from one side of the room apparently straight onto the helipad. A faded sign advised passengers to beware of rotor blades.

As I lowered myself into the safety of a seat I saw the lights twinkle outside a second lift. There was the same restrained ping and a security guard appeared, burly, menacing in his dark uniform, a bulky holster at his waist. Unperturbed Collingwood strode over to him flashing his ID.

"Just give us ten minutes alone," he said pressing a $10 bill into the gloved hand already hovering above the protruding trigger of an ugly revolver.

"Very good, sir. Thank you sir," he answered, his restrained aggression immediately tempered to grudging politeness. Then, muttering something into his walkie-talkie, he retreated back into the elevator.

Collingwood sat down opposite me. I kept my eyes focused on his face. Thankfully from a sitting position I was less conscious of the city traffic crawling 300 metres below.

As if reading the accusation in my eyes he said, "I have chosen this abandoned lounge because here we can talk away from prying eyes and without interruption. Now Benjamin what was the meaning of your note?"

"My trip to Peru gave me a clear insight into Inca Enterprises ..." I commenced.

"It's no crime to be a shareholder in a foreign company," he interrupted.

Ignoring him I continued, "You really worked a neat little arrangement, didn't you? Firstly you create precedent by agreeing an inflated fee with Ramirez for the supply to the Epicureans of South American delicacies. You then tie your successor into this arrangement. Next you claim your reward from the club. Then you set up Inca Enterprises and fly off to New York. But you sit here intending to receive future dividends from the profit made on the excessive level of fees the treasurer is committed to paying!"

Collingwood gave a smirk of satisfaction.

"Now, this struck me as very attractive. Indeed when Ramirez asked me to become a shareholder I was tempted. By the way, were you aware that the Ramirez had invited me to subscribe?" I added.

"When Ramirez took me to his island near Iquitos I became fully aware of the real purpose of Inca Enterprises. Of course I saw his breeding station; but he hardly disguised that fact that it was simply a front for other purposes. He also showed me the squalid orphanage you had set up."

"Orphanage? What do you mean?" Collingwood asked, a look of puzzlement on his face.

I wondered if there were certain things Ramirez had not divulged or which had not leaked from my account in the British Embassy in Lima. I decided to describe the foul wooden building hidden by the reed screen, the seething furry mass of rapidly breeding guinea pigs and the soiled straw bedding on which I had first seen the feral children.

He appeared slightly taken aback but then muttered, "I suppose if there is spare capacity Ramirez can use it as he likes. Peruvian standards are not the same as ours."

Taking advantage of this hint of doubt, my next words were cold and calculated.

"I also saw the stash of cocaine."

"You couldn't have," snapped Collingwood. "In any case the company had only just been formed. You conveyed the funds for my share capital as I recall."

"It was on my second visit," I added. "I have photographic evidence."

Collingwood gave me a knowing glance. "You are lying. For reasons which need not concern you, I suspect that is not the case," he muttered with a half smile.

"It is all safely stored on my mobile phone," I responded fixing him with my gaze.

I had been prepared for this moment. He was not to know that the phone had never left my pocket and that my last sentence was indeed untrue.

There was a pause. Collingwood glanced at his watch.

"Very well. What is it you want?" he asked.

"Just the million dollars that you owe me," I replied.

"What do you mean, I owe you?"

Again I was unsure how much he knew. I had assumed that he would have had some contact with Picard-Syme but from what he had said it appeared possible that they had not spoken since his departure for New York.

"Picard-Syme suspended both the activities of the Epicureans and your stipend as you termed it," I explained carefully.

"Did he indeed? When he telephoned, Quentin was lamenting the cessation of fine dining but I understood the reason for his temporary deprivation was the disappearance of the treasurer. Incidentally your position is now held by Justin Rhodes. In fact he has just winged his way here to discuss a supply for the delayed event, accompanied by the ever delightful Sabrina. She could have been in your Big Apple bed had you not deserted. I'm told that she speculated on the quality of your working class body but was sadly disillusioned by your working class unreliability. Her passion will be spent on Justin who will doubtless tell the unsuspecting Melissa that his exhaustion is due to the demands of his business trip."

I suspected he was enjoying this digression, content to steer me away from my purpose. But I pressed on.

"Picard-Syme denied ever authorising any remuneration, contrary to what you told me."

"Let's be perfectly accurate," Collingwood replied. "I recall a crackly conversation in which I said that he knew I had not received any payment for my efforts. That was all."

"So the US$1 million that I took to Peru on your behalf was actually an unauthorised withdrawal?"

"You can choose to put it that way if you wish. Unquestionably payment from the Epicureans was overdue."

"I understand, now," I said, Collingwood's duplicity becoming apparent. "That is why Picard-Syme forced me to reimburse the Epicureans."

"What do you mean 'forced'?"

I gave an account of the acidic onslaught from Picard-Syme and the increasingly menacing letters from his solicitors. I reminded Collingwood of his embargo on my e-mails and correspondence. He listened intently tapping the tips of his fingers together then finally attempted some dismissive comments, flashes of the old Collingwood emerging as he warmed to his theme.

"How standards have slipped since I left London. Hazzards collapses and your club chairman panics. Then he shelters behind lawyers!

"And Benjamin Turner becomes a philanthropist. He makes an unauthorised withdrawal to purchase an investment for his benefactor then, fearing the breath of a barrister, makes good by reimbursing out of his own funds. My only possible response is to say 'thank you'! Whatever you have done is your business and is of no concern to me."

I studied him silently for a moment before pricking his swelling bubble of pomposity.

"I anticipated that might be your reaction," I said icily. "I now intend to keep my appointment with DI Hunter. Check with Scotland Yard if you wish. He heads their drugs team – South America desk."

His mood darkened.

"How much does he know?" he asked.

"Very little at the moment."

I felt confident that my subterfuge was succeeding. I had ascertained that DI Hunter was the appropriate police contact. It would do no harm for Collingwood to believe that we had already engaged in some preliminary dialogue.

"I take it that you would prefer me to terminate the connection," I added.

Collingwood gave a considered response. "I can accept that Inca Enterprises may have a relaxed attitude to certain livestock importation requirements. For that reason alone and no other it will indeed be preferable if it does not attract official interest."

"I can guarantee that if you return my $1 million," I said emphatically.

"How do I know the value of your guarantee?" he asked cautiously.

"You don't," I replied. "You will just have to accept that a working-class boy's word is his bond."

He rose looking anxiously at his watch, becoming suddenly decisive.

"I shall sort out my remuneration with Justin. Picard-Syme panicked unnecessarily. After all, in a few weeks' time your former colleagues will again be summoned to board rooms to receive their gilded rewards. No doubt very soon the excellent new treasurer will be issuing more monogrammed cards. There will be ample liquidity to settle my stipend. I may even demand interest on late payment."

Then he paused adding, "You shall have your money, but there is one condition. We never have any further contact whatsoever."

"You can be sure of that," I responded with total honesty.

"You have had more than your fifteen minutes," he said hurriedly. "It's time I was leaving for JFK. Japanese Airlines do not wait even for directors of Grossman Brothers."

He strode towards the elevator and I followed, unsteady again now I was on my feet, clutching the chair backs to steady myself as I tried to blank out the plunging view over the city. The lift doors opened and we stepped inside, our images staring back at us as they reproduced themselves to infinity in the mirrors on the walls.

"My cheque-book is in my office," a few dozen Collingwoods mouthed at me.

But I did not trust him. I could envisage him handing me a worthless piece of paper then ensuring that any further clandestine access both to himself and Grossman Brothers was totally denied. There would never be a second opportunity to obtain redress.

"My expenditure on your behalf was in cash; I require reimbursement in cash." It was the turn of my lips to move and then to be imitated by the reflected lips of an army of Ben Turners.

The elevator stopped at the 57th floor where the directors' suites were located. He held the 'Doors Open' button.

"How symmetrical, how quaint," he said. "If you want cash that can be arranged although, remarkable and wide ranging as my abilities might be, I cannot conjure dollar bills from thin air at this precise moment. Come at the same time tomorrow and ask for my secretary. We part here. You can descend to the lobby on your own."

But at least he was more civil than on my arrival. He left me with both a farewell and a reminder.

His last words were, "Goodbye, Mr Forsyth."

19

Sunlight was slanting in narrow shafts down Broadway the following morning. But already there was a cold breeze in the air chasing the lingering autumn leaves in playful gusts, heralding the depression rolling in from the Atlantic as forecast on the Weather Channel.

Again I wore my leather jacket, hopeful that my task would be complete before the lashing rain swept in over Long Island. Relaxed in the knowledge that I simply had to make a collection from Collingwood's secretary, I strolled leisurely out of the hotel towards the subway. There was no great rush, neither was there any reason to linger. Accordingly I was early when, for a second time, I approached the skyscraper which housed Grossman Brothers.

I stood on the opposite side of the street and craned my neck to gaze up at the colossal futuristic structure. As I suspected the building tapered dramatically on its upper floors creating the impression of an unfinished pyramid atop the towering edifice. In the low glinting December sunlight I could even detect a reflective shimmering on the slanting windows of the 75th floor with which I had made unwelcome acquaintance the previous day.

Just before 11 a.m. I pushed at the familiar revolving doors once again, silently scrutinised by the security guard. I remembered to announce myself as Nick Forsyth and, feigning non-recognition, the ground floor receptionist unnecessarily repeated directions to Grossman Brothers on the third floor.

I had to wait at the Grossman reception desk while a call was made to Collingwood's office. Then I noticed the little red indicator light above the lift flashing furiously as it descended swiftly from one of the upper floors. A handsome lady probably in her late 40s or early 50s emerged. She marched over to me, introduced herself as

Collingwood's secretary and asked me to accompany her in the elevator.

It occurred to me that she would not want to count out $1 million in a reception area. Doubtless she was taking me to the 57th floor and the directors' suites. She said nothing, standing proudly upright like a sentry, her back a ramrod against the mirror, her reflection creating a brigade of guards. I watched the electronic numerals in the shiny brass panel flashing rapidly, anticipating the smooth barely perceptible deceleration after floor 50.

But we kept on moving upwards. The number 57 flashed briefly and spun onwards to 60 and then, to my increasing apprehension, to 70. Now at last the digits glowed more legibly. Number 72 winked, there was a longer pause on 73, but to my dismay 74 quickly disappeared and we came to a halt on floor number 75.

The doors slid open to reveal that once again I was below the helipad in the abandoned lounge, now suffused with sunlight. I hesitated, apprehensive and queasy, disturbed by the sudden glimpse of the bright city below. I had expected to be taken to an office, not to be exposed to light, space and height.

My escort said crisply, "I've been asked to reacquaint you with an old friend."

Then she gestured to some seats directly opposite where I could make out a figure impossible to identify clearly in the merciless glare.

"You can have privacy for your discussion. I'm on the 57th floor if you need anything," she added, stepping back into the elevator and leaving me to an uncertain encounter.

I tried to shade my eyes but the unrelenting beam created an impenetrable halo disguising the height, sex and physiognomy of this unexpected invitee.

"Justin?" I enquired tentatively.

Then the figure rose, slowly and ponderously. There was something uncannily familiar about the movement. Out of the yellow flood of light emerged a sardonic sound.

"We meet again Benjamin."

Despite the sickly heat of the claustrophobic lounge I felt myself shudder. The voice unmistakably belonged to Ramirez.

He slowly appeared out of the blinding backdrop, looking exactly the same as when we had parted company all those months earlier at the airport in Lima. Bizarrely he was still clutching my attaché case, the livid brown scar unhealed. He peered at me through his gold-rimmed spectacles, standing in a confrontational position, frowning slightly beneath his thick moustache.

Disorientated, my legs trembling, I struggled to retain my composure.

"What are you doing here?" I managed to utter, feeling shaken not only by the destabilising effects of height and glare, but also by the presence of someone who I had earnestly hoped never to see again.

"As ever I do what I can to assist the Honourable Crispin," he answered with a sickening grin. "I am given to understand that you are here to collect a substantial payment. Firstly, however, our esteemed friend thought I might like to ask you a few questions."

"I came here to see Collingwood's secretary, not you," I answered cautiously. "Anyway, why are you in New York and not Lima or Rio?" I demanded, trying to make sense of the situation.

"It is indeed fortuitous that our paths should cross in this city. It seems that the tastes of your erstwhile colleagues are equally gregarious in the New World as in the old. I have, as you might say, been killing two birds with one stone. Then by sheer chance a third flies into range." He sneered slightly and I noticed the flash of gold from the corner of his mouth.

"The Honourable Crispin was not slow to introduce his gourmet aspirations to his new colleagues on Wall Street. They too are soon to be acquainted with the culinary delights of cavia porcellus."

Ramirez had moved even closer now, leaving the case on a seat. I could smell the garlic on his breath and saw a speck of bread lodged in the coarse hairs on his upper lip. I tried to master my thoughts, to control my confusion despite the insecurity of this shabby eyrie.

He continued relentlessly.

"Bird number one is Mr Feinman. As is his name, is his nature; it will be a pleasure doing business with him. At least when he joined me for dinner yesterday he had the courtesy not to vomit over my suit.

"Bird number two is your successor, young Mr Rhodes. As I was visiting New York it was convenient for him to cross the pond and discuss arrangements, both practical and financial, for a much delayed event in London. I believe his delectable companion has a highly suitable venue in mind.

"Then, just as matters appear to be concluded, by remarkable coincidence in you fly as bird number three. I think you and I have a lot to talk about."

"I am not interested in any activities of the Epicureans either in London or New York," I said taking a long slow inhalation. "I came here for one reason alone. I am to collect $1 million owed to me by Collingwood. If you have it, please hand it over."

"I have your money," he answered. "Crispin telephoned me late yesterday morning. It really was most amusing. Although he is a fabulous financier he had an urgent need for dollar bills.

"However – and you will enjoy the irony of this – his only means of quickly obtaining banknotes was via myself. He had just seen me here in New York and, as you might recall, I also happen to hold a modest private account in this city. Collingwood arranged an electronic transfer and lo and behold when I stepped into the bank just an hour ago the helpful cashier counted out the exact sum in $100 bills."

"Then where is it?" I snapped.

"As it was my turn to be a courier the Honourable Crispin invited me to combine delivery with enquiry. I suspect you may be able to explain certain events which occurred several thousand miles south of here. Once I have received that information, you shall receive your dollars."

Once I had realised that the emerging figure was Ramirez I had begun to fear an interrogation. I wondered what he knew, what he had guessed and how much information had been fed to him through private channels in Lima.

He ploughed on mercilessly. "As you are fond of saying in your country, a little bird told me something. When I was back in Rio word came that you had appeared once more in Lima."

"Who told you that?" I asked.

Ramirez smiled grimly. "Raoul never betrays his friends," he snarled. "Not like some people I know. As I adequately demonstrated to you, Raoul looks after his people. As a result, wherever I have a business venture, there are many who notify me if something unusual occurs."

What he was saying did not surprise me. He was too subtle, too slippery, to commit any damning indiscretions.

"With great inconvenience I had no option but to amend my busy schedule and return to inspect my Peruvian enterprises personally. It is so tedious to have to travel so frequently to somewhere so hot and steamy but on this occasion it transpired that a visit to Iquitos was indeed essential."

His behaviour resembled a cobra's. He held me mesmerised, frozen with fatal fascination, before suddenly striking. "Who was the girl who stayed with you at Hotel Rosa?"

This venomous question caught me unawares. I thought quickly, my mind racing. Above everything I had to ensure the safety of Gilda and Rose.

"I don't know what you're talking about," I spluttered.

"Come, come, Benjamin," Ramirez snarled back. "There are several witnesses. Is it true that there was an uninvited guest at my island establishment? Should Inca Enterprises look to you to reimburse board and lodging?"

"It's none of your business who she was," I snapped back at him.

Instantly I realised this was a mistake. My response simply encouraged him to ask more questions, to dictate the agenda.

"Ah ha! So you don't deny it. And the child? Is it true that you have commenced a career in kidnapping?" He clicked his tongue viciously, the sneer spreading across his face. He was standing aggressively, hands on hips, gazing at me with cold eyes through his glinting spectacles.

This time I remained silent. I closed my eyes and willed myself to concentrate. He obviously knew that three of us had returned to Hotel Rosa but it was unlikely that he knew more than that. If I said nothing then his knowledge would remain incomplete and, more importantly, I would protect my new family.

"You are a great disappointment Benjamin," he continued. "I was so looking forward to our future business relationship. Instead you have turned to destruction. Are you jealous of my creativity?"

Still I said nothing, trying to shut out his voice, wondering if he genuinely sought information or was merely enjoying a sadistic indulgence.

"In the words of the song 'silence speaks a thousand words'," he said sarcastically.

Then he added, "Very well; you choose to be uncommunicative, but I really would like to know two things.

"The excellent river boatmen of Iquitos tell me that one of their number, a certain Pablo, came into a large sum of money. Now instead of driving a dugout canoe, he drives his own minibus. How much did you pay him Benjamin and what exactly did you require him to do? Was it he who started the fire? Surely you don't expect me to believe that was an accident? The rebuilding costs have been considerable."

For the first time since emerging through the lift doors I experienced a moment of relief. It seemed that Pablo had been true to his word and had kept silent about what he had witnessed. He was obviously shrewd enough to respond wisely to his unexpected reward. I relaxed slightly and opened my eyes again.

"If you won't answer that," Ramirez continued, staring at me defiantly, "then at least tell me what has become of Raphael. Where is he? How much did you pay him to desert his post?"

Again I felt a burden lifting. Ramirez evidently believed that I had bribed both Pablo and Raphael. I also recalled that I had made no mention of this detestable character in the account I had given to the British Embassy in Lima. He no doubt thought that Raphael had disappeared to squander a substantial sum of nuevos soles in the bars, brothels or gambling dens of the less desirable parts of Iquitos. I would not disabuse him of the notion. Ramirez need not know that the mute's silence would be total and permanent.

"Raphael was well paid," I said keen to encourage the misconception, adding in a moment of inspiration, "I am sure he has made a comfortable bed for himself."

Ramirez was still standing close to me, the scent of his aftershave mingling with his garlic breath. My unexpected response interrupted his flow. He seemed to think for a moment then, as if suddenly tiring, he backed away slightly saying, "You may have nothing to tell me but I have every reason to believe that you are responsible for a major attempt to disrupt the work of Inca Enterprises. You have not succeeded. You may have commenced a conflagration like a petty arsonist; but that is a mere flicker. Another commission to the industrious artisan in his riverside workshop and what has been destroyed has been replaced. Stocks have been replenished; already our furry delicacies are procreating, generating fine food for Mr Feinman. Be under no illusions Benjamin, your petty vandalism hurts no more than a pin prick."

When he paused I look directly at him and said calmly, "Please may I now have the dollars which Collingwood has entrusted to you?"

"In a moment Benjamin," he responded irascibly. "Naturally when I spoke with the Honourable Crispin I told him that I was perfectly agreeable to helping out an old friend. After all that is what friends are for as I was always taught to believe by my English teachers. He suggested that I gave you a small task before you collected your package. If you fail then your payment is forfeit to me by way of compensation for any damage which is your responsibility."

At least we had moved on from the relentless sarcastic questioning, but it was typical of Ramirez that there should be another sadistic twist.

"For goodness sake Ramirez," I snapped, "just hand over the dollars and leave me in peace."

"Tut, tut Benjamin," he mocked. "If you behave like that on the trading floor you will not strike many deals. But then of course your illustrious career has come to an ignominious end. Follow me."

He turned, pacing through the bright sunlight of the dusty lounge, beckoning me towards the stairs leading up to the helipad. I noticed that he was clad expensively but unfashionably in a heavy brown wool suit and brown shoes, brogues but made of suede and vaguely familiar.

As he moved I hesitated, alarmed. While I had been engaged in conversation, concentrating on divulging nothing, I had been able temporarily to ignore the sensations of unsteadiness and insecurity. The prospect of ascending to the roof of the building was terrifying.

Ramirez was hurrying ahead. Looking over his shoulder he called out enigmatically, "As you will see I have been shopping in Macy's."

I stood still at the foot of the short spiral staircase. Ramirez was already hauling open a thick glass door at the top, a blast of cold air already whistling into the stale and stuffy lounge.

"What's going on?" I demanded, "I'm not coming up there!"

"Then you are not going to get your money!" he answered with a cruel laugh.

I had no option. Tentatively I grasped the handrail and stepped slowly onto the curving stairs. Moments later I reached the heavy door and grasping it firmly for security emerged into the cold December morning 76 storeys high.

Although the low sun bathed the area already clouds were gathering in the east. The breeze was strong at this altitude the occasional gusts hitting my face like a sharp slap. Still holding on tenaciously I scanned the area in front of me. The very top of the building was perfectly flat apart from the small construction sheltering the stairwell. Several feet away was the perimeter of a thickly painted yellow circle inside of which I could make out a similarly painted letter 'H'. My eyes travelled slowly across this disused landing area reluctant to stray further, certain that it ended in an unprotected edge. If I ventured to the extremity I ventured to a sheer cliff, plunging 300 metres in a deathly descent to the street.

"For goodness sake Ramirez what are you playing at?" I shouted.

"You wanted your money. There it is. Departmental stores provide useful carriers. Go and get it," he replied, gesturing across the expanse.

With an unbearable tightness in my chest I found it difficult to focus on anything lying further away than the nearest arc of yellow. But then something caught my eye. Strengthening my grip on the door I forced my gaze onto a strange bundle on the far side of the helipad placed only a metre from the precipice. It was a Macy's carrier bag made bulky by its contents and held in place by one of the heavy ashtrays dragged up from the lounge.

"You mean my money is in there?" I gasped.

"Of course," Ramirez answered with a sickening grin.

"How do I know?" I demanded.

"Just look closely," he sneered.

With an effort I screwed up my eyes and stared. I could make out thick bundles of dollar notes wedged tightly into the bag secured with broad elastic bands, several of them poking through the curves of the handles.

Ramirez was now at his most sarcastic. "All you have to do is walk over there and collect."

This was no task; it was a torture. It was typical of Collingwood to spot a weakness and then exploit his knowledge mercilessly; it was typical of Ramirez to mock a weakness and then exploit his knowledge sadistically.

But I would not be beaten. Closing my eyes again I took controlled deep breaths and tried to remain rational. I told myself that if the package were on the opposite touchline of a football pitch I would have no hesitation in running to retrieve it. In terms of distance and a simple quick snatch what faced me was no different. It was absurd that I should balk at this minor challenge.

Cautiously I relaxed my grip on the cool glass and willed my right foot forward. I stopped, then moved my left foot beyond it. With my jaw firmly clenched, my whole body tensed, I managed maybe five slow steps. Now I was far away from safety. I could feel the wind harsh on my face; I could see the edge of the building perceptibly closer. Still I continued little by little, ungainly, swaying slightly, achieving another three steps, advancing another metre. With a wobble I crossed the near side of the yellow circle.

"Don't totter like that when you get near the edge!" Ramirez's voice stabbed like a stiletto into my concentration.

I turned and saw him standing away from the glass portal as if he had made a sudden advance towards me. I froze, incapable of moving either forwards or backwards. Having been so focused on the Macy's bundle I had not paused to reflect on my double danger. Not only was I unsafely exposed 76 storeys above the street, I was alone with the most detestable individual I had ever met. How easy it would be for him to creep up as I moved unsteadily to my objective and, with a slight touch, send me plunging into the void, spinning like a rag doll, a momentary flash outside the windows of financial minions staring fixedly at their computer screens.

"Don't come near me!" I screamed at him.

"I wouldn't dream of it," he shouted back. "As I thought; it appears that you have failed the test."

That angered me even more. Although trembling, desperately unsteady, I turned away from him and again fixed my gaze on the anchored package, trying to blank out the view of the lower buildings beyond, the sun winking at me maliciously from a thousand panes of glass. But my legs were rigid, locking me to the grey surface of the helipad. I crouched down, then lowered myself gently onto hands and knees. This was better. Immediately my horizon was limited, the sense of exposure diminished. I started to crawl forward. Carefully and deliberately I moved my right hand and then my right knee. I followed with my left hand and left knee. Cautiously I developed a slow momentum. With head down, eyes fixed on the concrete beneath me, I began to make progress. I did not care that I placed my flat palms on ancient streaks of oil or dragged my trousers through the clinging dust. Slowly and steadily I was moving forwards.

After a few moments I was traversing the yellow H in the very centre of the helipad. Still I crawled onwards, advancing 20 centimetres with every movement of my four limbs. At last, with grim satisfaction, I dragged myself across the far curve of the yellow circle. Now the carrier bag was only about 10 metres away; I could see the topmost wads of dollars trembling slightly in the strengthening gusts. I simply had to continue like this, on all fours like a dog, and within a few minutes they would be within my grasp.

From this crouching position I also saw with a sudden shock the very edge of the roof. Panting, aching, conscious again of the unfathomable drop beyond, I froze. Standing, my legs had locked; now in animal position all my limbs stiffened and refused to move. With searing disappointment I knew that even in a crawling position I was incapable of reaching my objective.

But still I would not be beaten.

Gingerly I lowered myself down even further, my legs stretched out behind me, my arms in front, until I lay completely flat. Now I forced myself forward, like a snake, sliding my chest and stomach through the grease and grime. Centimetre by centimetre the case came nearer. My hands and arms were filthy, my chin grazed, my gasping mouth tasted vile choking grit. Every part of my body was painful. My head was pounding; my stomach weak and watery.

This final slither seemed interminable. Mercifully there was virtually no horizon, only what I could see just in front of me. But equally there were no further landmarks. With supreme effort I willed my body slowly forward, squeezing the twitching vestiges of energy into my exhausted limbs.

My short shadow stretched in front of me. I raised one arm and the dark outline spread. The image of my fingers grasped the plastic handles before me.

I was almost there.

20

"What the hell is going on?"

An authoritarian voice yelled loudly from behind me. Instantly I dropped my hand.

"You're no goddam photographer!" it added.

Then I heard Ramirez. "You said I could have 10 minutes! I paid you well enough!"

"Are you suicidal?" The voice was obviously addressing me. "Get back. Move your ass now!"

Instinctively I obeyed. Unable to see behind but in no doubt that the command could not be ignored, I eased myself backwards like a retreating reptile. It was not until I was well within the yellow circle that I regained some control over my exhausted extremities and forced myself to turn and crawl to safety.

I hauled myself up clutching at the glass door. Ramirez had lost his composure. He was staring angrily at the rooftop intruder who now I recognised as the intimidating security guard from the previous morning. But any vestiges of purchased politeness had deserted him. He was agitated, gesticulating with his revolver already clutched in his thick grasp.

Relieved to achieve the comparative safety of the stairwell, I desperately desired the reassuring solidity of the ground beneath my feet. Trembling, I descended the stairs, pushing past the guard who began shouting, incandescent with fury.

"You said this was a photo shoot!" I heard him yell at Ramirez. "What the hell were you thinking?"

A shout of protest rasped in response. "I paid you $500 to leave us alone!"

I paused at the foot of the spiral stairway as a stronger blast from the approaching Atlantic front sounded mournfully across the entrance hitting me with its dying draught.

"What the hell?" came from the guard. "It's a goddam ashtray. What the hell is it doing there? Shift it!"

"Can't we just leave it?" Ramirez sounded worried, his confidence wavering.

"It's a goddam hazard. If that falls, I'm fired!" The guard was roaring now. "Shift your ass and fetch it!"

"Let's go. It's not important!" The voice of Ramirez faded into a whine of desperation.

"Shift your ass over there! Or must I make you move?"

I staggered towards the elevator. As another gust lashed the slanting windows of the 75th floor I thought I heard a shot, but the sounds were hurled away by the wind, distorted in a howling rage.

I was still breathing deeply, my chest heaving, my legs and arms shaking. I felt weakened with vertigo, humiliated, sickened that I had not seized what I had come for, cheated out of what was within my grasp. But I could take no more. I simply wanted to escape from the Grossman building.

As I groped along the empty rows of seats, my hand firmly clutching the back rests, I saw my attaché case where Ramirez had left it. Why should I let him walk off with it as he did before? He had stolen it once; I would not let him steal it a second time. As I passed I grabbed its handle, took the last few steps towards the wall and summoned the elevator.

Thankfully it came immediately. My descent was swift, unaccompanied and uninterrupted. I was glad to be alone unobserved except by the shiny mirrors reflecting a grotesque series of dishevelled ghosts wearing filthy trousers and black leather jackets smeared with grime. I prepared for a final ignominious manhandling, convinced this disreputable apparition faced violent ejection by the burly security guard at the revolving door.

But I emerged through the lobby without interruption, for outside was a scene of chaos. A yellow taxi was impaled on a sidewalk sign; cars were slewed across the road, their horns blaring; several women were screaming. A delivery lorry had screeched to a halt with an acrid stench of burning rubber. In front of its number plate I saw an unidentifiable bloody mass of flesh splayed like a burst tomato across the asphalt of the street; in front of a scorched wheel, a red stained brogue shoe made of suede. On the sidewalk I glimpsed a shattered marble plinth and a battered brass ashtray. A shredded Macy's bag was caught in a vortex. Pedestrians were leaping and gesticulating, snatching into the air at fluttering banknotes whirling in the rising breeze funnelling from Wall Street.

I turned and stumbled to the subway grasping a note blown into my face and stuffing it into my pocket as a pittance of consolation.

Fortunately I did not have long to wait for a train. Huddled into a corner seat I avoided eye contact with the other passengers who shrunk away from me in suspicion or disgust. We were at Houston Street before my breathing returned to normal and the trembling in my legs subsided. Idly I lifted my grimy hand off the scarred attaché case and slipped it into my pocket. I felt the paper of the banknote and with an overwhelming sense of disappointment examined the only vestige of the bundle which was rightfully mine.

There in front of me was the familiar face of George Washington above the bold capital letters spelling 'One Dollar'. But something was wrong. If Ramirez had brought the entire sum in this denomination he would have needed a hundred Macy's bags.

I turned the note over in my hand. On the reverse were the familiar images of the Great Seal of the United States, but beneath was a narrow pink strip bearing the words 'Play Money'.

Ramirez had indeed been shopping at Macy's – in the toy department.

I gave a loud involuntary laugh of surprise, again provoking wary glances from the few travellers seated nearby fearful of this madman. But rapidly overtaking the surprise came an overwhelming sense of relief.

It was another half hour before the relief became euphoria.

Once in my room at the Westin I was desperate to feel clean once more. I flung off my ruined jacket and trousers, stripped off all remaining clothes and hurried into the shower, turning the head to 'massage' and allowing the stinging jets to scour away my stale sweat and the foul contagion of Ramirez.

Refreshed, swaddled in a thick bathrobe, I sat on the bed. The attaché case was still where I had dropped it near the pillow, its gash smiling at me as if pleased to be home. I was certain that Ramirez would not have reset the combination. I spun the barrels until 2912 appeared. As anticipated there was a satisfying click and the lock sprung open.

A neat grid of dollar bills lay in front of me, broad bankers' bands concealing the portrait of Benjamin Franklin but revealing the denomination 100 on either side. I extracted a few notes, held them up to the light and turned them over. There on the back was the inscription 'In God We Trust' above the stately symmetrical Independence Hall. They were genuine.

My pulse quickening, I counted the number of notes in a bundle. There were five hundred. Then I counted the number of bundles: twenty. There was a total of exactly US $ 1 million.

I could not resist. I punched the air. But this was far sweeter than a bonus announcement. It was closure.

Neither could I resist the urge to communicate. I reached for my phone, set it to text mode and typed in Gilda's number. *Business complete. Leaving NY. Can't wait to c u . 5 days to go. I love u. Ben.*

Then I telephoned reception to request my bill and transport to the airport.